Uncle Neddy's Funeral

L.M. Pampuro

Uncle Neddy's Funeral
Copyright 2017by L.M. Pampuro

This book is a work of fiction.

Names, characters, locations, and events are either a product of the author's imagination, fictitious or used fictitiously.

Any resemblance to any event, locale or person, living or dead, is purely coincidental.

Cover design by the LMPatarini group

ISBN-13: 978-0692888759 (LMPG)

ISBN-10: 0692888756

For Steve

Uncle Neddy's Funeral

   Neddy took in a deep breath of air. A violent cough followed. Surrounded by darkness, he had zero perception, which, for him, was fortunate. His arms touched the silky sides, as did his legs. He tried stretching his feet to the end. It figured, where he didn't need it or couldn't use it, he had the space. His breath bounced back from the top. He could smell Mama's tomato sauce from breakfast. Leftover gnocchi and eggs made the perfect meal to get him through the day. With each exhale, his heart skipped.

   About an hour ago, the air became lighter, best he could tell. The stench had to be from his exhales. He tried not to smell, breathe. Leave it to Joe and Victor to come up with a plan that involved a disgusting odor. Those two could fill a room after one of Mama's meals. Not that Mama's meals were gassy, it's just those two needed no incentives to let one loose. Neddy's laughter broke into a coughing fit.

   "Ah, a minor inconvenience," he said. In the distance, he could hear hushed voices yet couldn't make out the conversation. The voices grew louder as Neddy assumed, people came closer.

"Be careful with this one," Victor's brogue came through clearly.

"Why boss," another voice spoke. "Ya think he can feel anything?" Laughter filled the room. Neddy strained to hear the paused conversation. A couple of awkward coughs filled the space.

"Just be careful," Ah, Victor used his I am in charge voice. Neddy knew the tone. His crew isn't following directions. Neddy smirked. "Think of this as precious cargo." Footsteps followed, growing weaker by the clank.

"I think the boss is getting weird."

"In what way?"

"He's worried about a corpse." Neddy smiled. He curved his temptation to knock. As funny as he thought it would be to make whoever jump at the sound, he knew better. Victor Cuzzuto would kill him.

"Victor got his job. Our job is to move the sucker."

"If Victor had finished the last job, we wouldn't be here, now would we?"

"Not our problem."

"When will the old guy retire…" Neddy banged into the side of the casket. His head bounced off the top.

"Ouch!" he exclaimed as he bit into his hand. The casket stopped moving.

"You hear something, boss?"

"I ain't heard nothing," came a quick reply along with a jolt. "Let's just finish this up. A place like this gives me the creeps."

Part One: The Funeral

"Brothers and sisters, we have come to say goodbye to our brother, Giuseppe Vittorio Vaffanculo."

"For crying aloud, did this guy even know Neddy?" Gia hissed in her sister's ear. The middle child of the Vaffanculo relations, Gia sat with arms folded across her black satin dress, in her opinion, a beautiful garment wasted at a funeral. Her eyes volleyed between the crowded sanctuary and the man standing at the podium. Her younger sister by a year, Amelia, stared at the priest with intent. Her eyes were tearing at the mention of her favorite uncle's name.

"Giuseppe was an exceptional man: father, brother, son…" as the priest paused a moment, Amelia glanced over at her ninety-year-old grandmother who sat playing with her false teeth. She nudged her sister in Grandma's direction. Grandma, dressed in traditional funeral black, included the customary laced veil, now thrown haphazardly over her head. Grandma Lena swished her teeth around her mouth, popped them through her lips, then caught the full set in her hand. Not a bit of spit followed. Without missing a beat, she'd place the choppers back in to start again.

"Oh, this is going to be entertaining," Gia smirked.

"Giuseppe was a fine man who loved his wife…"

"Which is he referring to?" Amelia giggled.

"…Adored his children…"

"Only those he knew about…" without missing a beat, Gia responded.

"…And was a wonderful son…" a "humpf" came from the direction of their grandmother. The girls watched their mother squat walk towards Grandma. She knelt in front of her, rubs the old lady's arm as she whispered something in her ear. Grandma turned around and flicked her wrist in her daughter-in-law's direction. The girls' eyes grew wide.

"We would get slapped," Gia pointed out to a nodding Amelia. Their mother just shrugged, stood fully erect, walked back to her seat. Her face was expressionless.

As the priest continued to extoll virtues her uncle never possessed, Gia looked around the crowded funeral home. Bright purple flower arrangements lined the wall then veered around the back of the casket. Family and friends sat, stood, and waited in the adjacent rooms, spilling outdoors under the canvass walkways to pay respects. She knew most of the folks around here all her life, some by reputation, most by some sort of relation.

"Giuseppe was a pillar in the community. He had a big heart…"

"Are you sure he's talking about Uncle Neddy?" Amelia said.

"I don't think this one had met him. He's new. Remember, straight off the boat from the mothership," The priest appeared to be moving around the alter to avoid stepping in something.

"Don't you mean Mother Land?"

"Ship…Land…Tomato…Tomato… What is the difference? The guy knows nothing about our family or the person he is talking about." Gia moved her right hand as she spoke, the same mannerism her mother and Grandma used.

"He knows some stuff…"

"Yeah, what is on the script. Aunt Neddy, the fourth wrote it up, or do you think she'd let the fifth in waiting do the eulogy?"

"I think she'd rather be reading the fifth to be's eulogy." As both girls began to snicker, Gia glanced up into their mother's warning glare. In silence, Angela Victorio Cuzzuto Vaffanculo held up one finger. Gia nudged her sister. She gave a head nod towards their mother. Elegantly she raised a second finger. Her dark blue eyes never wavered.

Both Gia and Amelia gave a slight nod, leaned back in their chairs. Both crossed their legs over their knees. They mirrored each other's worried glances, unconsciously tapping their bottom foot. Angela relaxed a little in her chair. To her left, her husband, Joe, snored quietly. Angela poked his arm. He would jump a little, smile at her, only to close his eyes again.

He held her left hand in his. Every so often, she would feel a gentle squeeze. *Ah, my Joseph, he works so hard at the restaurant. Still cleaning up his brother's messes.* She thought, *so he's napping. He is not disrespectful. It's his brother's funeral, not mine. He better not to nap at my funeral.* A laugh escapes from her lips. *Who am I kidding? I will bury him first. Here, a little nap hurts no one. Ugh – look at the line – I'm sure half are here because they love Neddy, the others want to make sure he's dead.* Her lips turned up into a discreet smile. *Iksch – This is all good. All these people here. This will help us with our situation. I wonder how many know?* She glanced over at her mother-in-law, who now moved from playing with her teeth to eating what looks like a pignoli cookie. *Now, where did those cookies come from?*

Crumbs float down the old lady's face. Angela nudged a tissue into Enzo's hand. She pointed towards the older lady. "Oh, for crying aloud," he proceeded to float down the row to the matriarch's side, causing as little commotion as possible.

"Mrs. V, you need to stop with the cookies," he reprimanded in a hushed voice the people in the back of the room could hear.

"I'm ninety years old…"

"You are not ninety, you are only eighty-five."

"The stunad caused me so much stress I aged five years." Enzo bit the inside of his cheek, yet the grin across his face gave him away.

"I understand, but still, it is disrespectful to be chowing down at Neddy's…"

"What's disrespectful is having this idiota talk about someone he's never met!" As the word idiota came out of the old lady's lips, all those in close vicinity did the sign of the cross. The gesture continued down the rows like the wave at a football game.

"Why are we blessing ourselves?" Breezy repositioned her swollen stomach to massaged her lower back against the chair. Because of her condition, the usher escorted her inside, only to be seated in the last row of the second room. She should insist on being moved upfront because she was part of the immediate family. Then again, in many ways, the back of the room had a better view. Her partner Harry stood close. Harry had a hard time with the overdone funeral, family obligations thing. He did his best to protect Breezy from the circus when he could. Today wasn't one of those times.

"I have no idea…" Breezy let out a deep sigh. Her foot started to tap.

"This is your side of the church." Harry gazed at his partner. He added a weak smile. She was getting cranky though he couldn't blame her. Somehow his kind, loving, beautiful girlfriend slowly turned into a raging maniac. At first, he thought it was just hormones, yet lately, after hearing about her father's mess of a situation, she got a bit dark. Being seated in the back row instead of up with the family will bring on a meltdown. He prayed it took place at home as he was hoping to leave here with as little commotion as possible.

Harry kept scanning the room yet couldn't see the person he labeled as his mother in law. He knew Wind would be here somewhere. She would show up just to make sure her ex's corpse is in the coffin. Neddy knew about the baby. They had gone to visit him after they found out. The reaction came in typical Neddy fashion, "To each his own, but keep in mind my beautiful daughter, your grandmother will take out a contract to kill him," at the same time, he pointed towards Harry. To Harry's relief, there didn't appear to be a contract out. Neddy's family all know they are not married, outsiders assumed with Breezy's condition, they are Mister and Missus.

Then there is Breezy's mom. She got too weird even for Neddy, from Harry's observations, that was hard to accomplish. The Vaffanculo's didn't talk about her. She is just referred to as Number Two.

Harry pushed to meet Breezy's mother. She finally agreed, yet warned that things would get strange—finally, Sunday dinner at her house. Harry had been to the Vaffanculo's for Sunday dinner many times. He enjoyed the loud conversations along with Grandma Lena's cooking. How bad could Breezy's mother be?

The house, the typical McMansion with the obligatory Italian style fountain spewing water in the front yard, appeared normal in a new money kind of way. He got ready for teased up hair, long nails, designer clothes, yet when the door opened to a naked middle-aged man with a protruding beer gut, Harry was stunned to silence.

They followed him to a back yard filled with other enlarged naked or semi-naked middle-aged people sitting around an in-ground pool/patio area. "Ug. Where is my mother?" Breezy asked over and over again.

Wind made an awe-inspiring entrance in a long gold toga. She bared one breast along with her left leg, while the other leg, the rest of her right side, covered by the cloth. Harry had been stunned, yet Breezy just walked up and asked when dinner would be ready. Her mother pointed to a long table close to the house containing fresh fruit surrounded by bottles of wine. Breezy excused herself. They left. There was never an explanation yet that Sunday dinner ended up being their most normal encounter.

Harry just wanted the priest to be finished, although even through the crackled speaker, it didn't seem like it was happening anytime soon. "Hey, Bree, I didn't know your dad played football…"

"He didn't. Joe played in high school, my uncle, I think." She took inventory of the people in the room. An audible sigh escaped, "Who wrote this anyway? I mean, if someone met my dad once, they would know he was not a sports guy. He liked playing with cheerleaders, not with balls, unless..." A few giggles floated into the conversation. "Anyway, the person who wrote this, definitely not wife number two or my Grandma, got their brothers mixed up...I wonder if whoever got them mixed up in other ways too..." A wave of people gasped and blessed themselves. Breezy smiled up at Harry, locking eyes.

"Must you do that?"

"Yeah –playing is fun." Breezy took in the crowd's reaction to her words. The pious ones pretended not to be listening. Yet, the position of their bodies and silence of their whispers said otherwise. She moved her body cat-like stretching from her lower back up to rolling shoulders and neck. With a giggle, "You know the sad part is no one knew my father's secret," she waited for a beat as the bodies around her leaned in to hear her better. Harry silently pleaded with his eyes for her to behave, "you know my dad, he always hated gossips and freaks." The crowd leaned away, yet not before a voice sailed above the shuffle, "I thought Neddy loved the freaks." Another wave of people making the sign of the cross spread throughout the room.

"They keep going at this rate, folks will leave with clear indentations all over their bodies from poking themselves," she laughed. Harry shook his head. "Besides love, I know my Grandma would enjoy this if she was sitting in the cheap seats with us. We'll need to tell her about it if we ever move to the front. I seriously should be sitting beside her. She needs me." A yawn escaped with the last comment.

Breezy's eyelids slid lower. "Wake me when it is time to move…" Harry took her hand and rubbed circles with his thumb. Harry loved it when Breezy slept. Soft snores vibrated from her lips. *Now all I need to do is keep you and our baby safe. I can do that. Ending this will help.*

"I wish I had known Giuseppe Vittorio in his vibrant days. Although even in the end, Giuseppe Vittorio made certain the church and his mother was taken care of…"

Lena placed her head in her hand. She chuckled silently. *Neddy didn't take care of her. Heck, Neddy could barely take care of himself. Everyone took care of Neddy.* From behind, the crowd viewed an old lady in grief for her son. From Amelia and Gia's view, the smirk and the head-shaking said everything. Grandma had once told them she knew all, so don't mess with her. After Gia snuck out late one night to meet her boyfriend, Grandma called her on it at breakfast the next day, mainly because Gia kept snipping at her mother. After several warnings about her attitude, Lena decided it was time to stop. *Why so tired, my Gia?* She had asked. *When I was your age, I could stay out all night and still be beautiful, not cranky, the next day.* When Gia didn't respond, Lena just gave a bit more information, *Even an old lady like me could climb up the fire escape in the dark.* The girls observed their mother spit her coffee into the sink while Grandma just sat with a half-smile spreading across her face. She informed her offspring the windows would be nailed shut until both girls were married off. Grandma responded with a sharp glare.

The girls learned when Grandma asks you to do something, you do it.

Grandma's little secret is Mrs. Delvechio down the road. Mrs. Delvechio has nothing better to do except look out her window, and for some reason, she doesn't sleep at night. She can see the entrance to the all-night espresso bar where the kids like to hang out—the night before she saw Gia out with Bobby Deluca, so she mentioned it in passing. Everyone in the neighborhood knew Bobby Deluca has the charm to lure any young girl out after curfew. Bobby reminded Lena of Neddy in his teenage years.

"At this time, I see there are many out there who would like to say a few words on Giuseppe's behalf. It is my honor to introduce the matriarch of the Vaffanculo family, Lena Vaffanculo."

Mama

Lena Vaffanculo stood up as straight as an eighty-five-year-old could. She scanned the crowd like a head of state. Her daughter- in- law rose to help, yet the old woman shushed her away with a wave of the hand before she could give assistance. This is supposed to be her son's funeral. She would immortalize him with the dignity he deserved. She knew eyes followed her every step. She was confident many of the seated wondered why Neddy and not her.

They were about to find out. The priest leaned over to offered his hand as she shuffled towards the steps. Fortunately for him, a dark veil covered her face. Otherwise, he would realize her disdain for his gesture. As she moved towards the podium, she glanced over to the casket. The cardboard cutout resembling her son comes across at peace. His hands folded in a prayer-like position. The funeral people had turned his lips up into the smirk he always wore when he tried to pull a fast one.

Neddy. Of course, Neddy would put her in this position. He, after all, remained her challenge child. Lena had shed all the tears she had for him during the two days of labor he put her through to be in this world. Today she would shed no tears. Lena grabbed on to the sides of the podium for balance. Again, her eyes moved to survey the crowd. "Con man, hitman, government men, and thieves, all present and accounted for," she mumbled. How appropriate.

With a deep intake of breath, she began to speak. "Benvenuti funneral di Neddy..." She turned towards the priest, "Il suo nome è Giuseppe Neddy non-si ass..." The congregation gasped as another wave of hands doing the sign of the cross moved through the room.

"Mama, parlando Enhlish," Joe's voice carried as his two girls snickered. Lena shot her granddaughter's a warning glance, followed by a soft smile.

"Excussee, I am Lena Vaffanculo, also known as Neddy's mother." She repositioned herself to leaning on one elbow and raised her right hand towards the audience. "I'ma here to talk about my Neddy. Just a little bit today. My Neddy, you know, he's a good boy. I know many of you don't think so. I mean, Neddy, he lied a little, so what." Lena shrugged her shoulders. Who was she kidding, Neddy lied like a rug. "None of you ever lie?" The mourners nodded in unison. "And yeah, he cheated a little on his women. Ok, he cheated a lot. I mean, otherwise, I wouldn't have four daughters-in-law just from him." The crowd snickered. Lena caught her granddaughters holding up five fingers each. "Ichk," she muttered with a wave of her hand. "My daughters-in-law think I think my sons are saints," she glances in the direction of Joe, eyes closed, his lips curled into a smile. Her eyes reach Angela's. "You see my boys they take after their father, God rest his soul." With both hands clasped, Lena blew a kiss towards the ceiling. "Giuseppe was one of a kind man. He never cheated. I know because if he did," she slammed down her hand on the podium as the audience jumped, "off comes his penis." The room fell silent. No one within earshot doubted Lena Vaffanculo would castrate anyone who crossed her.

"Today, today is not about my Giuseppe. Today is about my Neddy. So Ima going to tell a few stories and we'll see where this all goes. Ok? Ok." Lena gazed back at the casket, shook her head, moved her body back to focus on her audience. "When Neddy was a little boy, he used to do funny things. When I say funny, I don'ta mean haha funny, I mean you know, funny. Like he liked to go to the theater with me on Saturdays. Neddy would tell me how he was going to be a big actor like Sinatra, and I be going to see him at the movies someday." Lena wiped her hand over her eyes. "Can you imagine? Yeah – my

Neddy as the next Sinatra. You all know Neddy," she gestured towards the crowd with her hand, "Neddy wasn't no Sinatra. Could you imagine?" Lena started to laugh. Her snickers soon morphed into a cough. The priest moved in her direction. She waved him off as she recomposed herself. "Neddy is the dreamer of the family."

"Now, the theater thing bothers my husband. He dreamed of Neddy taking over the business so we could retire, maybe go back to Italy, But, who knows. Anyway, he also knew Neddy wasn't the right…" She let her words hang in the air. When Lena focused, again, the entire congregation nodded back at her. She smiled.

"He might not be the best at running Giuseppe's business, yet let me tell you the things Neddy is good at…" Lena smiled down at her granddaughters. "Neddy, he was good at makin' babies. His baby is here somewhere cause these two are Joey's babies. All my grandchildren are beautiful babies, and someday, they will make beautiful babies." Both girls smiled up at their Grandma. "Not too soon for you two!" Lena wagged her finger. "And my Neddy knew how to make a deal. Like the time he talked his brother into opening the restaurant," a gasp passed through the room. "Yeah, the restaurant they found him dead in," Lena waved her hand towards the crowd. "So what – Neddy died. You all are going to die someday…"

Lena readjusted her stance, so her right arm leaned on the podium. She gestured her left hand towards her audience. With a deep inhale, "So back to Neddy. My Neddy decides he's going to be an actor. So he starts taking lessons in New York City at someplace near Broadway. He goes and comes home on the train every day. Since he does, I always ask Neddy what he did at school today, like through regular school. You know, they come home, you give the kid a homemade cookie, and they tell you what they want you to know about their school day. Unless I got a call from the school. Then they come home, get no cookie, and a slap on the ass." Snickers vibrated through the room.

"So, one day, I ask Neddy what he did at school. He says, ma, let me show you. He gets down on the floor and just lays there, you know, like this," Lena puts her hands over her head. She turns her head sideways. Her tongue sticks out. "I say Neddy, what are you doing? And you know what he tells me?" Lena waits for a beat to look over the crowd, "he tells me, I'm dying Mama, I'm dying. I throw my hands up in the air. I tell him acting school is ripping him off. We are all dying, and even I know how to lay down!" Lena dabbed her eyes with a cloth handkerchief. "After that, he don't go back to acting school. He hangs around the house. Guiseppe tells him he needs to do something because he can't stay home. So Neddy decides he wants to be a lawyer because lawyers are just actors who get paid more, his words…"

Lena readjusts to the other side. "His father says we can always use a lawyer in this family," low laughter filters through the room, "so he tells him to apply to schools, and if he gets in, we will pay. Oh boy, did we ever pay! Law school is more of a rip off than acting school. Except you see Neddy wasn't all that smart –no, we can say it. My Joseph over there got looks and brains," Joe opened one eye. He curves his lips into a soft smile, "but my Neddy just got the looks. And as we know now looks without brains is well," Lena gestured back towards the casket.

"So, we send him to law school. For those who doubted, he actually has a B.S. degree in law from a real college. Giuseppe and I did not buy him a degree from one of those flies by night places on T.V.," another snort sounded from the pews. "Neddy had a degree in bullshit and was always a BSer. Just ask any of his wives." Lena smirked as the crowd agreed. "Anyway, we send him off to law school, and he comes back with a surprise…wife number one, what was her name?"

"Cloe…" A high pitched voice emerges from the front row, on the far side.

"Oh, you're here…"

"Yes, mother. I wanted to make sure Neddy is actually dead."

"Yeah, so do half the people in this room…Anyway, Cloe." She pronounced her name slowly. She completely moved her entire body to stare and smile in the woman's direction. "He comes home with Cloe not to introduce the family to his girlfriend, but to introduce his wife. Yeah – that's a how we met her. My Neddy goes to law school, gets a degree, but isn't a lawyer, comes home with a non-Italian wife…you see the problem. Neddy doesn't, though. He figured now he'd go to work in the family business. He had no clue as to what the family business is. Still, he was going to work with his father," Lena blessed herself, "Giuseppe says to him, Neddy, what are you going to do? Neddy answers, I am going to be your legal person. Giuseppe says Neddy, you don'ta have the permission to practice law. You didn't pass the test. And I love my son's response. He says papa, I only need your permission. Giuseppe being the family man he was, hired Neddy as the family lawyer. Until today I bet none of you knew he wasn't real."

Lena stood back and waited. Most sat with their mouth agape. Some even shook their head no. Her son had many secrets, yet most were not her's to tell. This one she could. She knew people sat wondering if the work Neddy did for them was legal. "Eh, maybe the work was legal, maybe not. You decide." As she focused on the concerned ones, she knew now anyone sitting there should think twice about messing with her famiglia. "So," her voice a little above a whisper, "Neddy wasn't who he said pretended to be. He was still a good man. I thinka Neddy just wanted to be loved. He did things for those he loved. How many of you knew Neddy sent money to an island every year to help people?" A few hands went up. Lena noted two mourners in the back, writing something down. "He did. He set up places for their people to read and study…"

Joe leaned into Angela. "He hid his money in the Caribbean…" he whispered. Angela didn't move. "Mama's going to have the I.R.S. in our faces if she doesn't shut up." Angela glanced around the room, her eyes stopped on the two men writing on note pads in the back. She righted herself to face back at the alter.

"Over my right shoulder, see the two gentlemen taking notes," she breathed into Joe's ear. "We need to hurry Mama up."

"And so, my Neddy gave money for books, to help people in the old country. He helped our village recover from the earthquake last year. He rebuilt our sister city's church. He donated toys every year at Christmas to the shelters here, and he gave to this church here too. He wasn't a bad person," she sniffed, "He was just confused most of the time. What is the saying…Joseph, you know, the saying?" Joe shrugged in his mother's direction, "He belonged in a toolbox? I don't know." Lena flicked off the crowd. "Neddy is with his father now. I get the sense they are both looking down on us smiling. At least I hope they are…" Lena threw her arms up. She shuffled away from the podium. When Joe rose to assist, she took her son's arm to allow him to lead her back to her chair.

Facing away from the crowd, Joe kissed his mother's cheek. "You are the best, mama." As he backed away, she gave a knowing smile.

Just take a look at my Mama, the woman is still beautiful even at her age! Between you and me, she scares the crap out of me! Everyone knows if Mama ain't happy... Is she eating cookies? Are you serious? My mother is chowing on pignoli cookies while the priest is talking at my funeral. I wonder who made those in my honor? Damn, I could really go for a cookie.

This is going to be a long day. Oh – wait...she's getting up to speak. This will be good. Mama's love their kids, right? She should tell people how wonderful I am. Yeah – I could listen to my Mama boast about me all day. I am going to sit back and enjoy –

Oh, man. Did she need to tell the Sinatra story? How embarrassing could this get?

Yeesh! How many times did I need to explain acting will always be my passion? It is important to me, you, the reader, understand my story. I never, I repeat never, compared myself to Sinatra. To even mention I would, is completely insane. I mean, we all know Sinatra is the man. I'm more like a Dean Martin than a Frank Sinatra. I could never be the chairman, yet I could definitely be the Vice President. You know the V.P. I am already a V.I.P.

Ok, so let me tell you about my Mama because the stunad writing this doesn't have a clue. My Mama is an *exceptional woman. The best. That was always problem number one for me. I compared every woman I ever met with her. You probably think I'm a mama's boy. That is part of the stunad's master plan. She's manipulating you, my gentle reader, to think bad of me. But hey, ask anyone, they will tell you, I am my own man. I made my own decisions.*

Only you, the reader, will pick up the entire story. I'm going to make sure of it. My Mama encouraged me to take the acting lessons. She loved telling all her friends I was going to be a lawyer. In the beginning, I was supposed to just do family stuff. Yet, when half the neighborhood is your family, you end up helping everyone who asks. You tell me how I could say no to your cousin's best friend who is like a sister to you? Especially when she had those beautiful brown eyes filled with tears.

At least I was on the right end. I could have been on the other end with the potential for something terrible to happen, not that this mess isn't bad, it's not really bad, at least yet. I hope Mama saw the tutaloocs in the back in the suits writing stuff down when she was talking about where my money was donated. I could never understand how my cash is anyone else's business yet...

It could be why Mama stopped talking. Wait – did my Mama just call me a tool?

Hey, writer – you could make her cry a little. I mean, I am her firstborn. She at least could clasp on the alter. Sobbed uncontrollably. In every movie I have seen, breaking down is what mother's do. Are you sure you are a real writer?

Ok readers...

The Brother

All eyes followed the priest back up to the podium. His expression changed from indifference to half-open eyes pairing with a slight smirk upon his arrival. "Thank you, mama **Vaffanculo**," he missed Lena's narrowing eyes. "What a beautiful tribute to your son, Guse, I mean Neddy." As he stood, head tilted to the right, the audience began to nod in the same rhythm as he. His smile grew if only for a moment. With a deep sigh, he continued, "Next, Joseph Vaffanculo would like to say a few words about his brother, Joseph." The priest made a grand gesture for Joseph to approach the podium.

Joseph leaned down to kiss Angela on the cheek. "Knock 'em dead," she whispered in his ear. Joseph stood, buttoned his Armani suit. He made his way to the podium. He briefly glanced over at the casket then back to the crowd. Joe focused all his attention on Angela, "Neddy was an idiot," the words slipped out as Angela narrowed her eyes. She mouthed, "Be nice," to her husband.

"But he was our idiot." The crowd nodded with approval. "Mama was right when she said Neddy was a good person..."

"Mama is always right," Lena barked back.

"...because he was. Neddy would give the shirt off his back to help someone. I can remember back when we were kids living off 8th street. There was a bunch of kids who would take Neddy's lunch bag. Now Neddy had the choice to bring in his muscle," the crowd responded with laughter, "but he wouldn't. I'd say Neddy, let me take care of this for you. Nope, he'd tell me. They need the food more than me. Look, they all are so skinny. I don't think their Mama feeds them, and besides, Mama's sandwiches are known to be the best in the neighborhood. That's the way he thought. They just need to eat more than him because why else would they take his lunch, right?"

Joe smiled. "I did take care of the situation, yet Neddy thought their mama learned how to cook because they stopped taking his lunch." Joe shook his head. "I always thought it was my job to protect Neddy even though he was older than me. As Mama said, Neddy got the looks without any brains. He saw the best in everyone, even when the person didn't deserve so. You can see why Neddy needed looking after."

Joe focused on his girls. He let his eyes drift over to his wife. How did he get so lucky? "It was Angela's idea to go ahead with the restaurant," she moved her head to keep going. "There were too many pizza joints and spaghetti houses. The area needed something different, she said. When I told Neddy, he was thrilled. He told me he found the perfect place, just perfect, so he thought. Perfect to condemn is what I thought when I saw it. The place was more run down than a squirrel on Main Street. My brother had a vision. Where I saw sheetrock needing replacing, he saw a large open space with a stuffed cow in the middle. Yeah, I said that he saw the cow before it was there."

"I saw a kitchen the health inspector would shut on sight; he saw a chef's paradise. Neddy had everything mapped out down to the black and white booth seats. Who was I to argue? Angela thought by doing this it would help put Neddy back on track to give him a project. My brother had been..." Joe stopped to mull over his words, "Angie?"

"Floating."

"Yeah, he had been floating. This would bring him back over..."

"Neddy had a boat?" Lena asked.

"Not a real boat Mama. Neddy had not been doing anything for a while, and in reality, Neddy was getting kind of weird. We thought a project would be a step for him in the right direction. Plus, I do like a good steak." Joe got a few laughs. "We get to the old factory, and we start to renovate. I put Neddy in charge because the whole thing is his idea. To be honest, our Mama told me about this, so I did." Lena gave her youngest son a smile. "The first day of work, I get a call from my brother. Joey, when is my help going to get here? I say what time you tell them? And there is silence on the phone. I ask again, Neddy, what time where they supposed to be there. Now I'm wondering what Neddy's been doing all morning, yet with Neddy, you never wanted to ask, because you really don't want to hear the answer. Besides that, the story would take too long. Anyway, you know what he says…" Joe gazed at almost every person leaning forward in the chairs, "he says oh…I was supposed to take care of the crew. I couldn't believe it. Who did he think was in charge? Yeesh. I tell him to call Victor and see if he has a crew and when can they start because we always call Victor, you know, keep it in the family and all…Neddy calls me back about a half-hour later to tell me we are all set. If we are all set, I think he means Victor set up the crew. They are on their way or at least are scheduled to come over and do some work. But no." Joe shakes his head. He glances in the direction of Angela to catch her with a wink.

"Angela and I go out to dinner with the kids to Enzo's place. Victor's there, so I give him the old nod hello. A few minutes later, he is standing at my table. The kids are yelling hello to nano, yet I can tell he's not happy. You all know his face when Victor's pissed…" The crowd glances over to and away from an elderly gentleman seated in the second row. Two muscle men in matching suits flank him. "...so, I excuse myself from the table, and we go to the office there to talk. Victor, I say, what's the matter? Can't you say hi to your granddaughters? He looks at me and goes, what's the matter with me. I want to know what the matter is with you? So now I'm kinda getting a strange feeling in my stomach. The same one where Neddy would come home from school, eat all the leftovers, and still eat a big dinner, so I ask Victor again what's going on. He says," Joe leans forward to the podium mimicking his mother's earlier position.

He smiles out at the crowd. "He says..." and he starts to laugh.

"I said, is your brother a dumb ass?" Victor Cuzzuto's voice boomed from his seat.

"Yeah, that's what he said. Is your brother a dumb ass? And I told Victor what makes you think so. And he replies--"

"Because he is doing dumb ass things." The whole room erupted in laughter. "You going to tell them what?" Victor smirked.

"Yeah, I'm getting there. You know how Neddy thinks, right those boys were just hungry and their Mama can't cook. My brother thought the guys who stand with signs on the side of the road that says will work for food really want to work. Ok, some do yet we know being in the restaurant business, some just want free food. Anyway, my dumb ass brother goes and rents a minivan, fills it up with these guys, has a dozen pizzas delivered to the job site. I guess Neddy figured he'd feed them and they'd do some work. The guys he brought over start to claim sections of the building as their own by laying down newspapers. When the pizza gets there, let's just say the scene took a different turn." Joe is smiling while Victor and the few others who heard the story double up. "The guys are yelling this is their island and for all the pirates and thieves to stay away. Others are locking themselves in the bathrooms and what will be my office. When someone tried to get in, they yell Mine! Mine! Mine!..."

"Tell them about the king…"

"Oh yeah – thanks, Vic. One of the men kept referring to himself as the king, and all the others would bow as they passed. Ok, so Victor tells me what is going on. I am furious. I'm trying to relax, eat a nice dinner with the family, and now this." Joe brings his hand to his forehead. "I call Neddy. No answer. I leave a message and go back to Angela. In as few words as possible to not upset my girls, who were upset already because nano ignored them."

"I did not ignore them. My princesses know I love them." Both girls turned to beam at their grandfather.

Joe shakes his head. "I explain I need to go to the restaurant, and I think I said I had a pirate problem…"

"Yes, you did," Angela jumped into the story.

"Victor volunteers to go with me because at this point, we both had an interest in what is going on over there. The two of us get to the site. The rented van, along with Neddy's car, is both parked in front. They killed Neddy, I say to Victor, and he says should we get more guys. I think for a minute, and we decide to check the place out first, so we walk around the side of the building, where the big window is. We look in to see…" Joe bursts out laughing. He tries to compose himself yet can't. Victor is laughing so hard he is holding on to his stomach. Even his escort's lips turned upward. A few others in the know wear smiles.

With a few deep breathes, Joe tries to continue, "So in the window," he holds back his laughter, "Is this huge gold chair…"

"The one now in the front of the restaurant," Angela adds.

"Yeah, exactly. And it's covered with green vines, white flowers, plastic grapes, and sitting high atop this throne is none other than Neddy in a bright purple robe. There are several people around him, music blaring, a long table covered with half-empty foil containers and pizza boxes." Joe inhales deeply. "I look at Vic, and he looks at me like what—"

"Joseph!" Joe smiles at his mother.

"Mama," he replies with a smirk. "We find a way in just as Neddy somehow gets a microphone. He starts saying I am Delicious, the god of wine, women, and song. Vic and I look around. We wonder what he is talking about because there isn't one woman in the place. We leaned against the opposite wall as he continued, you brought me here to make a festival of indulgence come alive. We begin tonight. Neddy swept his hands over the crowd. Confetti drops from the ceiling. Now Vic and I are looking at each other like Holy Crap! I'm wondering where he got the cash to do all this. I'm racking my brain, trying to remember if I gave the stunad full access to the checkbook or just the petty cash. As the confetti falls, all these guys start dancing around to Sister Sledge's *We Are Family* song. They are dressed in bedsheets and not much else. I look at Vic, and he looks at me, and he says, what do you want to do? I look back at Neddy and wonder what I can do at this point. He had a lot of guys dancing around, and to tell you the truth, none appeared quite right. So, we leave. The next day I ask Neddy about it. My brother looks at me like I'm crazy."

"Dude, he says, I hired Victor's crew to come by and do the construction, and then I had this vision. This glorious vision of a club instead of a steak house with blinking lights. A huge dance floor in the middle," Joe looks back at his brother, "and he adds, but we must keep the cow. I ask why Neddy and…" Joe pauses to laugh, "because we are going to call the place *Steak*." The crowd gives a nervous laugh. "Steak, I say. Are you kidding me? Where did this come from?

Now Neddy, with a straight face, always believing his own bullshit says from the pirate king, where else?"

"Tell them what happened next, Joey," Victor smiled.

"I'm getting there, Vic. So, what happened next was Vic, and I went back to the building in the morning, and the place was spotless. No homeless men, no confetti, no speakers were blasting music. There's a big empty, clean room. I looked at Vic, and he back at me, and at the same time, we both said Steak. It was manifest destiny, so to speak." Joe paused again to observe his brother. Eyes closed, hands crossed over his chest, the boy almost appeared normal.

"We opened *Steak* the nightclub with the cow on the dance floor and flashing lights everywhere. This was when Neddy met his second wife. Can I say that, ma?" Lena concurred. "So Neddy's working at the club, he's got a home life, things seemed to be looking up for my big brother." Joe wiped the water from his eyes. "But this is Neddy, so…it was only a matter of time before something happened. You know," Joe shrugged, "this is the charm of my brother. The club started to lose money. Instead of letting him fail, the family went in. We made a few changes like turning it into one of those restaurants during the day and exclusive club around 9ish. Neddy wasn't happy with any of it. He kept insisting the pirate king would be pissed. What he didn't tell anyone was the pirate king would want his cut too." Vic caught Joe's eye. He shook his head from side to side.

Joe paused to catch his wife, making the same gesture. Like father, like daughter. With a deep inhale, "So my big brother has moved on from this crazy life. Neddy," Joe brought his gaze up to the ceiling, "I love ya. I miss you. And I wish you the best…" with that last comment, Joe walked away from the podium. He wrapped his arms around his wife.

"You did good, Joey," she held on tight. "You did good…"

That's the best you got, Joe? I can't believe this. I saved your ass so many times, and this is how you eulogize me?

Ok, so the writer is totally against me! Damn, I knew folks favored Joey, yet this is blatant defamation of character! There are laws against this crap. I was trying to do something for humanity by hiring people who needed jobs. It was a bonus they were also willing to work on the cheap.

Want to hear a secret…the writer would never tell you this because she is biased against me. Yeah, you read that right, the writer hates me.

Could it be I dated her and she didn't make it to the wife list, who knows? The night the pirate king showed up, I think someone spiked the punch. I mean, I saw confetti and cows. I saw all sort of shit, yet in the morning… puff… it was all gone. Which is a blessing for all involved because Delicious is one crazy mother…

Really – you are censoring my clarifications. Are you kidding me?

Joey is the family favorite, obviously. I am the other brother, you know. Mama treats Bruno's son Enzo better than me, and he's not even blood. What's my point? My point was when I was a kid, the boys picked on me because the ladies loved me. Even back then. Those little turds took my lunch because their sisters liked hanging out.

In second grade, it doesn't matter yet in high school...let's just say I did better than Joey in the girl's department. Heh, heh, heh...My brother was our dad's favorite because he played sports. Joe got high grades in school. Me, not so much. I had fun. If I had a dollar for every time, my old man asked why I couldn't more like Joey? Me and Joey competed in everything, yet most of the time, he won. I was glad he didn't want to be a lawyer too, yet he doesn't have the B.S. gift I do. We all have our unique skills. He could never con people. We made a good team.

Steak was the first of its kind, yet does anyone give me credit, no. And you know why?

The evil writer will not pass on the creds. No problem, for now.

Look at Angela – the woman still looks stunning after all these years. She's tough like Mama, yet there is so much more going on there. Back when we were kids, Angela used to hang out with me. We used to smoke behind the stadium during football games. Not just me and her, there was a group of us, yet Ang was the only one in a cheerleader uniform. Use to drive Joey crazy.

He loved her the moment he saw her, so he says. I was thinking about asking her out for real, but before I could, she comes running back under the bleachers and tells us she got a date with Joey Vaffanculo. The girls all squeal as my heart breaks in two.

Joey told me she had asked him out. He just said yes to be polite, yet he knew I had eyes for her. Any way...water under the bridge. Look at them now. Angela is as beautiful now as she was when we were kids. And those girls… Gia is just like her mother. Watch out world! Amelia. She's not as ballsy as her sister, yet it's the quiet ones you need to worry about.

Ah -maybe not. This shows God has a sense of humor, giving Joey two beautiful daughters. I can't wait to sit back and watch as they torture him as teenagers. The older one already started. Heh, heh, heh…I mean, I took the blame yet Joey…See what I mean? Yo – reader! My brother isn't all as he appears. He should tell you about the times I saved his ass, but that wouldn't be Joey. It is always about Joey.

But he has secrets. Big secrets. His father in law keeps an eye on him for many reasons. God forbid he ever gets caught…

Joe's quick departure sent the priest stumbling towards the podium. He cleared his throat while making a grand gesture of glancing down at his wristwatch. He waited for a beat for everyone's attention, "Brother Giuseppe Vittorio Vaffanculo…"

"Una momento…" Lena began to speak, "Ur, one moment. Others wish to speak on Neddy's behalf."

The priest smiled as he moved swiftly to her side. "I realize if we keep going with the stories, you will not leave until morning. The line outside has grown and…"

"And we what?" Lena did not move.

"And I will see who else wants to speak," the priest hung his head as he made his way back to the podium. "Is there anyone else…" his voice commanded attention as a significant line formed down the middle aisle. From his perch, it appeared every person in the room had something to say. He had an engagement tonight. This needed to complete this spectacle, yet he knew enough from the stories he had been warned not to upset any part of this family. He thought about asking mourners to limit their stories. He watched Lena Vaffanculo command the room to think better of it. "Please come up and express your love for Giuseppe..." he gestured to the first person in line.

Amelia saw the long line immediately formed. "I guess Uncle Neddy was loved by lots," her sister snickered.

"Yeah – I bet most want a look in the coffin," she scarfed back. "I haven't met half of these people. Let's hope either Grandma or daddy makes them keep it short." Amelia moved in agreement. She leaned her body against her mother's arm.

"Mama, how long do we need to stay?" she whined.

Angela shifted her body to face the line and muttered something towards the ceiling. "Just a little while longer, love," Angela nudged Joe. He woke with a start.

"Are we done?"

"Hardly," Angela tilted her head towards the line.

An inaudible sound escaped from Joe. "Who are all these people? I recognize a few, yet it looks like everyone in this place wants to speak."

"Possibly, they are trying to appease mama?" Angela silently agreed. "Tadaloocs! There is no..." Angela giggled at her husband's reaction. When they focused back on the podium, wife number one jump the line. Both Joe and Angela caught Mama's eyes narrow. She glanced over at the two, "Really?"

"Oh, this should be epic," Joe said as he leaned back in his chair to enjoy what was sure to be entertainment.

Cloe (Number One)

She darted past the priest to grab on to the podium. The smile faded from her face as she met eyes with Lena Vaffanculo. The two women held their gaze as the congregation silenced. After a beat, the petite blonde began to speak. "Ok, for those who don't know me, my name is Cloe Vaffanculo, and I was married to Neddy first." She deliberately made a move to seek out wives' number two through four to give each a grin of disdain. She surveyed around for almost wife. "We seem to be missing one," she commented. In a clear voice, "Neddy loved me first. He always will love me. I am his first and only true love," A cough from the back of the room sounded like *bullshit*. "Neddy and I met while Neddy was studying law in the city. He was a gorgeous hot undergrad," she glanced back at the coffin, "and I, so, I worked in the city. We met, fell in love, took the train to Atlantic City and got married, all in the same day." Gasps could be heard throughout the chamber.

Cloe got a little glassy-eyed. "It was a bit spontaneous, but I swear we fell in love. I was working the morning shift at the club. The usual losers are sitting at the bar when in walks this gorgeous beast. He sits at the table in front of the stage. Our eyes lock on one another. I got so dizzy I fell off my heels! Seriously I almost broke my neck over this one!"

"Too bad she didn't," Lena muttered loud enough for all to hear.

"Mama!" Lena dismissed the reprimand with a wave of the hand.

"Well anyway, I finish my set and start to go on break when this one cuts off my way to the dressing room. The bouncers don't usually go for it, but for some reason, I waved them off, which is something I never do because let me tell you, there are too many wackos out there." Cloe twisted her finger next to her ear. "Anyway, Neddy offers to buy me breakfast. I laughed in his face. I told him I wouldn't eat the food in here, so he says well then let's go someplace else."

"That was my last set for the shift, I said to wait here. I went in the back, put clothes on, honestly I figured he had left in the four minutes it took me to do all this…"

"Bet it took less to take them off." Angela repositioned herself next to Joe's mother. It seems Enzo and the granddaughters couldn't keep her in line. Again, Lena gave a smile, this time waving off her daughter in law. Angela took Lena's hands in hers. They waited for the next slight.

"…but low and behold, when I walked out, there sat Neddy waiting for me. I got to admit, I was surprised. We went to the diner across the street and had eggs over medium with Italian bread toast. I couldn't believe we ordered the exact same thing! We both had iced tea too. Neddy told me how he was a student, and when I asked why he wasn't in class, he said because he was supposed to be here with me. I thought he was cute."

"After breakfast, we walked around the city a bit. He showed me his place. It was a room with a couple twin beds, a desk, nothing fancy. He explained he had a roommate, but the guy was always at the library, he basically had the room to himself. For some strange reason, I trusted Neddy. I didn't usually do, especially in my profession, because you never know what you are going get. Yet, Neddy was," Cloe paused to stare back at the casket, "Neddy was calm, yeah, calm. We sat and talked. He told me all about you all, especially his mom. He kept saying how much he wanted to make her proud." Lena made an inaudible noise similar to her son's. "I just fell in love with him because who doesn't want to make their mother proud. It was me who made the first move…"

"Surprise, surprise…" Lena muttered. Angela squeezed Lena's hands.

"I couldn't resist his lips, and I knew he's never come on to me…"

"If only she knew that was how he got all the girls," Joe leaned to whisper in Angela's ear.

"I went for it and wow! This was one of those kisses where you see sparkles dancing in front of your eyes. You just want it to last forever because when the kiss is over, you are

left breathless, dizzy even. It was amazing." She glanced at the priest, "You know what I mean?"

"Uncle Neddy kissed me, and it wasn't that great," Amelia whispered.

"Different kind of kiss," Gia smiled.

"Yeah, after our first kiss Neddy told me he loved me, so I said well if you love me, marry me and, well, he did. We took the train down later in the afternoon, I think it was the 3:09. We were married in a little chapel in the middle of Trump's place. Neddy rented a tux and me a dress. We got a honeymoon suite at the hotel. They played *Love Me Tender* for our song. It was meant to be because when they opened up the music folder for us to pick, we both pointed to the song at the same time. It was crazy! After we were married, we went upstairs and well…To me, this is the definition of a soul mate." She held her chin up triumphantly as the room went silent.

"Now I know why there was a Trump charge on his credit card," Joe shook his head. "He told me it was part of a project for school."

"It is a romantic story," Angela sniffed back. Joe was surprised to catch a glimpse of his wife taken with Cloe's story. The two never got along.

"We lived in a little apartment near his school. Eventually, we moved out near his parents. It was really important to Neddy to be near his family. They were his rock." The room fell silent. "I couldn't give him babies, we decided to adopt, yet it didn't work out too well for us because he didn't want a foreign kid. I guess I didn't either. It is tough to get an Italian kid. You have to worry about where in Italy, to quote my mother in law, his people are from, Let's just say it is all very complicated."

Cloe smudged mascara across her cheek as she wiped away a tear from her right eye. "It was hard…" she coughed back another tear. "After a while, Neddy found someone else. That someone else could give him babies, he left me…" Cloe twisted to survey her ex. She noted he had on the grin that always met trouble for those closest. "Neddy haunted me for years, especially with the occasional late-night telephone calls. Yeah – we kept in touch. He didn't call to hook up, although I know most of you are thinking otherwise. He called to talk or because he was high, or I don't know. One minute the phone would be waking me up. The next, my husband would be getting up for work."

She took in a deep breath before continuing, "Yeah, I married a really nice guy after Neddy left me," she bit her bottom lip, "ok, after a few years after Neddy left. Before I was kind of…" Cloe let the thought float out into the room. "My husband understood, sort of, Neddy wanted to talk. The few times we were all together, it seemed to be ok with both of them." Cloe turned back towards the casket. "Neddy, I will always love you. I know someday we will be together again." She blew a kiss, turned, and walked towards the family. She wondered why soon to be number five's seat was still empty, yet Cloe took a moment to hug each person and whisper, "I'm sorry," in every ear.

After she hugged Angela, without turning around, she walked towards the exit and disappeared into the sunlight.

Now I know what you people are thinking. You're getting all judging on me wondering why I married a woman like Cloe. There are a couple things this writer, and I use the term writer loosely, isn't telling you. First, let me say Cloe is a great person, a little needy, yet a great person. But who am I to talk, right? I mean, look at the position I'm in now. If she wasn't great, I wouldn't marry her. Bottom line…

Now let's talk about Cloe. I can't believe this stunad of a writer didn't tell you this! The reason Mama didn't like Cloe had nothing to do with her not being Italian or her last occupation. Yeah, I know, that is what he wants you to think. (Or she – I'm not sure about the writer…) Mama didn't like Cloe because she was married to me. I'm explaining the reality of the situation. Mama wouldn't care if I married Sinatra's daughter, she'd still hate the woman, or at least make her life miserable.

My brother Joey acts like he's the favorite cause he wants you to believe he's the one, yeah for our dead father, God rest his soul, but trust me on this, I am and will always be my mother's favorite child. Sorry…the end. No woman will ever be good enough for me.

Cloe may not be the reincarnation of DiVinci if you understand my meaning. Still, she has an uncanny way of knowing just what to say to make things better. Let me give an example; After we got married, I was nervous about meeting the family. I didn't have regrets. I was picturing the scene, and well, you've met them. This could go in many directions. I really wanted the family to like Cloe like they liked Angela.

Come on, reader, don't roll your eyes, you can see why – my family is crazy! In case you didn't notice, they married into crazy. Neddy nods towards Angela.

You get the picture. The best thing Cloe said when we headed down to meet them was, "Neddy, if they don't like me, then you can leave me. I will understand. Family is important to you." She brought tears to my eyes. That is the kindest thing anyone had ever said to me. She knew how important the family is to me. She was willing to walk away from our marriage. She even cried as she said it. Cloe just made me love her even more.

Come to find out the family was mostly ok with her. Cloe tried to learn from Mama the basics, you know, cooking, cleaning, all the stuff her mother never taught. Come to think of it, I never met Cloe's mom. She lived in Florida somewhere. Cloe always said she wasn't worth the trip. Being that my family is really tight, I ever wondered about hers.

Cloe also did her best to keep the marriage together even after the incident with number two. I'm sure you'll hear from her. Cloe offered to go to therapy if I thought it would help. At that point, I wanted out of the marriage. You know how it is.

Huh – thinking about this now, I guess I was the…hey wait a minute. Readers, see what the writer is doing! Why didn't I see this sooner? He or she is trying to get me to feel bad, trying to get you guys to think bad things about me. Let me say, don't let the writer manipulate your thoughts! I am a decent person. I gave Cloe a place to live after we split. I paid all her bills until she got back on her feet. At least I think I did. Joey had taken over the books for the business because I went on a hiatus of sorts…

Wait – he's doing it again. Damn writer!

Wind (Number Two)

Before the priest could maneuver back to the podium, a generously proportioned woman dressed in a flowing purple robe accented with several bright colored scarves, silver bracelets, long sparkling earrings, flew from the front row to the start of the line. She pushed her way to the podium. Those were waiting stunned by the spectacle. The woman squints her eyes in Lena's direction before inhaling deeply. She had waited over a decade for this moment.

With a deep breath in, "Hello. My name is Wind Vaffanculo, Namaste". She bowed her hands in prayer position. "In a past life, I was married to Neddy, and in this life, well, we were spiritually and physically entwined briefly." She waited for her words to sink in. "Lena Vaffanculo refers to me as number two," She shrugged. A few laughs came through the distance. "Neddy and I met at *Steak* one night. I am there in the physical sense with a couple girlfriends. That night a God strolled over to our table. He's tall, muscular, and for me, he had the right package. He tried to talk to one of my friends, yet the moment I locked eyes, I knew he was mine."

"A few things you should know about me. I may not be the most beautiful or posses the best body, yet I am a raging goddess in the bedroom". Wind paused a moment. She shut her eyes, took in a deep inhale. The release caused those close to jump. "As the moon rose, my spirit guide whispered to me Neddy *is* the one to sear the goddess a chosen one, after he went through all the other prospects, I took his hand to lead him back to my place. I did not ask anything about him. My spirit guide told me not to. I proceeded to light candles, spray patchouli, turn the lights down. We did a sacred ritual. We smoked some weed, or we might have eaten some out of the ordinary mushrooms, I'm not sure, it doesn't matter either way."

"What's special about some mushrooms?" Lena asked a smiling Enzo.

"My spirit guide took us both on a journey similar to the one he is now on. We explored the cosmos. We explored each other. We licked and sucked and drank up our nectar, and when we finished, we created what my spiritual guide referred to as the perfect being. One without flaws or judgments…"

Breezy's eyes burst open. She turned to stare at Harry. "Are you ok babe," he asked. His brow furrowed.

"Something is off though I can't figure out what."

"Is it the baby?"

"No, but she is kicking up a storm. She feels it too." Wind's voice came echoing through the room. The baby whacked her foot hard against the inside of Breezy's stomach. "Oh."

"Oh?" Harry asked.

"Mother," Breezy responded as she wiggled in the chair to stand. "We need to move closer." Harry winced. "Besides, I need to pee." The crowd parted around her as the couple made their way to the restroom. From his vantage point, Harry could see what would be his mother in law standing at the podium, almost preaching. When she said something about giving birth to perfection, he cringed.

This can't be good, he thought. *I must protect Breezy and the baby.* Harry moved closer for a better view. Wind appeared as he remembered, somewhere between the outer space, a hippie convention, and the Key West freak festival. "Neddy and I made a perfect being, yet in this human world, perfection sometimes gets mislead." Wind let her gaze fall on each of the Vaffanculo family. She did not move until they repositioned their focus. "Neddy was perfect when we met, yet along our journey, he became easily swayed by others into other places. Neddy would go off to gatherings for weeks, sometimes months at a time. He would visit the cosmos. He would forget he had an earthbound soul who needed tending. Neddy could not be corralled like a tamed horse, he needed to run free in the wilds." Wind raised her arms up to the heavens. Her sleeves were sliding back to reveal faded roses weaving up both arms. Around her neck, scarves moved with each breath.

She was a sight. Breezy stood next to Harry. "Yesch!" Breezy exclaimed. Harry smiled. She sounded like her Grandma. With a wave of her, hand Breezy lead Harry around the other side of the room, staying out of her mother's sightline. They leaned against a wall that brought her closer to her grandmother. Breezy whispered, "Grandma," She waited as the old lady turned to catch her eye. Their bond was extraordinary; both hers and Neddy's and her grandmother's. The rest, well, Breezy didn't want to put those kinds of thoughts out into the universe, at least not at her father's wake.

She closed her eyes to focus more on her mother's voice. *I hope I never end up like her. You never will,* her grandmother whisper back.

"When Neddy and I got back from Pluto the second time, not the first…" Wind rested her hand on her stomach at the same moment Breezy's baby kicked, "we settled into a nice little hamlet. We were happy, delighted. We decided it would be best not to be in the family complex. We needed space both physically and mentally from Neddy's family demands," Wind emphasized the word family, "we needed to bond with our perfect being."

"Unfortunately, Neddy needed to run the business here, we were never too far away."

"If Neddy actually ran the business…" Angela hushed him.

"Now Neddy is back in the cosmos," Wind winked at Lena, "we can all be sure someone or some being is looking out for us in this infinite universe. I hope Neddy ends up back on Pluto we may visit, although Saturn is nicer this time of year. He can visit the rings, swim in the stars. That is always fun." Wind gazed off into the distance. "Either way, I am looking forward to experiencing Neddy in another dimension. We can be together again without all the distractions. The way we are supposed to be one."

Wind command the audience, yet she faltered at times. Angela caught her wink at Lena. *Does she know?* She shook off the thought. She barely knew what was going on in the real world, never mind Neddy's. Wind danced around the casket. Every few minutes, she stopped to touch Neddy's folded hands. After a few convulsions, Wind threw her own up in the air while spinning in circles. The Vaffanculo family sat stunned at the spectacle.

"Where does your brother find these women?" Angela asked, a speechless Joe.

The priest grew paler with each turn. The woman gyrated, and ground around his alter. He muttered, "There has to be a rule against this," yet damn if he could remember one. Lena stared expressionlessly. *If anyone is going to stop the crazy lady, this one should. If I get involved…*

Lena stood then shouted, "Enough!" Wind froze mid-spin while the room became silent. "You did enough when you were married to my son. You're a botta compito." Lena's comment got a few signs of the cross yet mostly snickers. "You are being disrespectful to my Neddy again. You must leave! Now!" She pointed towards the door.

Wind stood still. She scanned the room, held her gaze with each family member. She descended the stairs, walked over to where Lena stood and embraced her. "I know," she said loud enough for only Lena to hear.

Lena showed no reaction as Wind made her way up the aisle to vanish out the door. "My lovelies," she addressed her granddaughters, "go downstairs where the food is. Sneak your nana a few more cookies."

"Mom will be mad," Amelia responded as Gia pulled her towards the stairs. Angela slid next to her mother in law.

"Mama?"

"I sent them for more cookies," Angela frowned. "Itsa ok. The dingbat said she knows, though Ima not sure about what." Lena felt a presence on her other side. "We must protect Breezy," she instructed as she turned towards her eldest grandchild.

"Hello, nana," Breezy leaned in for a kiss.

"Oh, my bambino! Look at my baby," Lena exclaimed. She hugged her granddaughter tight. "How are you? Where is Harry?" Harry waved from the side. His eyes wavered between Breezy, and the door Wind had exited.

"Is the nut job gone?"

"Oh, my Breezy – so disrespectful. True," Lena held up a gnarly finger to scold, "but disrespectful. We must always respect our elders." Breezy leaned her body into her grandmother's waiting arms. She smiled in the direction of Joe and Angela, who both returned her grin. Angela whispered something in Joe's ear. He rose. With a head nod to Victor, both exited. "Angela?"

"Men's room." A parade of people made their way up to the podium. Some thanked Neddy and the family for their help while others expressed condolences for the loss. Angela wondered why people couldn't follow instructions. Saying condolences in a public forum can't be necessary, yet once one started, the line grew.

Her father had disappeared with Joe, although his two escorts remained. "Bathroom my ass," she muttered as she stood. "I'm going to find the girls," she said to no one.

Gia and Amelia walked around the long table covered with food. "Gia, they made my favorite," Amelia pointed towards the round ceramic dish filled with gnocchi.

"Too bad, we are never eating."

"What do you mean?"

"Did you notice the line? All those people want to talk about Uncle Neddy, and they are going to want to eat too. We are never eating." Gia skipped around the table. "There are no desserts out."

"So," Amelia shoved a handful of gnocchi in her mouth.

"You are gross." Her sister grinned, tomato sauce dripping down her cheek. Gia handed her a napkin and kept looking. "Grandma wants more cookies. They got to be here somewhere."

"Try the kitchen." Voices echoed down the hall. Both girls went into the kitchen then ducked behind the pass-through. After a moment, Amelia whispered, "Sounds like dad and nano," to which she got a nod.

"Do you think she knows about…" Joe asked.

"Who knows! It could be Neddy. It could be the baby. There are too many secrets," Victor responded. Gia mouthed What about Uncle Neddy? To which Amelia shrugged.

"How long does the sleepy juice last?"

"We should be ok for about another hour or two. I'll try to persuade Gene to move the line along."

"Glad you are thinking. Could someone…"

"Already done, my son."

"Vic, I always liked your style." The two men's laughter faded as the girls stood up.

"What do you think they were talking about?" Amelia inquired.

"Who knows! Find the damn cookies — "

"Gia Enzo Victoria Vaffanculo, what did you just say?" The girls turned to their mother's thin shadow fill the entire doorway.

"I asked where the cookies are. Grandma — "

"I know what your nana wanted." Angela reached into one of the several bakery boxes stacked on the side of the refrigerator. She took out a handful of cookies then went back for more. "Hold your hands out," she instructed as she piled on the pignoli cookies. "Take some to your nana and Breezy. Then make sure to give Enzo and Nano a few."

"What about daddy?"

"Daddy can get his own cookies. Now andare!" Gia and Amelia darted out the door. Angela opened the refrigerator door, leaned in to pull back the plastic wrap on a plate of cannoli.

"Is it bad?" she turned towards her husband's voice as she took a bite of the sweet cheese-filled pastry. Joe leaned down to kiss his bride.

"No – I guess not," Angela managed to get out in between bites. "These girls—"

"I saw them leave. Do you think they heard?"

"Probably." Joe helped himself to a pastry as she went back for seconds. Powdered sugar streamed down his black suit and her dress. Angela wet a paper towel to brush the substance off both. "They'll be ok. They know not to ask.

"We should go back."

"We should."

"How many more?"

"Too many. Plus, number five is missing."

"Missing?"

"Yeah, as in not here. Don't worry, she'll show."

"Are you worried about Wind?"

"Nope," Joe threw his arm around his wife's shoulder. "Not at all."

"Daddy?"

"Daddy."

Ah, Wind. Now there is a character. The writer didn't do the woman justice because my friend, Wind, can only be described as an all-out whack job. Yeah, whack job...I think that is the right term. The gal is certifiable! Crazy! I guess she spiked my coffee with something the entire time we were together because once I ventured off by myself...

Anyway – she's a piece of work. The family hated her, probably because she kept them at bay. What she did was actually impressive. See Mama would call, and Wind would be all sweet and such on the phone so Mama would invite us over for a meal. You know how Mama likes to cook for crowds. Wind would say yes, then call back after a while to say I was working or something, and we couldn't make it. She would always add, "Maybe next time," leaving hope for a visit.

I don't know what she was thinking because I worked for the family. Mama would see if I was there or not by calling the restaurant. Obviously, I was never there because if Mama saw me, she wouldn't worry. Wait – who am I kidding? If Mama saw me, she would worry big time.

I was a mess. That's why I couldn't be around my Breezy – I didn't want to mess her up too.

Back to Wind…it was after one of her retreats, and I use the word retreat loosely, I figured out something was weird between us. We went up to Vermont to a gathering. This gathering took place in the Green Mountain National Forest. Beautiful place, lots of trees, you know, nature stuff.

We go to this gathering, and there are a lot of people. I mean a lot. People everywhere! Some were normal, again I use the word loosely, yet most were just out there. There was one group who only ate kale, but not any kale. They came to the park a month early to plant the kale. This gets better – one person spent the entire month camping by the kale, talking to the kale. The week before the retreat, they had a ceremony to explained to the kale why it had to die. There was a ceremony for everything at these things!

This group only eats their kale raw. They go there each morning, sit in a circle surrounding the field, each person apologizes for killing their piece of kale. This continues until everyone ate. Eventually, they invite others to eat too. But if you choose to indulge, you must apologize for killing the plant. I made the mistake of taking a leaf handed to me. My god – you'd think I farted in their circle.

Wind was mortified! She dragged me away before the kale mob could take their revenge. I don't know what they'd do, yet I am thinking leafing me to death. Oh man, after the lecture. Wind explained for hours how I embarrassed her and the family. The kale people are essential to our journey. They bring peace to our planet. Blah, blah, blah!

I think that was when Wind started to pull back on whatever she was slipping me. She told me I needed to stop *drinking her special tea for a few weeks to clarify my soul. After a week, I took off. I got in my car one night, and I just drove. Not sure where I ended up. This is how I knew she was a witch or at least had special powers. I'm sitting at a bar in some tiny town, I don't know where drinking a beer. The bartender hands me the phone, I say What, my usual way to answer. I hear Wind on the other end. She tells me to stop polluting my aura then she hangs up.*

I'm like holy shit! I freaked out and got the heck out of there. The woman is crazy!

Now hears the best part – Wind and I were never officially married, when I left her...I know everyone calls her Number Two, I guess when you make a kid together, she counts for something. Yeah – I left, and Mama somehow got Breezy.

I never question the power of Mama. When I came back, I moved to the third floor. I came home one day from work, the second bedroom is bright pink filled with stuffed animals, dolls, and a canopy bed. I walked down the two flights to ask what the heck. There in the kitchen is Mama and Breezy making pasta.

My gal gives me the biggest smile. "She's going to stay with us," Mama states. End of discussion. Wind would visit every couple of weeks. She sometimes took Breezy overnight. Mama made sure I was at work or anywhere else but her house when Wind blew in.

I never asked why or how...

Now I'm going to be a grandpa. How cool of a grandpa, am I! We had a family meeting. There Breezy was the one who decided she had to keep Wind away. I'm not even sure she knows about the baby, yet one never knows what she knows, if you know what I mean? If Wind would stay away, that would be best. I like Harry, my son in law. He'll do right by Breezy, probably better than I did as her father.

Breezy (The Daughter)

Lena half-listened to the condolences being offered. She gestured with her free hand as each ended, meeting each mourner's face as they exited the alter. She muttered the occasional "Thank you," yet for the most part, a wave of the hand is all the speaker received back. In between speakers, she received a squeeze of her hand from some of her favorites, a shrug of the shoulders always accompanied a slow shake of the head. Lena would offer a nod and shrug back.

"Breezy,"

"Yes, Nana?"

"Why don't you go speak about your father?" Breezy looked down at her protruding stomach. "Itsa okay. The crazy lady is gone."

"Are you sure, Nana?" Lena took Breezy's hand in hers.

"Tell a story from when you were little." Breezy glanced back at Harry, standing guard against the wall. "Breezy, I would not put you and the bambino in harm's way. I promise." Breezy pushes herself to stand position. She caught Harry's eye as he mouthed, "Are you sure?" Breezy used the same shrug gesture as her grandmother as she motioned with her head towards where Lena sat. Harry returned the nod.

His love wobble to the front of the line. She politely waited for the person speaking to finish, before moving towards the podium.

"My condolences," an older man said while exiting. She did not recognize him, Breezy repeated the hand movement she had seen her grandmother do. Her stomach gave a loud growl as her cousins return with handfuls of cookies.

"Damn," she muttered. "Save me some of those," she said loud enough for all to hear. Breezy got the attention of the full congregation, most had zoned out in hush conversations during the interval between family members. Two in the middle sat with pens poised ready to take notes. *I wonder if Nana saw them?* As if she is having a real conversation answered her own question with, *of course, she has.*

"Hi," her voice sounded weak. "Hi, my name is Breeze Rain Franchesca Vaffanculo, or as some of you may know me. Breezy. I am Neddy's only daughter." She waited for a beat for the fact to sink in. "I assume most of you knew yet I felt like I had to say it for those who didn't. My mother," Breezy kept an eye on the exit, "was wife number two. You just saw her, the whack job." This got her audience nodding with agreement.

"My nana thought it would be good for me to tell a few stories about my dad, and as most of you know, when nana asks you to do something..." Lena beams up at her eldest grandchild. "My dad – Neddy to most of you. My dad was a really decent guy. He would do anything for anyone. I know a lot of people say that yet with my dad, it was true." Breezy stumbled a little. Lena gestured for her to continue.

"The first time I remember meeting my dad, I was three or four. I see the confusion on many of your faces. My mom, number two, liked to move around a lot, and my dad got caught up in all her weirdness. They would go to yoga retreats and gatherings of, oh wait, I should use her phrase, oh yeah, like-minded people. Yeah, that was it. My mom would encourage my dad to take off then she'd take me to these places. It was a strange but fun place to be a kid."

"I'm out in the woods playing with my red ball, and this guy walks up. He calls me by my name. I knew who he is right away. Dad swooped me up in his arms, spins me around, and I think I puked." A couple people laughed. "Dad brought me back here to meet the family. My favorite part was when I met my nana because she gave me cookies." Breezy smiled at Lena. She envied her cousins as they stuffed pignoli cookies into their mouths. Her stomach growled. "I really love those cookies." Both stopped chewing.

"After a while, my dad and mom went their separate ways. That was okay. Nana came to our house one day. She told me I was going to live with them for a while because I had to learn to make pasta. Both were very important to me. Nana decorated a room in daddy's apartment for me. It was bright pink. Nana made sure I had every toy, or at least it seemed that way to me. Thank you, nana," Breezy glowed. "I am glad I grew up here because I went to church and school and got dance lessons. The best part, though, was Sunday dinner. For years, nana and I and Amelia and Gia too. We would all get together at nana's. She'd get a giant pot of sauce going before we left for church. We'd come back to make the pasta and stuff. Dad always made sure not to work on Sundays. As a matter of fact, neither did Uncle Joe, so the restaurant must be closed."

Breezy turned towards the casket. "Doesn't matter. Dad got really excited to become a grandpa. He and my guy get along great." She felt the baby kick. A tear made its way down Breezy's cheek.

"My last memory is when my dad stopped by our place last week. He shows up in one of those big contractor pick-up trucks. He pulled into our driveway and laid on the horn. Harry and I came running out like What The Heck! Our dogs are going nuts barking and jumping all over the place. It was crazy!" Breezy smiled.

"I'm about to ask him where he got the truck except dad yells look in the back. Harry and I walk around the truck. In the back in this humongous purple teddy bear. I mean, this thing is bigger than me! Dad says something for my princess. I say, dad, what am I going to do with a big teddy bear. And — " Breezy chokes back tears, " —he says not you – the princess. He points to my stomach." Harry jumped to Breezy's side, "It's okay. I'm okay." She squeezed his hand tight. "So his grandchild already got a big, purple teddy bear — "

"And a cradle," Harry added.

"Oh yeah, and a cradle, the pink dresser from my old room in his apartment. My gosh, there's a whole baby's room set up. My dad took care of us," She smiled up at Harry. Harry kept scanning the room. He locked eyes with the two men taking notes. One diverted, while the other broke into a slow smile. As one smile emerged, Harry's disappeared. "My dad's the best. I just wish— " This time, the tears came fast. Harry embraced Breezy and led her down to her grandmother.

"Was that necessary?"

"Unfortunately, yes. What did you see that disturbed you?"

Harry sighed. Of course, Lena Vaffanculo saw their every move. "Nothing." Lena held her gaze to his. "Just a couple note-takers."

"Already noted," Lena rubbed Breezy's back. "Why don't you take her downstairs. You two can get something to eat. I could hear your stomach from down here. It seems the younger two," Amelia and Gia were dusted in crumbs, "finished off the cookies I had them bring up. Oh, Harry, bring me some pignoli cookies, please."

Harry led Breezy towards the stairs. "Babe, can we please get out of here?" he pleaded.

"No, not yet."

"Babe, I really think we should —"Breezy silenced him with a flick of her wrist.

"Please trust me, Harry. If things play out right, we are going to be free." Breezy loaded her plate up with gnocchi. "Just trust me."

Harry helped himself to a couple meatballs. *Why does anything with this family need to be so complicated?*

"Give me a minute, please, will ya," Neddy choked out. "I just love my kid! I could listen to her for hours."

Man, how did I get so lucky? You'd never know she is the product of the whack job! Yessiree, Breezy is my pride and joy! I got to admit that I was worried when mama brought her home. I wasn't sure I could be the kind of father I needed to be but family, man, my family. They are amazing. Everyone pitched in and helped, especially mama and Angela. I still don't know what kind of deal with the devil mama made, yet she has her ways.

I was lucky, no, I was blessed. And now to be a grandfather! Wow is all I can say! She's got herself a respectable man too. Harry is amazing. I know he wanted to get her out of here before all this crap happened, but Breezy wants to be near family for the baby. Yeah – we may be brainwashed her a little. Mama taught her well. La Famiglia comes first – no matter what.

Obviously, this situation shows we stick together, right? I mean, the writer is at least acknowledging family must come before everything. The writer's an idiot, yet he/she might get this part right. Perhaps she is just getting lucky…

Not sure how Wind is going to fit into all of this. I don't think mama would cut her out of her granddaughter's *life entirely, yet I wonder. I guess she'll arrange supervised visits. Mama would take care of but maybe Harry and Breezy would just instead leave well enough alone.*

Who knows. Breezy did make her appearance after Wind left. I am sure something is up. Eck, who knows, she is just fighting with her mama again!

Oh, wait - look at Harry. He's keeping his distance to scan the room. I wish dipshit and dumbass would get out of here. They need to leave my family alone. I guess all this is partly my fault…okay, mostly my fault. Yet, not my fault at all?

Hey writer, could you eliminate those two. Poison their water or add a shootout outside the church? Oh, wait – that would be bad? I don't want to piss off god and all. I think this would be such a beautiful funeral without them. My family could relax a little. You know, not think about why they are here, maybe say a few nice things about me.

Especially Victor, I mean look at the guy, he's wound tighter than fresh Italian bread after the first kneading! Come on, this could be a nice funeral, everyone could eat some cannoli, eat a little pasta, you could make me look a little better. Get the make-up artist up here to touch up my face a little.

I get the impression she or he is refusing to listen. Instead of focusing on me, I can get double D's to go see about the writer. Now that would be funny. Yeah – they are taking notes on their writing. Making sure only the truth comes out…fact checking as they type. Oh, my now, I am laughing. It is not likely this is what is happening. Of course, if it did… that would be hysterical!

Okay fine. I'll go back to my fabulous daughter. Doesn't she look beautiful? Even with all the fat in the middle, the girl is still gorgeous. Thank god, she got my looks, and she got some brains too. My little girl is smart – she graduated from Columbia in the city. She was going to be a lawyer like her pop.

Now she's going to be a mother, hopefully not like hers.

Either way – my kid is a great person.

"Mama, how long are we going to let this go on?" Angela slipped Lena, another cookie.

"I don't know," she replied in between bites. "Til someone ends it?"

"In an hour?"

"Eh – an hour. Two hours – what does it matter?" Lena brushed crumbs off her dress. "We need to sit until it's over, capisce?"

"Yeah – I get it." Angela glanced at her children. Smarter than they let on, the two appeared to be fading. "I'm going to send the girls home with Enzo," she began, "They can meet us later at the restaurant or whatever." Lena waved Enzo over.

"What's the matter?" Enzo squatted in front.

"Nothing's the matter. You want to get out of here?"

"Mama, you can't leave – "

"Not me, you!" He waited. "Take the kids home. Watch some TV. Oh – and take a plate, you know, in case you get hungry."

"You don't want me to stay?" Enzo repositioned to see past Lena's shoulder to meet his father's eye. Bruno thrust his chin towards Lena.

"Enzo," Lena took his hands in hers, "I want you to do what is best for the family. Right now, it is probably best to take the kids home."

"I agree," Angela blurted. "I would, but I can't leave." She tilted her head towards Joe.

"Okay, I'm happy to help but—"

"Enzo, we appreciate you helping out the family at a time like this."

"No problem, but I swear on my mother's grave something weird is going on here," he said. "I'm not the only one. I heard two people talking in the bathroom. One told the other Neddy doesn't look dead. He looks like he's just sleeping. They creeped me out!" Enzo kept shifting his gaze between Lena and the casket.

"Who were these people?" Lena inquired.

"I don't know. I was in the stall and could only see gold flip flops—"

"Gold flip flops?" Angela shook her head.

"Yes – gold flip flops. And a loud voice. Like the gal had been yelling." Lena and Angela both indicate agreement. "They creeped me out, you know."

"Yeah, I know," Angela took her hand. "It was probably number two. She's a total whack job. I mean, who else would wear gold flip flops to a funeral?"

"Yeah – you are probably right. Anyway, I am happy to take the girls anywhere away from here."

"Good, good," Lena agreed. "Amelia, Gia," Lena waved the girls over, "Enzo is going to take you home. You two have had enough."

"Thank God!" Gia exclaimed.

"Enzo, don't forget to take a plate," she smiled at her granddaughters, "Make sure these two take some of the desserts, you know, a couple cannoli's, a few cookies."

"Thanks, grandma," Gia leaned in to kiss her on the cheek. She hugged her mother.

"Give daddy a kiss on the way out. Try not to be obvious." Amelia followed her sister's displays of affections as both scuttled towards the door. "Enzo, thank you again," Angela squeezed his hand. "For everything," with a wink.

"No problem." Enzo glanced back at the line. "You guys are here for a while."

All three disappeared through the door. Lena smiled up at the person speaking. One of the merchants from the neighborhood talked about Neddy sweeping his store when he was laid up with the flu. Lena approved of the kind stories. Enzo is right. The family is here for a while. Too long for this charade, as far as she is concern.

At least all her grandchildren were safe. Maybe Enzo will catch Breezy and Harry. He could take them to the house too. This will be better than we planned. Things are going to work out. I wish she thought of that sooner. Anyway. Is this guy still talking? She looked down the row. Number three and four sat side by side.

How lovely. Lena wondered where number five to be was? If Neddy was her true love, shouldn't she be here? Lena felt Angela take her hand. At least Joe married first-class. As long as I got this one here and Vic behind me, this will all be okay.

Lena smiled at Angela as she shoved another cookie in her mouth.

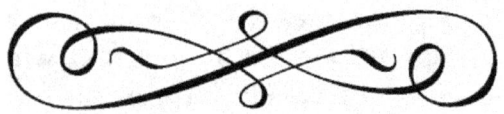

Meg (Number Three)

Number four observed the exchange between her ex-mother and sister in law. "those two were made for each other," she commented to no one.

"Oh, you mean evil one and two," came back from number three. "I always thought if you threw water on them, they would melt." A snicker surfaced from the row behind. "Okay, so let me confess, I actually got along with both, but I was only here a short time. Who's next, you or me?"

"We might as well go in order, so I guess it is you."

"It doesn't matter because I'm sticking around to make sure the cheater is dead and buried, so I am here…"

"Yeah – me too."

"You know, he doesn't look dead, does he?"

Her ex-mother in-law's eyes went black. She visibly shook. "Do we cut the line, or do we need to wait?"

"I think we should cut the line. We suffered enough being married to the jerk."

"You got that right," Number three rose from her chair, ran her hands over her hips to straighten her skirt. The person speaking finished, yet before the next person could get to the steps, she moved to cut her off. "Sorry, I'm next," she muttered as she forced her way to the podium.

"Good afternoon," she waited for people to settle. "My name is Meg Vaffanculo, and I am Neddy's third wife. Mama Lena refers to me as the normal one," Lena blew a kiss in her direction. "Neddy and I met at church. This church actually. I was visiting as part of a mission trip from my church in Minnesota. We were here for two weeks to help set up summer camps for the inner-city youths. I was fresh out of graduate school at the University. I hadn't landed a job yet, so my pastor suggested chaperoning a bunch of teenagers for a couple weeks would give me direction."

Meg turned back towards the casket. *Oh, Neddy. What did you get yourself into this time?* "My first day here, I am greeted by this incredibly striking man who is about my age. I actually thought he was the priest, and God was challenging me." Snickers went through the room. "What did I know? I was a young girl from the Mid-west. We think differently out there. I was shocked when Neddy asked me to dinner. Of course, I politely declined. I was partly responsible for twenty-three teenagers; besides, I had always thought priests couldn't date. A fact I later learned to be true," waves of nervous giggles prevailed through the room.

"Neddy asked me out every day for about three or four days. Every time he asked, I said no. The kids would joke when he showed up, my boyfriend was back," Meg let out an uncomfortable laugh. "I would explain with utmost patience how although both churches are based in Christianity, dating a priest was inappropriate, and their jokes needed to stop. The old priest here actually helped. He told the kids Neddy wasn't a priest. He helped out at the church on his days off. The kids thought Neddy must be a homeless person who worked for food. He seemed to always be on his day off. Back home, the folks who did the gardening, painting, cleaning, and such at our church were all down on their luck. This was the way the church helped them get back on their feet, with dignity, not handouts."

She paused for a moment. "Oh, wait – unless the person couldn't do anything. You know, if they were sick or something. Then the church just provides. We are all human, after all." Lena cleared her throat. "So back to Neddy. Each counselor got one day off during the two weeks. Mine happens to fall on a Sunday, so I attended the first service here, a new experience since I usually attend a different denomination. I sat with the kids than planned on exploring the city a little bit. This was my first visit to the East Coast. After service, the old priest asked what my plans were for the day. I explained I wanted to see the city because this is my first visit to the coast. Neddy popped out of nowhere to volunteer to be my tour guide. I started to decline, yet the priest thought I should have an escort because there are parts of the city that would not be safe."

"I reluctantly agreed. I didn't want people to talk. Looking back, I can admit that it was the best day of my life. Neddy took me to an amusement park. We walked along a beach. You all know how amazing seeing the ocean for the first time can be! Neddy took me to a beautiful park. We ate hot dogs on a bench. I needed to get back, so I thanked him. He asked me out to dinner again. I explained I had no free time left, yet I had enjoyed his company. Fast forward two weeks later, I get a letter addressed to me at my church. And it's from Neddy asking me to dinner. I called him to decline, but when he told me he was coming to Minnesota, I thought it would be rude not to show him the same hospitality he had shown me here."

Meg shrugged at her own thought. "Neddy and I were married for a little under one month. We went out to dinner that night and the next. After a week of dinners, he asked me to marry him. I didn't know about the first two. Actually, I didn't know much about Neddy. I was young. I took a chance. I was naïve and possibly a little stupid." Admitting she showed poor judgment hurt. She had a Ph.D. after all;

a higher degree had to indicate some type of intelligence.

"Mama Lena flew out for our wedding. We met in the church after the ceremony as she gave us her blessing." Meg smiled at her ex-mother-in-law. "It was a nice day. The parents all got along. We had a small party. Neddy, I went to the Wisconsin Dells on our honeymoon. It was all just a dream."

"We got back from the honeymoon, and I moved back East with Neddy. He had the business, and I didn't even have a job, so it all made sense, at least at the time. Our place was right below Joe and Angela's and right above Lena's. Family means a lot to me," Meg coughed out. "A real lot. I am grateful I got to be part of yours, even for a short time." Meg looked back at the casket. She took a moment to gather her thoughts.

With a deep sigh, she continued, "Please don't misunderstand me, I think Neddy is a virtuous person. If he wasn't, I wouldn't have married him in the first place. After a couple weeks together, we both realized we had made a mistake. On a Tuesday in August, I repacked up all my stuff, gave my new mama Lena a hug and kiss, and I moved back to Minnesota. That was it. There was no drama. We both agreed it was for the better. Mama Lena, I am so sorry for your loss," she caught Number Four's, Joe's, and Angela's gaze. "I'm sorry for all of our loss. Deep down, Neddy is, I mean was, a decent human. He had a huge heart. May he rest in peace."

Meg blew a kiss towards the casket as she walked back to her seat. Number Four took her into a hug while Lena reached over to hold her hand.

"You was always my favorite," Lena wept. "No offense," she addressed Number Four.

"None taken," Four whimpered back.

Oh, Meg – she still looks as beautiful as the day I met her. Look at those legs, yowza! Meg is incredible inside and out. She is also a perfect example of how someone with too much education could be incredibly stupid.

Okay – so that was probably mean yet hear me out. Meg is smart, one of the most intelligent people I know. We use to sit around and dissect Shakespeare, compare it to some concept of modern literature. My favorite argument being Stephanie Plum is a modern-day Hamlet. Oh my god – talk about getting Meg going!

If I really wanted an argument, I could bring up some pop culture figures, like Archer. I would make the same comparison. I am a master at taking senseless entertainment and applying whatever is on the screen to the classics. My Archer/Aristotle evaluation was legendary in our house. So much so mama thought we had an all-out fight. She came upstairs to split it up like she used to do with Joey and me.

You should see the expression on her face when she found out we were fighting over Archer. (Laughs) Mama asked, "Who is this Archer?" and when I pointed to the cartoon on the TV, I thought she was going to beat us both!

Meg was good for me. She made me think about things differently. She made me connect things others might not see. And most importantly, she understood the place of the pirate king. She didn't think I was crazy.

I didn't leave the apartment for at least a week after she went back home. I knew we weren't right together. I mean come on – comparing Archer to Aristotle? It would be selfish of me to try to keep her. The funny part and I know my readers will appreciate this, I drew up our divorce papers. Seriously – I did.

(Laughing) You get the irony, right?

Oh, in case you forgot…I'm not a lawyer! (Laughing) I take that back – the state of Connecticut says I am not a lawyer. My mama says I am, and I believe mama first. Crap – the writer is making me look like a mama's boy.

I am not a mama's boy! You've met my mother. She can be scary at times, so I always go with what she says. It makes life easier.

Back to Meg – I really loved her. After a stripper and a freak, I thought I had met Mrs. Right. Meg didn't seem to mind being at home or taking care of me. She always was primped and beautiful. I probably should introduce her to some of my academic friends (laughs), if I had any academic friends!

Damn if she taught until the babies came? With Meg, I am always second-guessing. I guess she is why I lean towards young and dumb now. The less a woman knows, and the better they appear on my arm; you get the picture.

I don't think I'm a dirty old man either. I just think the Cloe's of the world are more comfortable to live with than the Meg's of the world. And no one should need to deal with a Wind for more than one night.

I shutter…

Lena wiped the tears away on her dress sleeve. She let out a deep sigh. *This spectacle needs to end.* As soon as Meg left the podium, the line moved again. The next few skipped the alter to go straight over to Lena. "So, sorry for your loss," whispered with a squeeze of her hand. "Our sincere condolences," accepted with a shrug.

Joe observed as each person visited his mother. Some names came to him easy, while others he had no recognition of. The line moved like a good custard out of a pastry. When someone stepped to the podium, others quietly expressed condolences, return to their seats, or sneak out the back. If Joe didn't want to be here, he would have left long ago. *My babies are so lucky to be able to go.* Another face, another shrug, another thank you. Only Neddy could take up this much of his time with his stupidity.

He glanced behind him. Victor's chair is still empty, yet his two escorts remained. Joe gave the two a quick head nod. Angela sat straight up. His wife gave a slight smile to each mourner then replied with a quiet thank you. She was smart to send the girls home.

"How are you holding up?"

"Mensa mensa."

"Are you hungry?"

God bless this woman. She is just like my mama. Any problem can be solved with a little food. Please don't tell her what I thought. She'd cut my balls off. Seriously. "No honey, I'm fine. I just want this to end."

"Don't worry," she looked back at to where the two men taking notes sat. One was missing. She hoped he had left, and this one would disappear soon too. "It will all be okay. How much time is there left for Neddy?" Angela turned Joe's wrist toward her.

"About another hour. Can we get people to give condolences downstairs? You know, as they come in to eat?" Angela shook her head. "That could work, no?"

"I think [Number Four] wants to speak and of course, my dad—"

"Who's not here..." Angela spun around to follow her gaze. "I don't know when he left."

"He can't be far; Jimmy and Bruno are still here."

"Yeah, I see." Joe focused back on the line. "If Louisa gets up there and talks for a while, Vic would be back by the time she finishes. No one would say anything if he cut the line." Angela instructed. "You go talk to her." Angela made her way to where Neddy's fourth wife sat.

"That was beautiful, Meg," she smiled. "Just beautiful. Louisa, are you going to speak?"

"I was, but now I'm not sure."

"Not to be rude, but when are you going to decide?" Angela barked. "God, I am sorry, Louisa. The family, we are under so much stress. Neddy left a mess behind him, as usual. But hey, I don't need to tell you ladies about Neddy's messes. You lived through enough of them. Anyway, if you are going to speak, the family was hoping you could go next, then my dad will speak, and we can get to the repast." She locked eyes with Louisa.

"Repast? What about the burial?" Meg asked. No one spoke. Angela shifted her body to cut Meg off from the conversation.

"We decided to do the burial privately. So do you think—"

"Just give me a minute to figure out what I am going to say?"

"Sure, sure. Of course. Take your time, but not too much time."

"Five minutes?"

"Five minutes would be perfect." Number Four rose to head towards the hall.

"I think she's hitting the ladies' room," Meg commented. Angela slipped in the seat next to Joe.

"She went to the bathroom," Angela updated. "Said to give her five. Hopefully, daddy will be back then he can direct folks' downstairs." Joe closed his eyes.

Dr. Louisa Vaffanculo (Number Four)

Number Four emerged from the hallway under Angela's watchful eye. She wore a stiff smiled as she passed and proceeded to walk right up to the podium. Resting her arms on the side, Number Four waited for people to reclaim their seats. It didn't take long.

After, a quiet hum followed. Number Four cleared her throat to begin. "Don't worry, I'll be short," she smiled. "My name is Dr. Louisa Vaffanculo, and I am Neddy's fourth and apparently last, wife." She heard a whimper come in the direction of her former mother-in-law. "Neddy and I actually had his only local, normal wedding. Mama Vaffanculo insisted because Neddy deserved at least one wedding amongst the family in the church he grew up in. She and Angela planned the whole event for us. We got married right here, on this alter, in this church. We had our reception downstairs, where even on a day like today, I am certain there are tables covered with gnocchi, sausage, and meatballs, some chicken, some pasta, a few cannoli." She waited for a beat,

"You both did a beautiful job. It was a beautiful day. A fun celebration. Both Neddy and I appreciated everything you two did for us." Angela dabbed her eyes with a tissue.

"Neddy and I met in therapy." Louisa listened as a murmur floated through the room. "Please allow me to clarify; Neddy was in therapy. I was his therapist." The murmur continued, yet she noticed people now leaned forward in the pews. "I know this tale sounds cliché. Neddy was in group therapy for about three months before we started dating. We had an attraction from the start yet, I resisted because," she paused to ponder how to elaborate on her hesitation. Up until now, she appeared clinical, in control. "I resisted because I didn't think a relationship would be the right thing to do. Neddy convinced me otherwise."

"He had a way," Lena said.

"Yes, he did, mama Vaffanculo. I should elaborate. At that time, I was still a resident, working my way towards my M.D. My dissertation involved serial daters and how they were able to seduce women without any conscience. Now one would think with my area of study I would know to run away fast from a person like Neddy. And you would be correct." Louisa took on the stance along with the cadence of a college professor. "Usually, subjects show similar traits. In this case, they cannot visualize the effects of their actions on others. Serial daters see nothing wrong, leaving one love, and they truly believe they are in love for another."

"Concepts like a broken heart or mourning period in between relationships do not exist. This is where Neddy differed. First, when he volunteered for the study, he gave the reason he wanted to understand why he had been married so many times because, in his words, he didn't want to screw up the next one." The last comment got a laugh from the crowd. "I thought it would be a gallant effort on his part. Yes, he was worried he would end up alone. He wrote his purpose being there was to understand his past relationship patterns to hopefully break them. I found this fascinating." Louisa looked back at the casket. She smiled at the memory. When she peered closer, she swore Neddy smiled back.

With a shake of her head, she continued, "You can see this is not normal reasoning as the main attribute is not being about empathy for those around them. Neddy had empathy. He wanted to become a better man. This, I concluded, was a tribute to his raising..." She gestured towards mama Vaffanculo, who nodded back, accepting her compliment. Louisa glanced towards Meg in time to catch an exaggerated eye roll. "...Neddy had empathy. Neddy's problem and this is the technical term, he believed his own bullshit." A hush rolled over the room.

"After the trait of empathy became apparent, Neddy no longer qualified for my study because it became conclusive he could not be a serial dater. There is, however, and after note describing his condition forms a path for further study which will not be conducted by me."

"Neddy and I started dating soon after he was dismissed. He wasn't happy about being dismissed. I later learned he needed the compensation to pay an old debt, I am not sure to whom, yet it was imperative to Neddy this liability be cleared. He did get some compensation for his time, yet it was nowhere near the full twenty thousand dollars for completing the study." The gasp could be heard outside the church. Neddy needed money, and he owed someone twenty grand.

Lena glared in the direction of Meg, "It wasn't me." Angela glanced back in her father's direction. He shook his head no. Behind him, the second of the two note-takers got up and left.

"Neddy and I began our relationship, and six months later, he asked me to marry him. Actually, and this part is comical in a way, Neddy asked every week for the next six months until I finally said yes. He reasoned what difference could it possibly make if we were in love, and he didn't qualify for my study, so his love had to be pure. Even as an academic and future doctor, I fell for this argument. I guess part of Neddy's charm is his persistence."

Louisa took a moment to observe her dead husband. The smile seemed to fade from his face. She wondered if it was her imagination from the start. Neddy was at peace. Of course, she knew anything is possible when it comes to Neddy. She brought her focus to Bruno, who positioned himself to the left of Victor. Bruno brought his hand up to his lips, blew a kiss in her direction.

"I became Dr. Louisa Vaffanculo a year into our marriage. I figured Neddy's name should be on my degree since I had planned to be married only once in this life. My study was met with high praise from my colleagues. Neddy was very supportive. We made up a false meeting for my peers as it would be improper to be in any sort of relationship other than doctor/patient with a subject. Neddy decided he did actually need therapy. He did not share his issues with me, yet I did recommend him to a colleague. This colleague is the one who put Neddy into group therapy for addiction. I did not and still do not believe he was an addict. I diagnosed my husband with several phobias, the worst being a fear of failure that could be numbing at times, yet I repeat, I do not think Neddy was an addict."

"It was here he met the next one." Louisa looked around, surprised to see Number Five missing from the festivities. "Neddy explained his connection to this person went beyond anything he had experienced in the past. He also told me that he did not want to cheat on me and the only right thing to do, while he explored this chance, is to possibly temporarily separate. I wasn't comfortable with this solution, so I decided we needed to get divorced. The divorce actually became final two weeks ago, today. We were estranged for less than a year. I am not proud of the fact an educated woman like myself fell for a man like Neddy. Yet I believe part of Neddy's charm is he actually cares about other humans, and because of this, he needs to reach out and find the best in others. I am not bitter, Neddy, and I spent time together because he brought something positive to my life as he did to everyone here."

Louisa blew a kiss towards the casket and proceeded to her seat. Mama Vaffanculo embraced her in a hug. "Thank you."

"This is it." Mama Vaffanculo leaned back and moved up and down affirmatively. Upon seeing the gesture, Louisa relaxed a bit. "Thank heavens," she said to no one. She turned to catch Bruno and allowed her lips to give a slight smile in his direction. Her nightmare was almost over.

The exchange between her mother and ex-sister-in-law Number Four went on a little too long for Angela's liking. Louisa played the part well. For not the first time, she wished Neddy and Louisa had lasted. At least she wouldn't indulge her in this mockery of a funeral.

Some of the congregation had left, while others continued to offer their condolences to the family matriarch. Her father sat, waiting. He is to be the last speaker. One gentleman taking notes remained. She noticed the other partner had disappeared sometime during Number Four's speech.

Angela hoped her dad had taken note too. She caught Victor's gaze and gestured toward the podium. He held up one finger.

"What the heck is he waiting for?" Joe glanced over his wife's shoulder.

"He must see something we are missing." Angela rubbed her hands together. Joe took both into his. "We are in the home stretch. The only no-show is the latest." He stood and looked around the room. "As far as I can tell, the other whack job is missing in action." He sat. "Homestretch, baby," Joe leaned in to kiss his wife.

"Let's hope this is finally over."

Victor surveyed the interchange between his daughter and her husband. How could one idiot brother bring so much on their family while the other always seems to make the right decision? He looked back to see one of the note-takers still present and attentive.

"Where did dumb ass number one go," he whispered.

"The guys are following him. He left and headed down Main towards the restaurant. We got an eye on him."

"Good. Let's keep it that way." Victor fixed his tie and jacket. "It's showtime, boys." He walked with purpose towards the alter, stopping only to kiss Lena on the cheek. The line parted as he made his way to the podium. As the family predicted, the line for condolences disappeared, as those waiting found seats. Angela smiled up at her father.

With a cough, Victor began, "My name is Victor Cuzzuto. My beautiful daughter, Angela, is married to Giuseppe's brother Joseph." He waited for a beat before continuing, "Giuseppe, he's an interesting man. Joseph told the story about the pirate king earlier, yet that was not Giuseppe's only downfall. He married lots of women. Most are here with us. Giuseppe made a few mistakes in business," with this comment, Victor looked directly at the note taker. The man fidgeted in his seat as he exchanged glances with the back door.

"Even Giuseppe's mama confessed here on the alter Giuseppe was a bit...ah Lena, what did you say?"

"He's a toolbox."

"Grazie, Lena. Yes, Giuseppe's a toolbox." Victor turned back towards the casket to notice Neddy's middle finger is repositioned, He bursts out laughing. "Yes, Giuseppe is a toolbox, but he is our toolbox, right?" The congregation snickered. Victor's attention stayed focused on the back door. "okay, so now we got that straight I'd like to share how much Giuseppe, er, Neddy will be missed. Neddy was like a son to me. I looked after him after my dear friend, his father passed, Actually, I looked after the whole family. Neddy's father, Giuseppe, made me promise, and I kept my promise." Victor laughs again. "Joseph, I hate to tell you this, but your papa and I planned for Neddy and Angela to be married."

"Ewe!"

"Oh my dearest, I am so happy you and Joseph found each other. That is what makes mine and Giuseppe's plan so outrageous. Anyway, no matter. So Neddy was like my son. Since my beautiful daughter didn't really get into any mischief, Neddy was my challenging son. I can't tell you how many times we had to bail this kid out. Some days I thought it would never end."

"Anyway, I thought Neddy actually had got it all together when he married Meg. He did seem happy…" Meg had tears formed in her eyes. "And when he married you, Louisa, you seemed to get his demons under control," Louisa's tears followed Meg's. "The first two, eh! The only thing to come out of those two that is positive is Breezy. Thank heavens, the kid was smart enough to go off on her own."

Lena scanned the room for Breezy. *She must still be eating. Good for the baby.* Victor continued on. "There are times in Neddy's life when he is at peace. The prior mentioned, along with Lena, Joseph, Angela, and our princesses, brought Neddy peace. The other stuff," now Victor glared at the note-taking and did not waver. People turned to see who is getting his wrath. "The other stuff doesn't matter anymore. Not at all!" The congregation jumped as Victor's hand hit the podium. The priest awoke from his slumber in the corner.

"Neddy, er, Giuseppe, he made the lives of those around him better. We are all better people for knowing and loving Neddy."

Victor stepped down from the podium. He gave a quick wink to Angela as he bent over to kiss Lena's cheek. "That was beautiful, Vic."

"Let's hope this all works," Vic glanced back towards the casket. "Your idiot son gave me the finger while I was talking."

Lena looked to the casket with disgust. Leave it to Neddy to not appreciate a fiasco he alone had caused.

Damn Victor! You almost gave away the house. What an idiot, and he is supposed to be the smart one. Yeesh! Wouldn't you think a big-wig like Victor would know the concept of discretion? Man...I really should negotiate preapproval on his future speech. I wonder if he saw my middle finger go up?

Hee. Hee. Hee. Bet you all my winnings the coffin was his idea to make me learn a lesson. The lesson ha! These idiots do not understand the power of the pirate king!

The pirate king is a badass! I can't open my eyes, yet I am dying, no pun intended, to find out if this actually worked. I wonder if the king's men actually showed. They would try to be discreet, you know, fit into this crowd, yet knowing the kind of guys the king hired, something would be off a little. I can't tell you what, since I'm, you know, guest of honor, yet if the damn writer would pan the audience, you, my fair reader, would figure out who does not belong.

Figure these people would be rude and avoid extending condolences. Maybe they're dressed a bit different – hey, do you see any cheap knock off suits out there? Except for cousin Jimmy because his part of the family stayed out of the business. Still, everybody else should at least be in Armani. So, you know, cousin Jimmy is probably missing a tie. If his mama, my aunt Lulu (her real name is Maria, but nobody calls her that) dressed him, his hair should be tied back in one of those man buns, so it fools people into thinking he got it cut, but he didn't.

Cousin Jimmy – that guy cracks me up!

So what the hell is Vic doing now? I can hear people talking to mama. Yeah – condolences back at ya! Wait, who's speaking? Yo – readers…is Vic talking to the priest? Yeah? What's he saying? No problem, I can wait…guess Vic is using his inside voice. Probably telling the priest what to do. Vic likes to be in charge. I should be more agreeable to Vic because he kinda saved my ass, if you know what I mean…and at this point you're pretty intelligent, you probably do.

That was pretty interesting the thing about Ang and me. She is terrific arm candy, yet the woman is high maintenance. I mean HIGH MAINTENANCE! Joey, he's better at humoring her than I would be, and if we did get together – yeesh – she'd be number what? Two, or three? I don't think being one of many would go over well.

Oh – but dear readers, we wouldn't be conversing because if anyone hurt Victor Cuzzuto's daughter or worst if you personally pissed off Victor Cuzzuto's daughter… Has she done the look today? Angela got this expression where her eyes go from full of love to weapons of mass destruction. Haha, Bush should have had the Marines search Connecticut instead of Iraq. Here lives his worst fear. One look from that woman, and you knew you were dead. Dead, I tell you. Her beautiful baby blues would turn black.

Her face set hard, and her body stiff. The terrifying part is when she shuts up –you know you are fu –

What? Oh, I'm sorry! She got the attitude from somewhere. The only child of Victor Cuzzuto, I am sure, contributes. Her mama left her back in grade school. Nobody knows where she went – she just left. So, from then on, Vic was her sole parent.

Do you think Joey ever gets the look? Or mama? Oh, my (giggles) Angela is giving my Mama the death stare. Or better yet – teaching her the power of the death stare. Oh, wait…my mama already knows the power of the look.

Imagine if they teamed up. Hum…talk about a scary duet! Actually, mama and Angela seem to get along well. I wonder if she and I got together if they'd be as thick? My ladies and my mother seem to have, oh, what is the right word, oh yeah – issues. All the women in my life with issues. (Laughs and coughs).

Do you think when I see Joey again, I should bring up the me and Angela thing?

Vic straightened his tie and distended from the podium. He walked in a straight path to Lena and embraced her in a hug. "I am sorry for your loss," he said the words loud enough for half the congregation to hear.

"End this fiasco," Lena whispered in his ear, adding, "Thank you, Victor. And thank you for your kind words on behalf of Neddy." The later said so loud it repeated throughout the room. "Wake up the priest and let's go," she directed towards Victor.

Victor broke the embrace to walk back up the stairs. The person speaking stopped midsentence, yet Vic waved his hands up for him to continue. As Victor continued towards the sleeping priest, he heard a hurried, "Condolences to the Vaffanculo famiglia."

"Wake up, father," Victor nudged the sleeping form. The body shuttered as Victor glared into the now open wide eyes of the priest.

"Name of the father…"

"Yeah, yeah, yeah," Victor motioned with his hand. "The family would appreciate it if you could cut off the line and give final words. Direct people downstairs, to you know, eat a little, and we can be done." When he said done, the priest jumped up.

"No problem, Mr. Cuzzuto. Would any of the Vaffanculo like to read a passage?"

"Not at this time, father," Victor's lips turned up into a grin, "I think God heard enough about Neddy Vaffanculo, don't you?"

The priest motioned. He made his way over to the podium.

Rayleigh (Number Five To Be)

"Does anyone else wish to speak?" The priest rested his hands on both sides of the podium. He took a deep breath in...

"I do" A cold streak descended down Angela's spine as each click of the stiletto heels drew closer. Joe glanced at the rear of the church and quickly placed his arm around her shoulder to bring his wife into a protective hold. They had been waiting for this moment. His father-in-law broke into a sly grin. Soft murmurs are heard throughout the big, stone chamber. Parishioners turned to see who was responsible for the disturbance and bowed their heads. Silent prayers filled the room as heads bobbed from side to side.

"Sorry I'm late," the clicking sped up. "I had to stop at Morte's for, you know, two gourmet hot cocoas." She held the paper cups up as validation of her delay. At the same moment, her heel stuck in the carpet, and she fell forward towards the stairs.

The priest advanced as hot, dark chocolate splattered on his white robe. He stared, mouth agape.

"Whoopsie," the lanky brunette put down the two cups and pulled what little fabric available of her skin tight dress back down over her thighs. She righted herself, picked up the cups, and proceeded to climb stairs to the alter. "My bad," she continued to shake splashes of brown liquid off her hands. On her left, a diamond as big as a doorknob glittered. She sustained this motion as hot chocolate drops decorate the floor. The priest looked on, helplessly, as brown spots splattered the white, alter the carpet.

"What the hell is she doing?"

"I'm not sure…" Joe rubbed Angela's back. In most instances, this was a sure way to calm her anxiety. "I think she wants to speak."

Angela provided her husband with an exaggerated eye roll before barking, "Stop that!" He withdrew his hand to rest on the back of the pew. Angela turned her dark eyes in the direction of the podium, scrutinizing the female's every move.

The thin figure towered over the casket at the top of the alter. When she leaned in to kiss the attractive man lying in front of her, her bright red dress again rode up in the back, overexposing a little to those behind her. Even with the funeral director's cake of make-up piled on, Neddy's features were stunning. Yes, Guiseppe **Vaffanculo** was still a handsome man, even in death.

"Cuddle muffin, you are smiling," she grinned in return. "I brought the Morte's." Angela exchanged glances with Lena as both sat stunned as one of the cups disappear into the casket. A uniformed gasp spread through the church.

"What," Angela stage whispered to her husband. "Does she think Neddy needs a drink?" Joe couldn't help but smile, although this twist sent bocce balls bouncing in his stomach. Angela moved her hand to rest on his thigh. He engulfed hers with his.

Joe glanced at the back of the church in time to see a shadow moving in the darkness. He rubbed his free hand over his face and reached over to gently wipe away his wife's tears.

"Cuddle muffin." The figure touched the side of the dead man's cheek. "My cuddle muffin," she repeated with a head nod to a beat only she could hear.

Again with a stumble, her body fell into the podium, splashing more brown liquid. Her gaze went around the church as if taking inventory. With her left hand, she brought the cup of cocoa to her lips and took a long sip. She closed her eyes and smiled. Loud, slurping noises echoed throughout the church. Red lipstick stains remained on the side as she brought the cup back down. She placed the cup on the podium and released her brown eyes open.

"I gave cuddle muffin the full one," she explained to her wide-eyed audience with a shrug. She looked around the church, offhandedly began, "Yeah, for those who do not know me, my name is

Ryleigh. As far as everyone knows, the soon to be Ryleigh Orlando O'Connor **Vaffanculo**." She held her left hand out, so the diamond on her third finger sparkled in the light. The crowd gasped in unison. "Hi, Angela." Angela glared back at Uncle Neddy the not meant to be fifth. Ryleigh met her eyes, shook her head, and continued, "Yeah – anyway, so I'm obviously late, but I there was a good reason. I was on my way here, and the line at Morte's was huge, and I couldn't show up without Neddy's favorite..." she turned to stare at the ornate casket. "You pick that thing out?" She directed towards Lena, who could only affirm with a head nod. "Really nice. You always did have wonderful taste. Hi Joe," she gave, who was to be her future brother in law the old head nod.

Ryleigh closed her eyes. Both hands held the podium while her body started to sway from side to side. Her long brown hair extended beyond her small frame in opposite directions. The church fell silent as some leaned back to create as much space between alter and their bodies as possible, while others moved forward for a better view.

Ryleigh abruptly stopped, gave a quiet Mona Lisa smile, and released her eyes. Once adjusted, her gaze found a shadow loitering in the back of the room. A more immense grin formed.

"Ok, now all of you know me and Neddy were going to be married. Technically we are all related."

"She crazy," huffed Lena. "Related to her?"

"I didn't come around sooner because," he shadow in the back wag a finger, "well just because, but my point is… me and Neddy…," she giggled. "We kind of had to…" She touched her stomach, gave another glance back at the casket, and a quick swipe of both eyes with the front of her hand. Black marks left across her palms.

"Did she say she's pregnant?" Lena asked. "I'll kill him myself," she muttered.

Angela glanced back at her father. Someone's shadow moved in the back. Victor remained focused on Rayleigh. The woman's stomach had no bulge. *Neddy, couldn't be that stupid?*

"Anyway, me and Neddy, we were always close."

"So were we," Lena's soft voice caught Ryleigh off guard.

"Yeah – I know. Too close." Her eyes met and held for a beat. "Anyway, Neddy and I promised each other we would make sure our eternal sendoff would be a celebration, to celebrate his life, let me tell you about my Neddy… he was or should I say is," Ryleigh saw a middle finger go up behind the shadows. She smiled. "Yeah, Neddy is one cool dude. He can light up a room with his smile." Many people began to nod in unison. Ryleigh sensed a change in direction.

"If she doesn't shut up, she is going to blow this," Joe shrugged, yet his gaze focused in the back on the moving shadow. He readjusted his body to keep his view of the back of the room and Ryleigh at the same time. Angela leaned her body into his. Her eyes started to close.

"Neddy would do anything to help out a friend, even die…" a round of gasps heard through the hallway. "

"He did kind of die for his friend. You all know the story, right?" All began to nod no, except for Joe. "Ok, let me give you some details about how I lost my cuddle muffin. Yeah – that was my nickname for him. He called me Milady, although I don't know why. He started calling me Milady lately. Before, it was Venus, but he said the planet was burning out, and I deserved a more fitting love name. Anyway, that was my Neddy, always thinking about me." Rayleigh wiped a tear. "So back to the story; the night Neddy died he was making a connection for one of his friends—"

"What kind of connection?" a voice from the congregation asked. Rayleigh smiled. She knew she had the audience.

"He was connecting with another female—"

"While he was engaged to you?" Number three and four snickered. They both smiled, relieved to hear number five was no exception to Neddy's cheating ways.

"The slimebag," they heard someone say.

"Oh, not what you are thinking. I knew about it too. They weren't hooking up or anything. It was just dinner, I think. Yeah – he was definitely taking her to dinner. And after dinner, he was supposed to drop her off, but…" she gestured towards the casket.

"But why was he having dinner with her in the first place? Was she someone else's gal?" someone inquired — many "Yeah –why's" reverberated in the chamber.

"He was doing a friend a favor…"

"By having dinner with his girl? What kind of favor is this?"

"Let's say his friend is married," the crowd jumped back, "and the friend wanted to keep both the misses and the girlfriend in the dark."

"The bastard," a female voice exclaimed.

"And let's pretend the friend's wife discovered her husband's arrangement…"

"The whora," another female added.

"And since the wife could be a bit vindictive," Rayleigh looked intently into Angela's eyes. She waited for a beat before continuing, "The wife got more upset than most because you know —„ " she shrugged.

"No, we don't," a shout from the back. "What about his poor wife?"

"I'm getting to the best part. Hubby was hooking up with someone else while wifey stayed home and…I don't know – made the cookies."

"What is she talking about?"

"Who stays home and makes cookies?" Heads turned in every direction. Silent accusations flew across the room. The match had begun. Women stared down at their best friends. Beads of sweat glisten many male foreheads. Many women wore scowls, both for Rayleigh and most of their clueless husbands.

Lena locked eyes with Victor. "Take back control," she mouthed. Victor smiled and held up one finger. Lena gestured back, "One minute is all she gets."

"So now you can see how Neddy got himself in this jam." Ryleigh rubbed her hands together, satisfied. "I wanted to make sure you all knew he is still a wonderful guy, ya know…." She blew a kiss in the direction of the casket. "I am certain whoever spoke before me said my Neddy wasn't a saint, but…" Ryleigh sucked in air. "but he was a decent man. Neddy helped out everybody." She pointed her finger towards an elderly woman in the second row. "Maria, didn't he take out your garbage and grocery shop for you every week?"

The frail lady dressed all in black shrugged. "Oh, that Neddy," her head shook from side to side. "He da go to the market on Monday and take my trash on a Thursday. I call him any day – he goes for me. He never took any money although I tried to pay him. Neddy, he told me I remind him of his nana and to keep on making my special cookies." Lena held up another pignoli cookie for those behind her to see. Maria had made dozens for the funeral.

The congregation turned towards the frail old woman. "She's a widow," someone said. "She no, have a cheating man." Maria blush and smile as she gestured for Rayleigh to continue.

"The cookies. Yes," Ryleigh continued, ignoring the ongoing comments. "My Neddy loved his cookies." A loud snicker came from the back. She squinted to see who the culprit was. When no one person came into focus, Rayleigh again straightened her dress and brought her attention back to surveying the room. "And what about you," she again pointed into the crowd. This time her attention fell to an old man wearing a black fedora. "Didn't Neddy help you solve your little problem?"

The old man gestured with his right hand as he indicated yes. "Neddy, he solved my problem." His glare gave Ryleigh a shiver. Joe caught the old man's eye. He silently conversed with slight head nods, one towards the back of the room, another towards Rayleigh.

She watched the exchange from the podium and set her gaze on Joe. "What about you, Joe? Did Neddy solve your problem?" Ryleigh raised one sculptured eyebrow. Joe showed no emotion when Angela turned to him and asked, "What problem could your brother help you with?"

"I don't know what the crazy lady is talking about…"

Angela waited before whispering, "I told you if I ever caught you again, you'll be able to kiss your balls because you could hold them up to your lips." Angela turned a cold shoulder to her husband, yet took his hand in hers. Her gesture was visible only to those sitting close.

"Angi, trust me, it wasn't me. You know none of this is about us. She is playing with you. I'll tell you after, or you can ask your father," Angela sat back and crossed both her legs and her arms.

Ryleigh moved to catch Joe's eye. He returned her glare. "My Neddy helped many. I could name more, but there really isn't enough time." A sigh could be heard throughout the chamber. "As I was saying, my Neddy helps his friend. He helps old ladies," quickly adding, "no offense" in Maria's direction. She smiled over at Lena.

"Eh."

"And old men and whoever needs him. We can all agree to that, at least. Well, Neddy," she turned back to the casket and raised her cup, "I needed your help too." With tears carrying black mascara down her face, Ryleigh placed the cup on the white carpet of the altar and turned to leave. As she stepped off the bottom stair, the cup fell over and splattered the hot cocoa remnants. The dark liquid sank into the white carpet as the priest just stared.

Lena stood to block Rayleigh's exit. Rayleigh looked to the back of the church and returned the hostile glare at her future mother in law.

"Move," she said. Lena looked over at Victor and, with a gesture of his hand, returned to her seat.

Parishioners turned to follow Ryleigh's eyes to the rear of the church. A bright flash of sunshine followed a loud slam. The congregation jumped in in unison in their seats. Joe didn't move. He glanced over at Victor, who motioned yes.

The entire church followed Ryleigh's clicking heals and swaying bright, red rear end down the aisle. The sunburst in, and she too disappeared into the light.

Angela stared at the hard, wood floor. Her focused scattered. A thin line formed on her lips as she raised her head to give a quick head nod to the priest, who rose to continue the service. "I need to use the men's room," Joe whispered. His eyes focused on the back door.

"Now?"

"Yeah," he brushed his lips on his wife's forehead. Her eyes followed his body to the end of the pew. She sat stoic, glaring as the priest spoke while she repeated Ryleigh's words over again in her mind.

Joe returned moments later and gave the nod to Victor, the seats surrounding him now vacant. Angela glanced back with a slight smile. As she looked in Lena's direction, her mother in law sat with hands folded on top of her lap. Lena gave a slight head nod in her direction.

Could this nightmare be over?

My god, what is the matter with you? Do you want to get us all killed?

I'm talking to you, idiot writer! You are freakin' crazy, bring Ryleigh into this mess. She's a flipping whack job! Crazier than Wind! Oh – what! Was I supposed to know this because I met her in therapy? Really?

I may be a bit off-balance, but Ryleigh thinks the pirate king is real, and she killed me accidentally instead of the king, and that we should all bow to his every wish or some bullshit. In reality, she is the reason I'm sitting in this casket in the first place. She's part of, you know, the family, not my family, THE family.

I see the confusion on your faces, but trust me, her family is scary...really scary. Victor has been after them for years. I wonder if he set this whole thing up...you know he used me as bait to kill two birds. Victor Cuzzuto is pretty slick. I wouldn't doubt he would do it too.

Seriously – look at my family. They're all in on this, even my mama. Victor probably had arranged for me to want therapy so I could meet Rayleigh. Oh man – could he have organized all my marriages to keep Angela and me apart because he liked Joey better? That would be crazy, yet Victor can do it. The man moves more strings than a puppeteer.

Crap!

Getting back to Rayleigh. She seems all cute and dingy, but she is sly. That girl came up with some outrageous schemes, and did you catch the sparkle of her rock. For the record, I did not buy it. She thought the ring I had bought was too, what was the word she used, too pedestrian? I don't know. She said it was unfit for a peasant yet would agree to marry me if we could use her great grandmother's ring, which we had to steal from her aunt's house, which is no big deal because her aunt is eighty-seven. When she goes, Rayleigh gets the rings. We were speeding up the process without killing her aunt.

And the pirate king would help. The pirate king is a personal friend who owes Rayleigh a favor. A favor for what? You don't want to know, but I can tell you that's why Victor wants to nail her and her entire family. It really is a sick obsession for him.

Even I think so.

Ug…I need to wiggle my toes. At least they left me barefoot. Oh, man, this feels wonderful. I hope the rest of me isn't moving. Ah shit. Writer, you can't allow them to give me more drugs. It won't work.

Oh – wait…this is good stuff. What did Victor just hit me with? Yeah – the writer did right by me. Woo-wee…

"Would anyone else like to speak?" Silence fell over the room. The priest turned to every corner, waiting as if he expected someone to pop up to volunteer. "Okay then…"

"Wait!" The sun's rays filtered in through the side entrance, temporarily blinding those in the front. Silhouetted by the white sparkles, a figure emerged from the shadows. "Thank you," she muttered as she walked past the priest and stood at the pulpit.

"Who I am is not important," her arms rose towards the ceiling. The ruffles of her robe reflected colors of the rainbow back into the sanctuary, blinding several in the process. "You do not know me…" Joe glanced over at his mother, rosary beads in one hand, mouth moving in silent prayer. "…I am here to help you say goodbye to Giuseppe Vittorio Vaffanculo. He will be missed by most in this room. The rest should leave in shame as you are only here for the spectacle."

Many moved uncomfortably in their seat, yet no one moved. Eyes focused on hands in laps, the floor, the ceiling, anywhere except the direction of the voice.

"Giuseppe Vittorio Vaffanculo or Neddy as so many referred to him," she said his nickname with disdain, "is a blameless person. He tried to please too many during his time here, yet no one saw this. Most saw a reflection of themselves or who they needed Giuseppe Vittorio Vaffanculo to be at the moment. He was a chameleon of sorts as he functions only to please others." She pointed towards the back, "Think about this as you cultivate how you will remember this man."

The priest took a step forward as the mystery woman turned in his direction. "Sit," she instructed, and he obeyed. He proceeded to look at his hands and mumble the same prayer as Lena.

"Giuseppe Vittorio Vaffanculo wanted only the best for all. He tried to see the world as a place that needed his help, and he tried only to assist with love." She waited for a breath and continued, "We all lost loved ones, some we are happy to see end suffering while others leave us with heavier hearts. Each person who walks the earth is responsible for one another. Create those bonds to lift those around you. When we lift others, we also lift ourselves. And when those choose to leave, they take with us a small piece of our hearts. They take with us a small piece, yet they leave us with memories and stories. As long as those stories are told, people are not forgotten, and they live, filling the small hole left with love."

Heads nodded in unison. Lips moved in silent prayers. "Tell Neddy's story!" A bright light flashed, and the figure disappeared.

Whoa – that was sure some good quality stuff. Hey, writer? Did ya put it in the holy water so everyone would see her? Zowee!

"What the hell!" exclaimed the priest. He crawled over to the pulpit. His hands, now covered in silver sparkles. As they moved in the sign of the cross, silver sparkles floated. "Amen!" he exclaimed.

The white sheet blocking the view of the casket is placed on the closed container. With a nod from the pulpit, the congregation rose. The priest began with *The Lord's Prayer,* while four large men maneuvered the casket down the stairs. Lena Vaffanculo covered her face with a black veil. Other female family members followed. As each squeezed out of their row, they turned and knelt towards the alter.

Bright sunlight provided a temporary release as the family dissented into the summer heat. They walked single file to the line of stretched, black, limousines, and starting with the third vehicle, family disappears from view into the cool covered wagon.

Out in the hallway, Breezy bowled over with laughter. "Now we played them all," she gaffed. Harry helped her out of the gown. Glitter flying in every direction. "I can't believe no one noticed my size." Harry wiped glitter off his hands. He picked the sparkles out of Breezy's hair.

"Vic said to create a slight diversion," Harry reminded her. Breezy flicked her wrist in return, the same gesture as her grandmother. Harry shoved the gown into a big green garbage bag. He added in Breezy's light purple wig. "Okay, we are done." He threw the bag in the back of his Denali, came around the passenger's side to help Breezy up in the seat. Harry went around to hop into the driver's seat.

"We need to get out of here." Harry turned the SUV in the opposite direction of the crowded street. The crowd faded in Breezy's rearview mirror. Her surroundings faded from urban to rural. As her eyes began to close, Harry heard her mutter, "Please let this nightmare be over," right before falling asleep.

For Lena, the mess unfolds through the tinted limousine window. Off to her right, an unfamiliar face directed people like a maestro leads an orchestra. Some in uniforms, some in jeans, while others dressed for the occasion in a suit and tie. She folded and unfolded her hands.

"Don't worry, mama," Angela said. "This will all be over soon. Most will go downstairs for free food. Daddy will take care of the rest."

"This seemed like such a good idea at the time," Lena commented. "Now, I don't know. Neddy, he ain't too bright."

"Do you think he'd develop a problem following instructions?"

"This is Neddy we are talking about. I don't know. It looked like Vic gave him another shot up there," Lena shrugged. The thought of someone drugging her son didn't bother her as much as it once would. She put her head against the window. *That was the problem,* she thought as her free hand slapped the side of her head. Nothing her son did or required surprised her anymore.

She meant the toolbox comment. She loved both her sons equal, yet this whole escape seemed like something out of a bad movie. This is all too much, even for Neddy.

"You alright, ma?" A rush of warm air entered the car. Joseph took up the entire doorway. "It should be over soon. Victor's guys are everywhere." He backed out and shut the door.

Lena and Angela sat in silence. "Breezy?"

"She left after the girls. Harry is with her. Breezy is safe. Both of them are safe."

"What about your girls?"

"Home with Enzo and their new friend, Gio."

"Who is this, Gio?" Lena demanded.

"He works for my dad. Daddy thought, under the circumstances, it would be better to send a friend back to the house with the girls, just in case." Angela stared out the window, taking in the scene. "Can you believe one freakin' idiot caused this mess?" When

Lena didn't respond, she continued. "I mean, are men really this stupid?"

Lena snickered and gestured around their space. *Were men really this dumb? Look around.* Instead, she commented, "Apparently so."

The two sat in silence as people they recognized mingled about while others slipped away, hands behind their backs. One of the note-takers from inside the church, spat on the car as he ran by. A familiar female lay on the ground a few feet away. Her voice carried through the window, "Victor, you bastard. You promised! I will make sure you die next time!"

Jimmy came into view. He shoved something into her mouth and tightened the plastic ty on her wrist behind her back. Her face scrunched up in their direction. Angela sat expressionlessly.

"She won't get near my dad or anyone else for a long time," her voice came out monotone. "I can't believe Neddy was going to marry her. Idiota!"

Victor appeared nowhere in sight.

Lena took a deep breath. "How did we get here?" she waited, in silence, for Angela to answer.

UNCLE NEDDY'S FUNERAL

Louisa sat at the kitchen table, laptop open, working on a case study of her latest client. She heard the front door slam and heavy footsteps in the foyer. "Hello, love," she called. The returned mumble could only be her husband's. She studied her handwritten notes; according to the website *Stalker,* the key to this situation not becoming violent is Louisa's ability to remain calm.

The sound of water hitting against the tile sounded down the hallway. Neddy had started his shower with the door open. Louisa rose to walk towards the bathroom. "Neddy, are you okay?"

"Just peachy," came a quick reply. Louisa waited for more. "Mama mia...Molto bene..." Neddy shouted in Italian. As he sang, she walked back into the kitchen and changed tabs. Her other project had been too emotional to complete. Yet, after what she witnessed tonight, she knew it would be necessary. Not long ago, Neddy would be in her bed after the club closed, yet before she awoke. During the past few months, Neddy's arrivals home got later and later.

She spoke to him about this several times. "Neddy, why can't you do the early shift?" she'd ask, and the answer always came back, "Because of Joey, he has kids."

At one point, Louisa suggested she could do her research at the club. That way they could spend more time together. "You'd never get anything done. It's so loud there!" Truth be told, Louisa had been content to be at home. This gave her time to finish her observation reports, so when Neddy got there, she had his full attention.

Neddy had wanted Louisa's full attention. He would get up and make breakfast for her so she could go to the clinic with a full belly. He took care of some of the chores around the house, although Louisa suspected his mother did most of the cleaning.

The water had stopped. Louisa went back to the tab titled *The Split*. She had already sent resumes out and had several phone interviews with a few prestigious institutions. She thought hiding in academia would be a better fit for a while. There she could get lost amongst a large faculty, continue her research, and teach a few classes. Louisa even called Meg, Neddy's third wife, who was a Ph.D., to see what she thought. The two were not friends, yet Louisa needed to know the signs since she ignored them when it was Meg on the other side.

Ithaca wanted to see her next week, which meant she had to confront Neddy about her findings. Last night the alarm woke her at exactly midnight. She left her warm bed to visit the bathroom for a quick shower. Her clothes lay on the vanity: black pants, black shirt, black sweater, and black hat. She had read an online article about stalking and being the ultimate student, decided to follow their instructions to take zero chances of being seen.

After consulting several websites, her plan seemed simple enough. Louisa would park around the corner from the club. She located a spot earlier in the day with full visibility of the front door. Neddy always left by the front door. He had the valet move his car before they left so he could exit onto the main street verses in the dark, back parking lot. To get the exact spot to park her car will be her first challenge. She hadn't yet decided if she would watch from the vehicle or sneak into the club. She remembered Neddy had complained the staff tended to be lax about locking the entrance after they exited.

Her refection showed dark circles and a few wrinkles where none had appeared. Since Rayleigh O'Conner or whatever she called herself, starting taking therapy, things kept breaking around her. Her philosophical differences with Dr. Von and the rest of the staff at the Center justified her actions this night. She shoved the last piece of her burnt Siena hair under her cap. "Now is the time for truth. I am seeking truth," she kept repeating.

Lena heard the front door open and close. She got up to look out the window, only to catch Louisa getting into her car. Lena glanced at the time and climbed back into bed. Where Louisa is going will not be her business unless it involves her son. She liked Louisa, but, after all, Lena only considered her family by marriage. Of course, knowing her Neddy, he is doing something stupid again.

As luck followed her, the parking space was vacated as she arrived. Louisa watched the night crew exit one by one. She had been sitting in the car for over an hour. First, she saw what she labeled as the regular clubbers leaving. Most had smiles on their faces, a few sported a disappointing glare, and a few appeared intoxicated to her. She concluded these were the people out for a good time.

One of the bouncers threw out about five guys, all who hopped into an S.U.V. parked across the road from her. They left hooting and hollering! Louisa's education would not allow her to stereotype. Yet, she couldn't help but note the similarities in dress, hairstyle, body type, and attitude of the occupants. These she concluded were the troublemakers. They were out for a good time, usually at someone else's expense.

The bouncers appeared next. Louisa made the observation they sported the same appearance as the troublemakers, yet did not display any of the attributes she wrote down earlier. After a series of high fives and handshakes, all left except one, who disappeared behind the door. The same person walked out a few minutes later with a half dozen women all dressed in black skirts and white tops. They were followed by two men she recognized as the bartenders. The lone bouncer walked with the group to the corner. He stood and waited until a flow of headlights emerged, walked back to the entrance. "He must be a nice person to do that," Louisa yawned.

She finished her coffee and needed to get rid of it. For a second, she considered using her empty cup. "How low can I go," she commented. "Screw this." Louisa got out of the car, walked across the street, to try the club door.

It had open with ease. "Idiots." The ladies room had already been cleaned. Louisa did her business. She didn't flush the toilet or wash her hands for fear of being discovered. The later bothered her more than the flush.

"Good night, boss," she heard a male voice. He sounded like he stood right outside the door. She leaned closer. No answer. The front door slammed. Louisa walked out into the bar area. Two lights are shown; one out of the door crack from Neddy's office, the other from a *Crown Royal* display on the bar. She moved at a slow pace, stretching each step out as she followed the wall.

The door had a limited view. She tried to reposition herself in different places for a better look, first stepping back into the dark, when this didn't work, creeping closer. The only visible item appeared to be a red dress, crumpled on the floor. Her heartbeat so loud she swore Neddy could hear her coming. Louisa moved to the opposite side of the door to nudge it open a little further.

On the couch lay two bodies. Her husband faced her with his eyes closed. His shirt open and pants around his ankles. On top of him, a naked woman rocked back and forth. Neddy smiled. Louisa could not look away. Her fascination she could only use to explain voyeurism. The woman threw her head back. When Louisa saw her face, she stepped back out of view. Her hand covered her mouth as she bit into her thumb to keep from screaming.

Louisa was not considered to be a tough woman. The short debate between interrupting and leaving concluded with her taking a photo with the small camera she had brought, another suggestion from the stalking website, and sulking back into the dark. The one rookie mistake, as they referred to this online, and release of tension came as she slammed the door behind her.

The noise vibrated down the quiet street. What Louisa had discovered; she could not keep secret. And if she had, she would be living a life she did not want. She looked around the small apartment. "Everything got a reason." She wiped her palms on her night robe. When the bedroom door squeaked, she shouted, "Neddy, we need to talk!"

"Now?" came echoing down the hall.

"Yes, now." A couple of thuds followed as Neddy made his way to the kitchen. He plunked down into the chair across from Louisa and stared off into the distance. He didn't meet her eyes. Louisa noticed the bags and face stubble, something her handsome husband appalled. The red mark on his neck broke her heart.

"Neddy, I got an offer from Ithaca to go teach," she blurted out. Louisa took in a deep breath. Her hands shook.

"That's a long commute."

"Yes, I know." Louisa went silent. This whole situation was her fault, well at least she thought it could be. During the ride, back from the club, she considered her situation. She sent him to Dr. Von and arranged for him to be in the group study. She knew part of the research required her husband to be the only male. Every one of her fight or flight senses rose when the new one joined. Yet when she saw a red mark, "I think we should go our separate ways." There she said it.

Neddy stared off into the distance and waited for some kind of reply. He sat there, and for a moment, Louisa wondered if they could work this out. The hum of her laptop, combined with an all-nighter, began to invoke a rhythmic breathing pattern. She considered a cup of coffee yet thought better. "Aren't you going to say anything?"

"When did you find out?" This was not what Louisa expected. Her stomach began to ache.

"Tonight."

"Tonight?"

"Yes. I went to the club after hours…"

"But you said you had an offer from Ithaca. That happened all tonight?" Neddy's voice had a rough edge.

"I had my suspicions before, so I called Meg—

"You called Meg? I didn't know you two were close."

"We aren't," the response came quick. "I just—

"You just what?"

"I just wanted to know the signs." Neddy just stared at her. He knows. She knows. "I have an interview next week at Ithaca…"

"And what. If you get the job, you would pronto leave?"

"Neddy," she waited to get his full attention. Her eyes floated back to his neck, which he moved his hand to cover. Louisa took in a big inhale, "This," she pointed back and forth, "This isn't right. I—

"You what?"

"I think we should split up." There she had repeated it. This time with a force. Her husband shifted in his chair.

"Why? This seems to be working."

"Working for you, Neddy." Louisa poked his neck. "You get what you want, but I get nothing?" She shifted her body position to match her husband's. "Is she a waitress? Is that why you are always at the club?" Neddy hesitated, shrugged.

Louisa waited for a beat, stood, went back towards the bedroom. She soon reappeared carrying a suitcase.

"I guess I didn't have a chance?"

"Neddy, you lost your chance when you chose the whore over me." In two longs steps, she stood at the table, proceeded to stuff her laptops and cords into their case. "I'll return the car as soon as I get settled," she shifted direction towards the door. "I should confess I had hoped the symptoms Meg and I spoke about were all my imagination."

"Louisa, why did you go to the club tonight?" Neddy's voice became a whine.

"Because I wanted to be wrong." Louisa grabbed the bag in the hall and shut the door behind her with a loud slam.

"You're going to wake up the whole freakin' house," Neddy mumbled. He put his head down on the table. In a matter of minutes, he heard the door creak open. "Change your mind already?"

"Change my mind on what?" His mother's voice caught Neddy off guard. "Louisa left early today," she commented as she began to gather up the coffee cups to place in the sink. In the same amount of time, it took Louisa to leave, the kitchen filled with the smells of egg and bacon. "Neddy, what else do you want?"

"Things to be normal." Lena stopped to look at her son. She saw the tiredness in his eyes and as her gaze drifted. Lena reached over and slapped the side of Neddy's head. "Mama, what the heck!" he exclaimed with a jump.

"No number five Neddy" she screamed

"What do you mean?" Neddy yelled back. "What did Louisa tell you?" Lena pointed at her son's neck, which his hand flew up to hide.

"Louisa told me nothing," she said, "What did you do?" Her hand went up to hit him again, yet this time Neddy ducked away. Lena turned to grab a wooden spoon out of a jar on the counter. She raised her hand again.

"Mama, what are you doing?" Both turned to see a half-asleep Joe standing in the hallway in his boxers and a t-shirt. "Mama?"

"Your brother's an idiot."

"Ma, I didn't—

"Don't you lie to me!" She raised the spoon again.

"Okay, okay," Joe separated the two. "Breathe!" He pointed to chairs on the opposite side of the table. "Someone tell me what is going on," he looked around, "and where the heck is Louisa?"

Mama pointed at her oldest son's neck. "Stunad! Stunad!" Joe followed her crooked finger to the red mark.

"Oh, Neddy," he said as his head shook. "We warned you after Meg—

"I know. But this time, it wasn't my fault." His mother reached across the table and whacked him on the hand with the spoon. "Ow!" With one swift move, Joe grabbed the spoon and threw it across the room.

"Joseph!' Lena exclaimed.

"Not saying he doesn't deserve this. Just saying not now, mama."

"Humph," Lena crossed her arms and went back to glaring.

"I want to hear how this isn't your fault."

Joseph waited. His mother got up to fetch the wooden spoon, arrive back at her chair, re-cross her arms, armed with the object.

"Louisa got a job offer in Ithaca. She was going to leave me, mama!" Lena looked back at Joe, who shook his head. "I had to do something. She was—

"She was doing nothing," Lena spat. "Who is this whore?" Rage filled the silence.

"She is not a whore mama, and for the record, came on to me," Neddy said. Lena went to raise the spoon. Neddy's eyes followed as she placed the object on the table in front of her.

"She came after you? Who is she? Because of this, she works at the club, she is fired."

"No, she is too classy to work in a club. Her name is Rayleigh, and she's in my therapy group."

"Therapy group?"

"Yes, for my addiction."

"You're addicted to something?" Lena screamed. Her hands began on the sign of the cross.

"I'm a serial dater." Both his mother and brother froze, then fell over with laughter. "No, really. This is a real thing. I go to meetings and see a real doctor…"

"Tell me about these meetings," Joseph asked.

"I go to the place Louisa works or at least used to work, and I sit in a group with Dr. Von, and we talk."

"How many are in the group?"

"It started with me and three others. Rayleigh joined about a month ago…"

"Thank god," Lena turned towards Joseph. "He can fix this, right? I mean, men make mistakes and Louisa…"

"I can't fix it, ma," Neddy interrupted. "I think I love her." Lena grabbed and raised the spoon. "No, really, and we are a better fit because you know Louisa was my shrink, but Rayleigh is a patient too. She's like me." Lena threw her hands up and looked to Joseph for help.

"She's like you?" Joe picked at a piece of bacon.

"Yeah, you know. She has a serial dating issue. Actually, a guy was coming in the club she said was her ex." Neddy paused and looked up at the ceiling. Both Lena and Joseph's eyes followed. "It doesn't matter. Louisa wants to go teach in Ithaca, and I am staying here. She doesn't want me anymore, which is the best for the situation, right?" Neddy got up from the table, "And if you don't mind, I need to go lay down. There is too much on my mind."

Her oldest left the room. A door slammed shut. She looked up at Joseph, "What do we do?"

"Mama, there is nothing we can do. You know Neddy. Once he gets an idea in his head." Lena shook her head. "Yet, something sounds off."

"Even for your brother?"

"Yeah – even for my brother. I know Louisa. She loved Neddy. There is no way she would pack up and leave. Plus, we may have a few other problems at the club. Just for S and G's, I am going to ask Victor to check out this Rayleigh."

"Joseph, do we really need to bring Vic in on Neddy's affairs? He just finished with one problem…"

"Why not? Vic brings us in on his. I'll stop by the café on my way in. This gal must be something for Neddy to cheat on Louisa."

Lena looked down the hallway towards the closed bedroom door. "Yeah, she's something." Lena got up from the table to follow her son out. "This is too stupid, even for Neddy. Talk to Vic and let me know."

Louisa decided she needed to get out of town as quick as possible. Yet, she wanted to take all her research files from the institution. At seven in the morning, the halls still appeared pretty empty as she made her way back to her soon to be old office. Once in, she logged on to her computer, she proceeded to download the selected files onto a flash drive.

Louisa kept glancing out the door and checking progress back at the screen. "Come on, you antiquated wreck," she whispered. She opened one desk drawer at a time, systematically emptied notebooks, pens, post-its, and a stapler into the canvas bag she brought. The contents of the last drawer vanished as the flash drive signaled the file download to be complete.

Louisa smiled. "Screw these bastards. I warned them this would happen." She proceeded to highlight and delete every file with one exception. Her resignation letter remained the only icon beside an empty trash can. Her smile faded as she changed her screensaver from her wedding picture to the message.

"I think they'll get the hint," she murmured. Louisa hiked the bag upon her shoulder and headed for the door. Voices coming from down the hall caught her off guard.

"I thought our agreement was for you to join the group. I fulfilled —

"Shut up and get in your office."

"I never — "

"That's your problem Doc, you don't think…" Louisa remained in the shadows until she saw the two figures disappear in the direction of one of the group therapy rooms. The voice sounded too familiar for comfort. "Could it be Von?" As she tiptoed down the hallway towards the observation area, the voices grew loud again.

"Now you listen — "

"In here." A door slammed hard. Louisa walked around the corner to sneak into the observation area. A chill swept up her back. This is where she'd sit and watch Neddy's therapy group, The Nedettes, as she referred to the circus. Dr. Von may be the attending doctor, yet Neddy ran the group.

Two figures stood in the middle. Louisa recognized one as Dr. Von, Neddy's current therapist, and in her mind, the cause of the mess that is her life. Earlier in the week, she had pleaded with both Von and later their boss to pull Neddy from the study. Von had told their boss he had a groundbreaking concept in relationship therapy hanging in the balance, and Neddy's presence was needed to complete his research. He had added his results would bring prestige and money to the institution. Like so many Louisa had encountered, the later got their curiosity going.

It was then Louisa had threatened to leave. Neither had seemed to care. When she sent her resume out in a rage, she did not expect any response, especially not the same day. Ithaca happens to be the open door she needed to move forward.

The other male, she tried to place. Where had she seen him? It was no matter. The scowl across his face told Louisa everything she needed to know. Whoever he was, he was mad. And he was mad at Von, so that made him and Louisa cohorts.

Lip reading had never been her forte. Louisa turned down the volume and turned on the speaker.

"I told you Rayleigh would be part of the study. I kept my end of the bargain." Von crossed his arms and waited.

"And I told you, you would get paid when I am good and ready."

"I never agreed to these terms," Von responded. "You said the money would be transferred once she got it. Well, she is in, and I want my money. Otherwise—"

"Otherwise, what?" Louisa leaned closer. *Is that a gun?*

"Otherwise I'll go to the police. I got enough on both of you…"

The stranger's laughter filled the room. Louisa watches the gun slip back into his pocket. "That's funny. You'll go to the police. Doc, there is so much on you, your head would spin. The way you bilk this institution alone could get you ten years for embezzlement. Seriously, how stupid are you?"

Von glared back at his opponent. At one point, he switched his view to the two-way mirror, and she gasped. *He knows I am here.* She grabbed her bag off the table and ran out the door. Her shoes clambered in the hall along with the fire exit door slamming behind her. Louisa got to her car yet did not exhale until she passed the line at the employee parking garage.

She pegged Von as an imposter to her profession about a month after Neddy had begun to see him. Her instincts had proven correct, she had a choice to make. Her suitcase sat in the back seat of the car—a gentle reminder her decision had already been made.

Joseph drove by the club and headed into the back parking lot. There were already two cars there, yet the parking space closest to the door remained empty. He backed in, yet sat for a minute. Angela wanted more of an explanation, yet he had none. "Neddy messed up," he had told her. "Stunad!"

He poked his head inside the kitchen. The Grateful Dead melted into the sounds of pots banging and his head chef shouting obscenities.

"Marco, I thought this stuff was supposed to calm you down," Joseph greeted.

"It does," Marco smiled, a butcher knife dripping with blood held tight in his hands. "Imagine what I would be like without all this passion."

"I got to go see Vic," Joseph explained. He grabbed a mouthful of the chopped vegetable slaw as he moved, adding, "Wow, that's delicious. Keep serving that," as he stepped back out the door.

A brisk walk down the street had Joseph at the café. In the back booth, he could see Victor holding court. He walked inside and up to the counter. "Uno espresso por favor," he instructed.

"And give him more biscotti," he heard from the back. Victor didn't miss a thing. Joseph waited for his drink, which came accompanied by a plate of fresh biscotti. He walked to the end to join his father in law.

"Joey, to what do we owe this pleasure," Victor Cuzzuto greeted him the same way as when he was a little kid.

"Can't I just come to enjoy a cup of espresso with you," Joseph placed the plate in the middle of the table. Victor gave a slight nod of the head. Immediately the two men sitting opposite him excused themselves. Joseph took one of the vacated seats.

He gave the nod to the remaining man, standing outside Victor's booth. "So, Joseph," Victor spoke before he even took a sip of his drink. "My Angie tells me you have troubles."

A smile spread across Joseph's face. Of course, she had. When would he learn father and daughter had no secrets. "Could be a problem," Joseph shrugged. "Could just be Neddy."

Victor's guard laugh turned into an unnatural cough. "Ah, Neddy. What did your idiot brother do this time?"

"Where do I start," Joseph took a small sip. "This morning Angie and I wake up to my mama and Neddy having a shouting match. It seems Louisa left—"

"Louisa, left?"

"Yes, she got an offer to teach in Ithaca."

"Ithaca," Victor turned towards the man standing, "Do we know anyone in Ithaca? Find out." The big guy disappeared through a side door. "Please continue."

Joseph shifted his weight. "So Louisa left because Neddy was cheating — "

"Oh my! Is there a number five?"

"I don't know. Vic, this is all weird. I got money missing at the club, at least I think I do, and somehow," Joseph paused for a moment. "You know, Neddy."

"Do you think the missing money and number five are related?"

"Please stop calling her that. Mama would beat you with a wooden spoon," Victor laughed so loud heads turned in their direction.

"Sorry, Joey. It's your father, God rest his soul, referred to Neddy as an idiota so often nothing the kid does surprise me. Do me a favor," Victor leaned in and lowered his voice, "send me what information there is on number five and any other material you think I should know. I'll see what I can do. But remember, I am trying to retire so…"

"I get it." The big man appeared again and said something in Victor's ear.

"Joey, do we want Louisa to get this job or not?"

"Things will probably be better for Louisa if she gets away from Neddy."

"Done." Victor turned back towards the big man, "Tell him, gratzie, and I will be in touch." He focused back to Joseph, "Louisa has the job. Email me at my business, and I will take care of the rest. Anything else?" Joseph shook his head no. "Gratzie for the biscotti. Give my love to my princesses."

Joseph rose to leave. "You know Vic, the princesses are almost teenagers, are you sure you should retire?"

Victor sat back, "Oh Joey, it is your turn now. I already took care of my Angie. I know you can take care of the princesses." At the door, he turned to see the two who had left when he arrived back sitting opposite Vic and Vic giving detailed instructions.

If anyone could help this situation, it was his father in law.

Doctor Von walked to his office, excited to jot down notes after the morning session. He had watch Neddy leave for coffee with the girls and wanted to share his new developments with his colleagues. The women had adopted a male quickly. Is it because he appears broken (which he wrote in air quotes) or because he is safe and off-limits (both earned additional air quotes) because he is currently in a committed relationship or so he says?

Von had heard Louisa cleaned out her office sometime between last night and this morning. Rumor had it she left her resignation letter as a screen saver. "How passive-aggressive could she be?" a colleague had said. Von was happy to see her go. Now he could conduct his research in peace and not worry about the high and mighty Dr. Louisa Vaffanculo getting in his way.

When he finished his update, he noticed his secretary's chair appeared empty. She must be off on errands again. The woman spent more time gossiping in the building than doing her job. He shut his door with more force than necessary. For privacy sake, he closed the blinds on his only window. His office simmered in a light shade of dark.

He proceeded to look in his coat closet, behind the small couch, and under his desk. When satisfied, he produced a small key to unlock the bottom drawer of his desk. He reached under the file folder, past a banded stack of twenty-dollar bills, to take out a small cellphone. "The winds are blowing south," his words sounded hollow, yet this, he was told to be the procedure.

"We can expect rain," the voice on the other end came in almost a whisper.

"The session went well."

"What does this mean?"

"Giuseppe Vaffanculo could be a future ally?"

"He fell for the bait," laughter filled the receiver. "This will almost be too easy. Yet does he have access to his family?"

"Based on the stories he told today, they are close. There is only one problem…"

"The marriage?" When the doctor didn't comment, the voice continued, "It won't last. How is the new patient working out?"

"I forgot to ask you what type of insurance do they carry?"

"Are you stupid?" The voice rose. "She is just a new member of your group."

"I know, but I thought since she is here…"

"Since she is here, what?" the voice growled.

"Well I might as well because this is going to mess with my research —"

"I don't give a shit about your research! Now she is officially in the group, make sure you pair her off with Giuseppe."

"Pair her off?"

"Whatever you do to partner them up. Just make sure she ends up with Giuseppe."

"Anything else?" Doctor Von sighed. His backers did not understand the point of his work. When he publishes his new research, his new book will become the authority on relationships. A guaranteed New York Times bestseller. He would make millions telling lonely people how to meet their soul mates. Doctor Von laughed.

"Something funny?" He forgot he still had his contact on the line.

"No, sir," came as an automatic answer.

"As I said, the quicker my contact and Giuseppe become an item, the better."

"Got ya."

"The deposit will be made in two installments. You got Giuseppe acclimated to the group. The first went in today. You'll get the second when my contact confirms they are together."

Before the doctor could speak, the line went dead. He placed the phone back and locked the drawer. The key disappeared into his pocket. He stood and opened the blinds, his office now drenched in light. He pulled out the top folder on his desk and stared at an architect's drawing. He picked up his desk phone and dialed the number printed on top.

"Please add the rumpus room on top of the pool house," he listened intently to a response. "Cost is not an issue. Oh, and is there a discount for cash?" He hung up and expressed reserved amusement. His wife and kids are going to love the changes.

Louisa looked at the cardboard box of files resting on her passenger seat. "Was it worth it?" she contemplated as she drove the winding back roads that lead to tranquil Ithaca, New York. A large truck sped up behind her. Louisa's heart clichéd, and her breathe resumed as soon as the truck passed. It soon faded from her view.

Being part of the Vaffanculo family had never been easy. Between Neddy's jealousy for Joseph and Lena keeping control of family matters, she often thought she didn't have a chance to fit in. There were the other times. The family meals with the nieces running around or when she got to spend moments alone, talking to Breezy. Although she wasn't her mother, Louisa felt a bond had been formed.

An unexpected tear escaped from her eyes as she came over the hill and pulled into the Ithaca College visitor's lot. Louisa took a moment to take in the bright white brick buildings and long enclosed hallways. "I hope the only chill up here is from the weather," she said out of earshot as she grabbed her briefcase, exited the car, heading towards the administration office. Upon opening the door, a fair-haired student worker greeted from behind the desk.

"Doctor Vaffanculo, I presume?" Louisa indicated, yes. "We've been expecting you and are so excited you will join our staff." Before Louisa could correct the young lady, she grabbed her briefcase out of her hand and hurried towards a paneled door. "Please wait in the conference room. I'll let the others know you arrived."

Louisa quietly said, "Thank you," as she moved out of view. The conference room had a long-paneled table down the center, surrounded by several high back chairs. Louisa moved her briefcase to a chair with a view of both entrances and waited. The stillness of the room, combined with mental exhaustion, brought deeper breathes, moving into a rhymical pattern.

She rose from her chair and stretched, to fold forward. As she touched her toes, the door flew open, and several older men in suits with ties bearing the school logo entered. Louisa stood at the same time the voices ceased.

"I do that in my office also," one of the men commented.

"There are studies that show getting blood flow to your brain is beneficial," the other chimed in. Before Louisa could comment, he added, "I am Doctor Simon and my colleague Doctor Chaim."

"A pleasure to meet you both," Louisa gave her best *please hire me* smile.

"Oh no, the pleasure is ours, Doctor Vaffanculo. Am I pronouncing that correct?" Without waiting for an answer, Doctor Chaim continued, "We are thrilled you are joining our department."

"Joining the department? I thought this was an interview?"

"Oh, no need," Doctor Simon waved his hand in the air. "With your background, we'd be crazy not to hire you." Doctor Chaim sent a warning glare. "We are looking forward to you joining our team. Will you be continuing your relationship studies here?"

"I am hoping to," Louisa hesitated with a long breath. "The study was almost complete before I left the lab. I left…"

"We do not need to know why. As long as you'll be continuing your work and publishing as a member of our college's faculty, you are all set."

"Really?"

"Why, yes. Your studies are important to us. Can we assist in getting you settled, or do you already have accommodations?"

"Yes, I mean no. I mean, I need a place, at least a temporary place."

"Done. Currently, a visiting professor's apartment just became vacant. Would on-campus work in the short term? Okay, I will instruct Jenna, our receptionist, get you settled, and we can meet in the morning to go over logistics."

"Wow, sounds great." The fair-haired student appeared again and led Louisa out of the conference room.

Once the door shut, Doctor Simon instructed, "Is this all we needed to do? Get her a position and a place to live?"

"I think so, at least at the moment. I can check with Vic."

"Damn, beneficiaries!"

"At least this time we got someone with credentials." Both men laughed.

Neddy woke up in his bed, alone. He shook his head. His lips curved upward. It was all just a bad dream. Neddy rose out of bed and proceeded into the bathroom. The counter, usually covered with Louisa's hairdryer, brushes, and combs, was empty, apart from a single strand of her hair. He walked over to their closet and flung open the doors. One side contained his shirts, pants, shoes, and a small four drawer chest. The other side had a few wire hangers and some worn sneakers.

Neddy stared as the space for a beat before circling back into the bathroom. He took a shower and dressed. On the kitchen table, a stack of papers lay in the center. Neddy glanced at the attorney's name on top and smiled. "So, she wasn't planning to leave me, huh?" he muttered. A quick look told him all he needed to know. *Make sure she signs these before this becomes yet another problem.* His mother's handwriting stood out.

Maybe Louisa hadn't planned this, yet his mother appeared ready for it. "She never believes in me," Neddy said as he tossed the papers into a kitchen drawer. He left in a hurry. First, he went to the restaurant. Joe was out, the staff informed him. Neddy slipped into the office. In the bottom, right-hand drawer, he withdrew about a grand from the petty cash piled inside.

He drove over to Rayleigh's penthouse. When he tried to enter, the doorman informed Ms. O'Connor was out. Feeling frustrated, Neddy drove down Main Street towards the clinic. Heart pounding, he entered the facility. As he walked down the hallway, whispers erupted in his wake. He moved in the direction of Doctor Von's office, stopping short at the sound of familiar voices.

Neddy stuck his head inside the door of the therapy room. Inside, Doctor Von sat in the middle of his therapy group. All present except for him.

"Oh, Neddy," Doctor Von called. "Please join us. You are late. We were starting to get worried."

"Late?" Neddy stumbled to a chair. "I didn't…"

"I called the house. Louisa didn't pass on the message?" The doctor's smile punched his gut. *How could he not know?* "Either way. You are here now, and that is what is important."

"Yes, I am here, but," Neddy tried to formulate the words.

"But?" Rayleigh sat opposite. "Neddy?" Neddy smiled. His eyes met hers. "Neddy, are you okay?" Rayleigh asked.

"Yes. Yes, I am." Neddy sat in the empty chair on her right and took her hands in his.

"Victor, Louisa is all set."

"Thank you, Bruno. That is good." Bruno left Vic's office. Victor returned his gaze to the big whiteboard stretched across the back the wall. Photos scattered, some with writing, some not. "Ah," Victor scoffed and moved his attention to the papers across his desk. He picked up the file titled *Neddy 4* and moved it to this bottom left-hand drawer setting it amongst the N's, all of which started with Neddy.

Family business completed, Victor tried to concentrate on his latest predicament. The Marker appeared back in town. Vic warned the first time he would only give the guy one chance to escape. Records indicated he left for Tucson, yet the photographs showed something else.

Victor Cuzzuto paced around his small office. On one wall, a corkboard stretched, filled with photos of various people, all taken from a distance. Post-it notes scattered throughout. Names listed and crossed off. Half sentences with scribble only he could understand. He stared at a blurry photo of a man in a red fedora. A quiet knock on the door broke into his thoughts.

"Hi daddy," Angela, his only daughter, stuck her head in. "I have a surprise for you!"

Shouts of "Nano! Nano!" filled his space as two curly-haired girls jumped around. "Nano looks at our new dresses," Gia, the older of the two, exclaimed as she and her sister spun in circles.

"Don't we look beautiful?" younger sister Amelia added.

"Oh, you two are the most beautiful girls I have ever seen!" he exclaimed. Although the girls were getting older, they acted like little children around Vic. His daughter told him this was a ploy so he wouldn't make someone watch their every move. Victor didn't think his princesses were that smart.

Then again, their mother at their age had spunk. He smiled up at his daughter, who, with one quick motion, moved the pistol sitting on his desk into the top drawer.

"Nano, want to come to lunch with us?" Gia asked. She looked up at her grandfather with the same deep brown eyes of his daughter.

"Of course, I would love to join you for lunch with the most beautiful girls in the world! How can I say no?" His granddaughters danced around his office. "Would you do Nano a favor?" Both motioned yes, "Would you save me a seat, and I will meet you where?" He looked over at Angela.

"Daddy's," the girls shouted in unison.

"At daddy's restaurant in, oh, twenty minutes?" The girls stopped dancing and stuck their lower lips out. "Oh, my princesses, I promise to be there in twenty." Victor hurried the girls out and whispered to his daughter, "Thanks for hiding the gun."

"Yeah – don't leave it on your desk next time," Angela shot back. Victor went to reply and shrugged. He waited for the sounds of his granddaughters to fade in the hallway, looked back at his chart. He went in his top desk drawer, took out the gun, and placed his pistol back in the holder. His gaze focused on an attractive female about Angela's age. The date on the photo read yesterday.

"You are the mystery in all this, aren't you?" He muttered before heading out to join his family.

Within a month, Neddy had Rayleigh coming to family dinners. As with past Neddy women, Louisa was soon forgotten. Lena stood in the kitchen as the two circled around the dining room table, which was set up temporarily during Christmas after Gia was born. Between all the family, more space was needed.

The table never got put away. The family grew. People died. People born. Lena looked over with pride, at least until her eyes fell on Rayleigh. Rayleigh rarely spoke, at least to Lena. She only speaks her replies in Neddy's ear. Later Neddy will share what she had said, yet Lena couldn't figure out why the woman didn't talk.

"Okay, everybody. Sit. Dinner is ready," Lena announced.

"Mama, this is the best sauce you ever made," Neddy proclaimed as he shoved another forkful of spaghetti in his mouth.

"Better than yesterday?" Lena Vaffanculo joked back at her eldest son. "And you eat!" Lena exclaimed as she put another scoop of pasta on Neddy's girlfriend's plate.

"Oh, mama!" Rayleigh comes back with, "I can't eat another bite. You spoil us!" Lena smiled back at the compliment. *Could her gut be wrong with this one,* Lena thought. *Tonight. She decides to speak to me. This is progress.*

Maybe now Neddy would give her another grandchild, a boy this time. She loved his daughter Breeze, although being over twenty, the girl challenged her constantly. Joey had one still at the adorable stage, yet this too would be over soon. His oldest will soon have his hands full, if not already. Lena decided she'd like another grandbaby to cuddle.

Neddy's laughter broke her thoughts. She looked over to find her sauce all over his face. "Didn't I tell you I could eat mama's sauce like those contests on TV?"

Rayleigh sputtered in between giggles, "That was a pie-eating contest!" Lena threw a clean towel over to her son.

As he wiped the red sauce off his face, she asked, "Neddy, no work tonight?"

"Joey is doing the dinner shift. I am relieving him around seven, so he could tuck the girls in."

"And, my grandbabies are…"

"At the restaurant. You know he always takes a break to eat with the family."

"And where is my other grandbaby?"

"I got Breeze running the hostess station until I get there." Neddy saluted in his mother's direction. "All present and accounted for."

"Please, Neddy," Lena asked, "Let her go by Bri or Brianna. Breeze is — "

"Her given name, mama."

"Humph," Lena dismissed her son. Neddy stood to help his mother move the dishes over to the sink. He leaned down to kiss his mama on the cheek as he passed. "Molto Grazie."

Neddy arrived at the restaurant at precisely 7:07. Late enough to make an entrance yet not so late, Joey would be in a panic. As he walked through the front door, his brother greeted, already in his jacket. "Busy night. The dining room should start to clear in about an hour. Bri still has a few stragglers at the bar waiting on tables. You should be able to make the switch by ten."

"By then, there will be a line too. Hey Joey, you came up in my therapy today." The comment stopped Joe at the door. "Yeah – we were talking about sibling rivalry and stuff. The ladies asked if you were sane and single."

"And what did you say?"

"I said no to both," Neddy cracked up at his own joke.

"Yeah – unless you want to piss off Angela…" Neddy stopped laughing. "I suggest you stop talking about me in therapy. Why you still doing therapy crap anyway? You got another woman at home. The business is working. Wasn't that a Louisa thing anyway?"

"It started with her, but I think therapy works for Rayleigh and me, too." His brother flinched at the mentioned of Rayleigh. "I don't know, Joey. I don't know. Anyway – go home to your girls. Enjoy your family. My turn to run the joint." Joe left with a wave as a young girl caught Neddy from behind.

"Hi, Daddy," Breeze said.

"Hello, princess. Uncle Joey said you did fine tonight."

"Daddy, this is pretty easy work. By the way, some guy at the bar is asking for you." Breeze peeked through the doorway. Neddy right behind her, still out of sight. "Far corner, looks like a dork."

"Breezy, be nice!"

"He's wearing jeans with a suit jacket. Hello…dork." Breeze turned to help an older couple standing by the hostess station. Neddy watched the guy from a distance. He didn't look familiar, though that didn't mean anything. A lot of people came by and pretended to know him. When the restaurant converts to the club at ten, many people come in and know Neddy by name. He smiles and waves, sometimes he remembers the face, most times not.

He caught the bartender's attention and gestured towards the man. Santos shrugged in return. Neddy walked around to the man's blindside and tapped him on the shoulder. "Giuseppe Vaffanculo," the man had a thick Italian accent. "I hear you are asking for me."

"Is there a place we can talk in private?" the stranger asked.

Neddy hesitated yet instructed for him to follow. Again, he caught Santos's gaze and gestured towards a private dining area. The bartender nodded.

"So what can I do for you?" Neddy asked upon entering the cove. The stranger looked him up and down before sitting in a chair facing the doorway.

"The pirate king isn't happy," the stranger stated. "You owe us a payment and didn't show up to his court tonight." Neddy flinched. "I am here to warn you, Neddy. This is the first, and the last time you miss the King's court." The stranger rose to leave. On his way past, he bumped shoulders. Leaning in, he repeated, "This will be the last time."

Neddy sat down in the chair the stranger had vacated. A minute later, Santos poked his head in. "Everything okay, boss?" Neddy waved him off. He stared into his restaurant to watch Breeze as she moved from table to table. The stranger stopped her on her way back to her station. He whispered something in Breeze's ear, and her smile froze. She looked over to catch Neddy's gaze. When she turned back towards the stranger, he had disappeared.

Breeze finished her rounds and headed towards Neddy. "Who was the ass?" she waited while her father ran his hands over his face. "And don't lie to me. I don't have time for it."

Neddy looked up at his daughter. "If you don't want me to lie, why ask the question? You already have your answer." Breeze opened and closed her mouth a couple of times. While she had an internal debate, Neddy asked, "What did he say?"

"You want to know what he said? He said to enjoy my time with you because you weren't going to be around too much longer," she tapped her foot. "and neither would I because you're first. If it doesn't work with you, I'm next and maybe even nana or Uncle Joe."

Neddy winced at the mention of his family. "There is nothing to worry about. We all are going to live long lives, except for your nana because she is already old." The last part got a smile from his daughter. "Now, go back to work, and Rayleigh will pick you up at nine."

"Nine? Dad, I'm only working until eight," Breezy said. Neddy smiled. Crisis adverted. "And I don't want Rayleigh to pick me up. She either asks a lot of questions or doesn't talk at all. Either way, she is creepy."

"Breezy, be nice." Breeze turned to greet a customer.

"This conversation isn't over," she wore a tight smile as she added, "Right this way," to the couple.

Neddy let out a sigh and moved into his office. The room reeked with coffee and cigar smoke. Either Joe had a rough day or his father in law, Victor, had stopped by. Either didn't bode well for Neddy. He made two quick calls. The first to Rayleigh, to let her know he would take care of Breeze tonight.

"I really don't mind. I'm coming to the club anyways."

"No, no, I got this," Neddy replied. "I will see you later."

The second call went to an old friend. "What the hell do you want?" the raspy voice barked.

"King, please forgive me," Neddy groveled. "I was having dinner with mama — "

"I don't care if you were dining with the Pope."

"You know who my mama is?"

"I do. Neddy, you should know by now Lena Vaffanculo or any other member of your family does not scare my organization or me. You—"

"Owe you money, yes, I know. I would like to stop by later tonight and pay you."

"What do you think I am? A twenty-four-hour Dunkin Freakin' Donuts?" he barked back. "You will meet me tomorrow at the café, say two."

"But King, I have therapy--"

"You'll need more than therapy if you don't show." The phone went dead. Neddy let go of the breath he held in one "whoosh!" He waited for a beat to composed himself. With a painted-on smile, he worked through the restaurant crowd, only stopping to give a quick kiss goodbye to his daughter.

Neddy watch heads turn as Rayleigh entered the bar. She sauntered through and waited for the customer who occupied the last stool in the corner to move. Neddy observed she didn't even ask. He watched her through the bar mirror for a minute. He turned back into the office to finish the books. Large piles of cash scattered over his desk, yet he couldn't count. All he could think about was her.

He had arrived twenty minutes late to therapy to find Doctor Von alone, talking with a tall, muscular brunette seated in the circle of chairs. They sat with their heads inches apart and spoke in low voices. Neddy let a cough to announce his arrival. The woman stared him up and down. She ran her tongue over her lips.

"Oh, sugar. You need to come to sit next to me," she purred. Neddy glanced over at the doctor, who diverted his eyes. He sauntered over to the chair opposite and sat. One at a time, the rest of the group walked in. Each gave the new girl the mean girl stared down and sat down, the first two next to Neddy, arms folded, leg crossed. The third took the empty chair and placed it in a space closer to the other two.

Breaking the silence, "Okay, so we can see there is a new member to our group," Doctor Von said. "I'd like you all to welcome Ryleigh Orlando O'Connor, our newest member." When silence persisted, he added, "Rayleigh, why don't you tell us something about yourself."

Rayleigh adjusted herself as so Neddy got a full view of her cleavage. "You know my name," she sighed. "Let's see what else I can tell you. I'm a sex addict," Neddy sat up in his chair. "Raised a nice Catholic girl so every guy I wanted to screw I married. It seemed easier than living with the guilt." Instead of turning away, they had moved, ever so slightly in her direction. Rayleigh smiled to hide her glee. "So I've been married," she started counting on her fingers, "four times so far —

"You really got married so you could get laid?" Susy, the short brunette, asked.

"And only had sex four times?" Neddy added.

"Yes, to the first question, no to the second. I have had a lot of sex," her eyes met Neddy's, "I like sex a lot, and when I find the person I want to indulge in sex with, let's just say I have only been divorced once."

"You don't need to get married to get laid," was added.

"I know, but I was raised Catholic, so I believe in the ten commandments, including not having premarital sex and such."

Doctor Von took notes. The change in the attitude of the original group came quicker than he had expected. His advice to Rayleigh to make her ailment about sex had worked. Bringing in multiple marriages and Catholic background seemed to pay off too. The doctor wondered if he should take his research in a new direction. How far could he push this group to get the results he needed for the book?

"Hey, Doc," Neddy interrupted his thoughts, "Do you think my upbringing could be part of my problem. I hate to blame mama," he added to the group, "I love my mama. She's the best!" The ladies all smiled and moved in unison.

"I don't know, Neddy," the doctor responded, "you are dedicated to your family. Do they pressure you to do things you may not want to, or are there any hidden tensions?" Neddy didn't answer. He gazed off into the distance.

Rayleigh jumped in, "My mama never liked my first husband," she explained, "or my second. She said they were…"

"Unsuitable?" Neddy jumped in.

"Yeah, unsuitable, although my mama wouldn't use that word, she said something to mean the same."

"Mine too," Neddy exclaimed. "Though she did grow to like my third, and she definitely likes my current." Neddy smiled into the two-way glass. He never knew if Louisa was watching, yet

he made the gesture frequently during sessions, ever since Louisa admitted to her visits.

Rayleigh turned back to the mirror, yet kept quiet. She half-listened to the chatter of the three females. A soft smile formed on her face. She caught the doctor's eye, and he winked in return.

"Hello, darling," Neddy jumped at the sound of Rayleigh's voice. "Did I startle you?" She noticed the piles of money were scattered on his desk, and Neddy had bills stuck to his arms.

"No, no," he adjusted himself. Picking up, straightening the piles of money, added, "I think I fell asleep." He stood to meet Rayleigh, bending over to touch their lips together. "Did you need something?" he smiled.

"No," Rayleigh turned away. "I am bored. Can we leave soon?" Neddy glanced at the clock on the wall. It read five past midnight.

"I can close early, say another hour?" When Rayleigh pouted, he added, "Or you can go home, and I will meet you after two?"

"I'll be sleeping," she muttered.

"What?"

"After two will be lovely, Ned." Neddy leaned in for another kiss. He watched Rayleigh disappear out the door.

Louisa stood in front of the grand lecture hall to stare out at the many blank faces in the chairs. She observed some had their laptops open, yet most wore headphones. Her latest challenge seemed to be providing entertainment as well as information to these brilliant minds. How much has changed since she sat in those chairs?

She pulled up her PowerPoint presentation, "So what we see here is how the human being brain can fool itself into believing a fictional situation if it is in their best interest."

"Can you give us an example," a voice rose from the darkness.

"Why, yes, I can. How many of you have ever been in a relationship that the person wasn't committed to the same degree you were?" she quickly added, "No need to raise hands. This probably happened to most of you. Anyway, if subconsciously you knew this, yet chose to think you could change the other person—"

"—Or make them love you?" This time a female voice asked.

"Yes, or make them love you when you tap into this portion of your brain. We, psychologists, study this phenomenon before Freud, yet our conclusions vary. According to your text..." Louisa went on to explain the dated material in their college textbooks compared to recent studies completed in the field. "Are there any questions?"

"I have one. Do your tests come from the text, the lecture, or both?"

"Both." Louisa's smile froze.

"Will you post your PowerPoints on Blackboard?" A different student asked.

"No." An uncomfortable silence prevailed.

"Why not?" This voice sounded whiney to Louisa.

"Because you should pay attention and take notes. Ask questions. Don't just sit there checking email and texting friends." She waited for a beat to continue, "This class is not a requirement for any major except psychology. The material covered can and will be relevant to your future studies. I want active learners."

Louisa glanced down at the clock on her computer, "Have a wonderful weekend, and please don't do anything stupid." She turned off the projector, removed her flash drive, and logged out of her account to the sounds of shuffling chairs and student complaints. *Ah, academia,* she sighed.

"Doctor Vaffanculo?" The correct pronunciation of her last name startled her. Not for the first time, Louisa wished she had not changed it when she married.

"Yes?" She recognized the student. His graying hair made him appear a bit older than the typical college kid, which could mean either veteran or trust fund.

"I have a few questions I didn't want to ask during your lecture. What are your office hours?"

"They are on the syllabus."

"Yes. Yes, I see. I was wondering if we could chat. Perhaps now? My other classes are during your official hours."

Louisa glanced over at her empty wrist. She had stopped wearing a watch a decade ago, yet the habit remained. "Of course, I have a few minutes." She lied. Louisa had set time aside to complete her serial dating paper. Yet, she knew in her current situation, students, administration, department demands, and finally, her research appeared to be her new reality. "Do you mind following me to my office? We can chat along the way?"

"Sure." The student followed Louisa's quick pace thru the building and up to the third floor without speaking a word. She opened her office door, hit the lights, and pointed to a chair on the side of her desk. He waited for her to sit. Enzo got up to close the door.

"Excuse me," Louisa stood.

"Doctor Vaffanculo, this is a personal meeting. I'd like privacy." The word privacy hit her in the stomach. Her heartbeat increased, yet she sat back down and unlocked her desk. She pushed open her bottom drawer with her foot—something shiny layout of her reach.

"Okay," Louisa waited for a beat. "What would you like to discuss?" The twenty-something leaned forward in his seat. His eyes moved around her entire office, locking on the open drawer. He smiled.

"Doctor Vaffanculo, my name is Enzo. My father, Bruno, works for Victor Cuzzuto. He wanted me to let you know if you needed anything, to let me know."

"Your father works for Victor?"

"Yeah – he is like an uncle to me." Louisa kept an eye on Enzo as she opened an excel file and searched his name.

"Maybe because of the connection, you'd be better off taking the class with another professor?" Louisa observed Enzo's mouth open, and his eyes got a faraway look. His smile took over his entire face as laughter filled in the room.

"Oh, no. No, Doctor Vaffanculo. I don't think you understand." He snickered louder. "I am a good student. I'm not asking for anything. My dad saw you on my schedule and said Vic always had a soft spot for you and I can't remember the other one — "

"Meg?"

"Yeah, Meg. Because you two were smart enough to leave what's-his-name. Anyhow, I am not asking for or expecting anything special. I earn my grades." Enzo sat up in his chair. "We wanted you to know if you needed help, someone was here." He stood to leave, yet paused at the door. "If you really think there is a conflict, I will drop your class, yet I hope you don't. Psychology is my minor. I am pre-Law here because, as you know, my family could always use a lawyer." Both Louisa and Enzo laughed.

"I think we will be okay, Enzo. Yet at any point, if I start to feel — "

"Just tell me, and I will drop the class, no questions."

"We have a deal." Louisa stood and extended her hand.

Joe went through the receipts from the prior evening. The restaurant held its own, yet their money maker, Steak, Neddy's nightclub, appeared to be way down. He remembered a line forming when he left last night. The people waiting out front were dressed like their nightclub crowd; young and in designer wear. He would need to talk to Neddy about this yet today he had the more pressing matter of meeting his father in law.

Victor said he needed to talk. Joe had been with Angela Cuzzuto long enough to know this could be anything from *I want to take the family to Disney in the spring* or *Somethings up, and we need to be extra cautious.* Joe loved his wife, yet there were times when her family carried way too much baggage.

He left a note for Neddy regarding the money, headed out to the expresso bar down on the corner. He arrived to find Victor sitting in the last booth by himself. Two expressos already placed on the table with a plate of biscotti in the middle.

"Joey," Victor exclaimed as he embraced his son in law in a hug. "I am so glad you could make it."

"Come on, Vic," Joe sat in the seat across, "is there a choice?" Both men broke out in laughter. "What's going on?"

"What? No, how are you? What's new?"

"Okay. How are you, Vic? Anything new?" The sarcasm in Joe's response could be heard throughout the café. A few patrons at the bar turned to see who would dare speak to Victor Cuzzuto with that tone.

"I'm fine, Joey. How about you?"

"Vic, I don't mean to be rude, but I am running a business over there, and if I don't finish the books from yesterday, I don't get home on time to spend time with your daughter and granddaughters. I'm a little—"

"Stressed. You're a little stressed. I get it." Victor lowered his voice so only Joe could hear. "Look, I was trying to make this look like a social call because I didn't want you to come by the office, you know? So a couple things. First, and I'm sure you heard about this already, Ang brought the girls by, and I had my gun on the desk," Joe tried to speak yet Victor continued, "Ang put it away in my top drawer before the girls got a look. I already heard it from my daughter so…I just wanted you to know."

"I appreciate this, Vic. You know what I am going to say – no guns around the girls. This should be common sense, yet somehow I understand how it is not." Joe took an appreciative sip of his espresso. "Anything else?"

Victor stared directly into Joe's eyes as he spoke, "I got something big going down, and I need you to be more observant over the next few weeks."

"Observant of what?"

"I don't know – new people at the club," Joe stared up at the ceiling, "the girls having new friends who recently switched schools, you know stuff like that."

"I'm supposed to be suspicious of any new people who show up in my life in the next few weeks? You do know I own a restaurant, right?"

"Yeah – I know. It's just I want my family to be," Victor paused and took a bite of a biscotti, "safe. I want you guys safe."

Joe sat there and let what Victor had said sink in. "Safe, huh? Vic, I can't wait for the day you retire!"

"After this is settled, I think I might do that. I'm not as young, you know." Joe finished off his drink and got up to leave. "Oh, and Joey, not a word to Angela."

"You don't want me to tell my wife? Your daughter? Are you nuts?"

"Joey, this will worry her. Give me a little time. I think I can fix this. If not and we need to, we'll tell her."

"Great."

"Oh, and Joey, let me know if I can do anything to help out with your stress." Joe exited the café.

Joe paced the bar area. Employees and patrons alike stayed out of his path. He wore a scowl and visible aggravated annoyance. For the tenth time, he glanced at his watch. 7:15. Late again. A small commotion by the entrance alerted him to his brother's arrival. In two steps, he stood next to the glowing man.

"You are late," he barked. Adding in, "Again."

"Didn't know we punched a clock here, brother," Neddy returned.

"It is courtesy to be on time. And what are you, resident wise ass?" When Neddy didn't answer, Joe barked, "Office, now." He turned and stomped in the direction of his office.

Neddy stood and watch. He finally turned towards Breezy and asked, "What crawled up his ass?"

Breezy shrugged her shoulders. "He's been this way since I came in. I tried talking--" Neddy held up his hand to cut her off.

"Not your job, princess. But unfortunately, it is mine." He kissed Breezy on the cheek before proceeding towards the office. Unlike his brother, Neddy stopped at tables, chatted to customers, and greeted most by name before slipping through a discreet side door. Inside he found Joe, sitting at his desk, papers thrown everywhere.

"Neddy," he spoke in a calm voice, "Sit." Joe pointed to the seat opposite his. Instead, Neddy went over to an old couch. He sat with flare, taking the time to fold both his legs and arms. His smile now disappeared, Neddy gave his brother the same stare he received.

He waited.

"Neddy," Joe wrung his hands together. He reached over to a single sheet of paper and slipped it in Neddy's direction. The paper took flight and landed on the floor next to his brother's foot. "Take a look at this and tell me what you see." Neddy bent over. He picked up the paper containing a spreadsheet of receipts over the past two weeks. "I included the graph to make it easier for you to understand."

Along with a series of numbers, Joe had placed two graphs on the page. One showed a number of people entering the club. The other showed revenue by each night. The club appeared to be up people and down money.

"So," Neddy threw the paperback.

"So?" Joe turned away. "So Neddy, how can Steak have more people and bring in less money? Do we need to fire a few bartenders? Or what?" When Neddy didn't answer, Joe continued, "Neddy, we are not talking chump change here. Best I can see, in the last week, you and I lost fifty grand. Fifty grand!" Joe's voice grew loud. "Fifty grand is about two hundred thousand a month!"

"So, we've lost a few bucks."

"Really, Neddy? That is what you are thinking?" Joe look intently at his brother, "I want to know where is our money going?"

"Don't worry about it, Joey. I got this under control."

"If I'm losing two hundred grand—"

"We—"

"Then, no, this is not under control." Joe hesitated before asking, "Neddy, what is going on? Are you paying off Louisa?"

"What does Louisa have to do with this?"

"I don't know, Neddy. I was trying to come up with a valid reason. I was going to talk to mama—"

"Talk to mama? What are you nuts?"

"Neddy, I need to know what is going on. That is all. Just tell me, and I can help."

"Joey, when have I ever let you down?" His brother opened his mouth to speak, "Wait, don't answer. All I ask is you trust me, okay? Just trust me."

Joe didn't say anything. He slammed the sheet of paper on his desk and got up. With his index finger in Neddy's face, he said, "Fix this. Or I will," and walked out.

Neddy sat on the couch for a few more minutes. Of course, Joe would find the discrepancy. He crumpled up the sheet of paper and tossed it in the trash. This appeared to be the least of his problems.

Every man's head turn as Rayleigh strutted into Steak. She grew to love the attention she drew here in the United States. The bright blue dress and silver stiletto heels helped to accent her muscular body. A push-up bra and big breast helped too.

She walked the entire length of the bar and turned, like a model on a catwalk. The two men vacated their seats, offering it to her with a full gesture of the hands. Rayleigh smiled and accepted the last chair, her chair. Here she could observe the entire restaurant. Santos made his way down to where she sat.

"What can I get the lovely lady this evening," he purred. Rayleigh gave him the once over. Tall, sandy blonde hair. Very athletic and attractive looking.

"I'll save you for another time." The bartender scratched his head, she ordered, "I'd like a glass of white wine," and gave a smile to melt him away. He placed the glass next to her and moved back down the line. She thought it was odd he hadn't stayed to flirt, yet that would be best, at least for now.

Neddy appeared out of a side door. She watched him speak to his daughter, who played hostess then walk around the restaurant greeting customers. Every person he met, he smiled, shook their hand, and said a few words. When he finished in the restaurant, he headed up to the bar.

His smile vanished as he spoke with a man at the opposite end. Whatever the conversation, worry lines began to appear around Neddy's forehead and eyes. The other man pointed as he spoke and got up to leave with most of his drink still sitting on the bar.

Neddy ran his hands, threw his hair, and put back on the smile as he greeted each bar patron. She watched in the mirror as he got closer. Rayleigh crossed and uncrossed her long legs. About halfway down the bar, her mouth formed a soft smile as she took a slow sip of wine. A quick peek back to the mirror confirmed she had caught his attention. She appeared to be staring off in the distance as he approached.

"Hey, don't I know you?" Neddy asked. Rayleigh turned her entire body in his direction as she uncrossed and crossed her legs, brushing up against Neddy as she did.

"I'm not sure. I'm new in town and only been to a few places," she smiled. One glance into the bar mirror told her others were paying attention to their exchange.

"No, I would never forget such a beautiful face. Just give me a minute." Neddy leaned in and gave her a full kiss on the lips. "Ah yes, I remember you."

"I don't remember you," she turned her lips into a sly smile. Neddy leaned in for a longer kiss. He could feel the stares, yet did not care. When the kiss broke, Rayleigh breathed, "How are you?"

"Better now. Would you like to see my office?"

"Not now, Neddy," Rayleigh turned away. "Besides, don't you need to work?"

"Ah, work. This is a family business. I am the boss." Neddy gestured into the room. "I say we work in my office."

Rayleigh leaned in so close Neddy could feel her breath on his ear. "Later." Neddy backed up and looked at Rayleigh. She smiled when his eyes lit up with awareness.

"Promise," Neddy commented.

"Of course," Rayleigh winked.

Neddy responded with a nervous chuckle. "Yeah, later." His eyes went back to the other end of the bar. The seat where the king sat now housed a buxom blonde and her date. He turned back to Rayleigh, "Stay here. I'll make sure you find your way home."

Rayleigh lowered her eyelids and brought a toothless smile to her face. "Anything you say, love."

Victor walked down the main drag and into a plain white van parked opposite Steak. He greeted each man with a head nod before asking, "What is the status?"

One man removed his earpiece and shrugged. "Nothing, boss," he said. "Your son-in-law had no visitors today. The brother had two." The man rifled through a stack of notepaper. "Okay, there was the guy, what's his name, we've been watching already and some broad in a tight blue number."

"A guy and a broad, huh?" Vic noted.

The other man, hunched upfront with binoculars, chimed in, "We are waiting on a positive I.D."

"When did you send the information up?"

"About midnight, I think. Yo – Bruno, when did you send stuff over to the hacker?"

"Yeah – around midnight," Bruno answered. He rested the earpiece on his left ear while drawing his attention over to Vic.

"You couldn't use the program?" The two men glanced at each other and back at Vic.

Both nodded no. "Okay. Would you send the photos to me? I'll take a crack at it."

"Boss, you don't need to do that," Bruno moved towards the computer. "We got this for you."

"I know you guys do. I want to see if I can work the program, you know?" Both men laughed.

Victor gave another head nod and exited. He walked passed the restaurant and crossed the street. In front of the apartment building, he paused to greet a few passing by, before entering the main door. He rode up in the elevator four floors and exited.

He knocked on apartment 4-B and waited. The door opened to reveal a small formal living room. On the opposite wall sat a bank of windows, overlooking Steak and its parking lot. Vic walked towards the windows and took a seat in a high winged back chair. He clicked his ring on the arm while waiting. People mingled up and down the street. Most he recognized as family or friends.

A few minutes later, a plate of hard salami and cheese is placed on the table next to him, along with a glass of red wine. "Grazie," Vic comments to the servant, who is already out of the room. He picks at his food and watches the door of Steak. "Come on, reveal yourself," he said to no one.

Victor watches Bruno leave the white van and walk the same path he had vacated. Within minutes there is a knock. Bruno takes a seat on Victor's right, his body occupies most of the worn couch. Neither speaks.

"You're not going to like this," he finally states. "The guy from last night. He was in here a couple nights ago, too, except he left with a paper bag.

"What was in the bag?"

"Don't know. I was thinking of money, booze, or drugs. Not to say Joey's dealing because he was already gone for the night. I think this guy and Neddy are connected somehow."

"Is Santos still giving you reports?" Bruno pointed to a piece of paper on Vic's desk. "Let's keep him on the payroll."

"You know Victor, this set up goes beyond the family if you know what I mean…" Victor shoved the last piece of salami in his mouth. "We all love Angie and the kids, but this," he gestures around the room, "this is above and beyond, even for you." Bruno rubbed his hands. "I mean, you got Enzo up at school, keeping an eye on Louisa too." When

Victor didn't speak, he got up to leave. He got as far as the door.

"The van is too obvious. We can get rid of it – at least for now. Move the observations up to here. I want to know who the man is. The broad will probably be Neddy's fifth or sixth, who knows."

"I thought he was married?" Victor rolled his eyes. "Right…"

"So we get rid of the van. Can we get the computer set up here?" A crash of dishes comes from the kitchen. "Rosy doesn't mind us taking over her place. Rosy, how does the Marriott for a week sound?" A small Italian woman sticks her head out of the kitchen and smiles.

"Can I order room service?" she asked.

"Whatever you want," Victor waved. "We send Rosy here to a hotel, maybe pay her a little for using the place. You can bring in the setup."

"Got it, boss."

"Oh, and Bruno," Victor stood, "When you get rid of the van and get rid of Tweedledumb too." Once out the door, he let out a long sigh. Working for Vic is tough enough without doing his dirty work for him.

Rayleigh handed Neddy a glass of Pinot Grigio and directed him over to the overstuffed white sofa. She watched him watched her in the window's reflection. Her gaze moved to the corner to catch the soft flash of the hidden camera. After a long sip of wine, she turned in Neddy's direction, catching him staring at her almost exposed breasts.

"So," she comments with a head nod.

"So," Neddy returns the gesture. When Rayleigh scoots closer, Neddy jumps up and pretends to look out the window, "So tell me again how'd ya get the place?"

"I don't know," Rayleigh responded breathily. "Hubby number three had money, and number four was a realtor. I forget which one decided I could do with this place." She walked to Neddy's side, "But it is way too big just for me." Rayleigh allowed her dress to slip off her shoulders. From Neddy's view, one perfect breast pointed in his direction. She reached up to place her hand on his shoulder. "Would you like a tour?" She turns him to face her. "This place is much better than your office, no?"

Rayleigh allowed the other shoulder to become bare. When Neddy turned, she appeared naked from the waist up. "Do you like the view?" Rayleigh took a quick glance at Neddy's crotch to admire her work. Her smile came easy.

Neddy glanced at his watch. It was after three. The Pirate King would not be pleased again. "Rayleigh, there are family issues…"

"Family comes first…" Rayleigh arched closer, so close Neddy could hear her pulse. "Family always comes first," as she reached her arms around his waist.

At her touch, Neddy jumped. "Rayleigh, I really should go." Neddy turned towards the door.

"I suppose I understand if you need to leave," she pulled her dress back into place.

Without a word, Neddy placed his wine glass on the side table and left. Once back in his car, he stared up at the penthouse. Rayleigh's outline appeared in the window. His crotch reacted again.

Rayleigh sniffed her underarms. Hands-on hips, she stood at the window to watch the red brake lights disappear down the street. "That was a wonderful performance, darling." With a deep inhale, Rayleigh turned towards the voice behind her. "Now, do I get to take advantage of the matinee?"

She squinted her eyes to softened her glare. Lex stood naked in the doorway, leading to her bedroom, long and hard. "I didn't know you were here," she sighed. "What would you do if we made it to the bedroom?"

"Kill you both," he promised. "Or maybe kill him and use you." When Rayleigh didn't respond, Lex's voice softened. "Actually darling, I would make passionate love to you until you forgot about him and all the others. Then it will be you and me as it is supposed to be."

Rayleigh allowed a soft smile to form as her eyes half-closed. With one move, her dress fell to the floor. She pushed past and gestured for Lex to follow as she disappeared down the long hallway.

Neddy arrived at therapy, only to find the group huddled around Rayleigh. Her sobs came roughly as her mascara ran down her face. The group rubbed her back and took turns to hug her. Doctor Von stood up to approached Neddy at the door.

"Rayleigh's ex-husband is giving her troubles. It looks bad."

"Which one?" Neddy asked.

"Not sure, but she's been here for over an hour. First, to quit therapy, as the girls arrive, crying and babbling. Group today will probably be a little different."

"Of course," as Neddy approached, he heard snippets of conversation. "Oh, Rayleigh, you can stay with me." "Or at my place. I got plenty of room." "You should contact the police…" With the mention of the authorities, Neddy watched Rayleigh howl.

As Neddy joined the group, Rayleigh lunged into his arms. Neddy saw the others didn't show any objection.

"Oh, Neddy," Rayleigh sobbed. Her hand brushed his crotch, "My ex showed up after you left last night and trashed the place. He threatened to kill both you and me even after I told him nothing was going on." She punctuated the statement with another howl. "I don't know what to do!"

Neddy waited for the Doctor to respond. A shrug followed. "There, there," he spoke in a whisper. "Uh – Doc?" Rayleigh repositioned her body to lay her head in Neddy's lap. The other females gathered around to massage her back and offer support. Most men would be in their glory, yet Neddy stared at the doctor, pleading in silence for help.

Doctor Von stood. "I think under the circumstances," he announced, "group will not take place today. I suggest we reconvene at the same time tomorrow." The females loosened their embrace, yet Rayleigh tightened her hold on Neddy. "We can make up the session. I will assist Rayleigh from here." Neddy went to move as Rayleigh turned her face towards his zipper. She rubbed her nose along its path. To the others, she appeared to be hiding her emotions. Neddy peeked down to see a soft smile along with Rayleigh's brown eyes, half-closed, meeting his.

He jumped. She fell off the couch. "Neddy, what the heck!" One of the females shrieked as the three rushed to help Rayleigh up. Neddy noticed the doctor staring at his crotch, which his pants had become very tight. He turned to hide his reaction, yet the mirror on the wall only shown the truth.

When all had calmed down, Doctor Von reiterated, "We should break now," Neddy now the focus of his glare, "and we will talk to tomorrow." He placed his arm around Rayleigh and led her towards the door.

"Thank you all for your support," she muttered as they parted. Inside the doctor's office Rayleigh flicked off her shoes and plopped on the couch. A grin took up most of her face. "Told you it would work," she crossed her arms in satisfaction.

"I don't understand why you need the charade. I mean, you two are already sleeping together."

"This is why you are where you are, and I am," Rayleigh sat up tall, "I am in a position to pay you a lot of money to create this illusion. Don't worry. We are almost done."

"Thank heavens!" Doctor Von walked around his desk and shuffled papers before he sat.

"I think the session went well," Rayleigh said. She repositioned her purse on her lap as the doctor moved around her.

"Yes, that was interesting," Doctor Von countered. "With females, it can go two ways. The fact they rallied around you," The doctor scribbled with intent, "this puts some of my theories into a new light." He continued to write as he spoke, "Common enemy, bonding, intentions…"

"Uh, doc?" Rayleigh interrupted. "Doc!" Doctor Von stopped writing mid-sentence. "You need to team Neddy and me up so I can get over my fear of males." The doctor snickered. "No, I am serious. Once you do, I promise," she slid closer. Doctor Von's eyes widened, "to get your second payment." He relaxed a bit, yet his body still appeared rigid.

"I will call Neddy today. Set up another session for the two of you," he still wrote as he spoke, "until we get all this done, you should lay low."

"No shit," Rayleigh responded. "Call me as soon as you get things set." She got up to leave, hand on the doorknob, and stopped. "Remember, doctor," she met his eyes, "our arrangement may be terminated at any time."

Doctor Von watched the door close behind her.

Neddy waited in the men's room down the hall from Doctor Von's office. When he considered the mirror, he swore he saw the outline of a person. Months ago, the shape would be Louisa, yet now she was gone. His mama had pulled the divorce papers out of the drawers and threatened Neddy with no more meals unless he signed. "You need to get this over with," his mama didn't mince words. These were the same she used with the others.

The door to the doctor's office was slightly ajar. Neddy listened, and when silence returned him, he knocked.

"Come in," Doctor Von called. "Oh, Neddy. Glad you are here," he gestured to the chair next to his desk. "You are the man I want to see."

Neddy took the seat. He saw house plans laid out across the desk. "You moving Doc?"

"Oh, no. No," Doctor Von scooped up the plans. "Just doing a bit of remodeling."

"Yeah – when we did that to the restaurant, it ended up costing us a small fortune."

"You're telling me. I almost fell off my chair when they gave me the price to add a hot tub. But the kids wanted it and for the family —"

"You do."

"Exactly. You do." Doctor Von waited. "Neddy, I wanted to talk to you about the group today."

"Me, too, doc. I mean, what a messed up deal?"

"Actually, I thought it went rather well. The group bonded further and seemed to help one of the members out of a jam." He let that thought sink in as he rearranged papers.

"I'd like to add a few sessions for Rayleigh to help her get through this mess."

"Divorce is never easy." He shifted in his chair. "I recently signed the papers for Louisa and me…"

"Neddy, wonderful news." Neddy winced at his enthusiasm. "I'm glad you understand and now in this position, Neddy because I was hoping you would join us."

"Join us?"

"Not us, us, just myself and Rayleigh for the extra sessions. You are a male who has been divorced four times."

"Three times," Neddy corrected.

"Three times, going on four. Whatever. and I believe you and Rayleigh got some sort of trait which perpetuates this activity."

"I don't know about Rayleigh, but every time I got divorced, it was because the current wife noticed me hanging around with another woman more than I hung out with her. You know Doc, this probably isn't the best idea. I think you should find someone else. Maybe someone not in the group…"

Doctor Von admired his pool expansion as the bathhouse fade off the plan. "No, Neddy. I think working with a female of multiple divorces will give both of you a new perspective on your situation." He glanced back to see a sauna in the new bathhouse.

"I don't know Doc. I mean, Rayleigh and I started hanging out a bit, and I think we should be in different groups. Because, you know…"

"I don't understand, Neddy. If you and Rayleigh have become intimate," Neddy cringed, "I would think you would want to help your lover. Seriously Neddy, unless your intentions are not— "

"No, they are— "

"Then, of course, you would want to help her." Neddy moved his head up and down. "We can pick this up in our private session tomorrow. I am so glad we had this chat."

Neddy got up and walked out the door shaking his head as he tried to figure out why he agreed to this plan. "Rayleigh will shoot this down," he said.

Bruno made the drive to Ithaca in under four hours without any speeding tickets. He had one short conversation with a cop in Roscoe, yet they parted the best of friends. Victor had taught him well.

He strolled up to the main building with anticipation. He loved visiting his son at school. As Bruno surveyed the lobby, his smile faded. He moved towards the receptionist desks. She held up one finger while she continued her conversation.

"No, you turn north in Binghamton." Bruno only caught one side, yet he could hear the frustration on both ends. "Yes, this will take you at least another forty minutes. I don't care that the space is less than an inch on your road map…" Bruno laughed aloud. The receptionist jumped in her chair. "People are waiting at the desk. Call back if you think you are lost. Thanks." With a significant sigh, the young woman brought her attention over to Bruno, "May I help you," she purred, now wide-eyed.

"Yes, please," Bruno replied. "I am here to meet my son—

"Dad, you are early!" The receptionist's head moved back and forth between the two handsome men. She opened her mouth to speak as Enzo cut her off with a "Mille gratzie" and a smile. The two vanished towards the parking lot.

"It is so wonderful to see you!" Bruno embraced his son in a tight hug. When he broke the hold, "Where are we off to?"

Enzo hesitated. "There is a famous restaurant in the mall. They write cookbooks and everything!"

"Cookbooks, huh? What kind of food because if it is Italian—

"I know…nothing compares to home. No, actually, the restaurant is vegetarian."

"Vegetarian? What is this fancy liberal arts college doing to you?"

Enzo smiled. "No, dad, they serve fish too. I really think you'll like it."

"Ah, Enzo, you are so like your mother." When the two fell into a silence, he added, "she would be so proud."

The hostess leads the two to a table by the window. By habit, Bruno pointed to a less visible table, and the hostess obliged. Once seated with his back towards the wall, he took in the exotic printed wall hangings and embroidered pillows scattered about. The space reflected the earthy vibe of the staff.

"Tell me about school. How do you like it so far?" Bruno rested his elbows on the table. His Enzo had a glow. His boy appeared healthy.

"Ah, school. What can I say about the school," His father's smile vanished, "No, no, dad, school is good. You know me. I am doing well in classes and..."

"And what?"

"The only place I have trouble is keeping an eye on...Dr. Vaffanculo! What a nice surprise!" Louisa dropped a folder, scattering papers upon hearing her name. Enzo jumped up to help her retrieve the contents.

"Oh, hi, Enzo. Fancy meeting you here." Louisa looked up to meet Bruno's wide-open brown eyes. His lips morphed into a smile, "Bruno, what are you doing here?" He stood to give her a soft hug.

"Ah, Bella," he replied, "I am here to visit my Enzo. Seeing you is a bonus. Please join us." Bruno gestured towards the empty chair next to his.

"Oh, thank you, but I need to —

"Just for a drink." Bruno caught the waitress's attention and signaled her over. "Please..."

The waitress took Louisa's order for a plain green iced tea and disappeared. Louisa moved the chair to create space and sat with her briefcase and papers on her lap. For a moment, no one spoke.

"How is my Enzo doing in your class?"

"Oh, I'm sorry," Louisa started to stand. "With privacy laws, I can only talk about Enzo's progress with Enzo. Nice bumping into you —"

"Excussee, I mean, I am sorry," Bruno stuttered. "We talk about you. How are you?" Bruno sat forward in his chair to study Louisa.

"I am good," Louisa replied at the same time a sizeable green tea was placed in front of her. "I am doing my research and teaching, as you probably know."

"Do you do anything else?"

Louisa thought for a moment. "Once or twice a week, I come here. Enzo knows this because we ran into each other before." She held eye contact with Enzo for a beat. "Other than this, I manage to stay off the radar."

"Stay off the radar," Bruno repeated. "Louisa, you should do something fun. Enzo, what is there to do around here?"

"Dad, my version of fun may be different —

"Fine." Bruno cut him off with a wave of the hand. "Louisa, I am up here for one night —

"You are?" Enzo injected.

"My Enzo forgets. Anyway, seeing you already ate lunch, would you like to accompany us to dinner?"

Louisa vacillated, "Bruno, I appreciate your offer, yet I have work to complete," she held up the overflowing folder, "so I must decline. Although I thank you for the offer." Bruno's smile faded. "Actually, I think I'd better go. I thank you for the tea." Louisa exited before anyone could object.

Enzo watched his father's eyes follow her out the door. "Well," he commented, adding, "Are you really staying for dinner too?" When Bruno didn't respond, Enzo started to babble, "I know where she lives on campus. Maybe we could stop by. I mean I am her student and —

"Enzo, this is fine. I was surprised. That is all. Now, do you really want to eat here or should we go somewhere else?"

"Yeah, let's go to the brewhouse. I think that would be more your place." Bruno threw a ten on the table, and the two exited into the flow of the street.

By the time Louisa reached her apartment, her shakes had turned into anger. She slammed open a drawer in the kitchen and threw to-go menus, a hammer, and several screwdrivers up on the counter. From the back corner, she pulled out a small card. With one swoop, Louisa dumped back in the rest of the contents.

As she reached for the phone, it rang. "Hello," her voice cracked.

"Louisa, this is Bruno," his voice remained calm. Louisa didn't speak. "I am calling to apologize for surprising you today. Apparently, Enzo knew you frequented that restaurant yet didn't share any information with me. Please believe me when I say our meeting wasn't planned by me."

Louisa spoke in a steady cadence, "I appreciate the call, Bruno. I am okay. Thank you—

"I am leaving this evening," he began again, "My son has plans."

"Of course, he does," Louisa's voice softened. She glanced down at Victor's card to reconsider contact. "Enzo is a good boy," she mumbled.

"Yes, yes he is…most of the time. I am going to some farmer's market—

"At the vineyard?"

"Yes, I think. Anyway, I am going there, heading back home. Louisa, again, I apologize."

Louisa placed Victor's card back in the drawer. "I hope you enjoy it. I have never been."

"As a friend, do you want to follow me out there? Can we see the market, and I will head home? This way, neither one of us needs to do this by themselves?"

Louisa hesitated to answer, "Okay. I will meet you in the lot in ten." She hung up the phone to stare at the closed drawer. *How did that happen?*

The view from the penthouse offered a stunning panorama of the city, yet Rayleigh sat on the couch. Her reflection in the mirror kept her attention. She held her wine glass in different positions and tilted her head back to take a sip. Her green dress cut to show off her breasts, of course, yet it also had a slit up the side to give a full view of her tone thighs.

She glanced over at the Tiffany clock she had set on the end table. He was over an hour late. As she refilled her glass, the bottle of wine she opened earlier, now had splashes left at the bottom. She rose to go get more as a male's reflection caught her attention.

"You look ravishing, darling," his voice brought chills. His English accent emphasized the word ravishing.

"You're late," Rayleigh responded. She tapped a beat with her bare left foot.

"I am, but I bring rather useful news," Rayleigh crossed her arms. "If you aren't interested," the Englishman turned to leave. Before he took a step, Rayleigh appeared at his side.

"Useful, you say?" she purred.

"Beneficial news," he cupped her chin to raise her mouth towards his. "Our friend is in debt."

Rayleigh turned her head away. "So how will this help us? I already know about Neddy's personal problems. The hack comes in the bar almost every night. I only care about getting Victor Cuzzuto off our back, permanently."

"Exactly. Neddy is in debt to a small-town crook. If we can take care of –"

"Neddy would owe us—"

"Exactly. Big time. We can get rid of his problem and him—"

"Can help us set up Cuzzuto to get rid of ours." Rayleigh's lips broke into a huge smile. "Do you—"

"Yes, I do," she waited. "We take care of this pirate king—"

"Oh my god! Is that this chump's code name," Lex Oxford concurred, "Are you kidding me?" Rayleigh went over and plopped on top of the couch, exhaling a fit of laughter.

"Yeah – so we need to find out when the pirate king and Neddy will be together. Neddy must see you off this guy for him. If he is a witness—"

"He's more likely to help us—"

"Even if he doesn't want to!" The mystery man fell on top of Rayleigh. She watched in the reflection as he kissed her neck and slid back the top of her dress. She ran her hands up and down his back. As he brought his head up to kiss her, Rayleigh expanded the plan to include yet another problem could be eliminated.

Victor arrived at Joe and Angela's to the smell of scampi and his granddaughter's screaming, "Nano's here! Nano's here!" He wrapped his arms around both girls in a giant hug as Angela came around the corner.

"Gia! Amelia! Stop! You are going to hurt Nano!" she leaned over and planted a kiss on her father's cheek. "Hi, daddy."

"Hi, Angie. Is Joey home yet?"

"He should be here any minute, and so should Lena and Louisa."

"You got Louisa down from Ithaca?"

"Yeah. She said she wanted to hand-deliver some papers and talk to Lena. I don't know about what. Do you want to share daddy?" When Victor didn't reply, Angie knew better than to push her father. "What can I get you to drink? Glass of wine?"

"Small one, Angie. I need to go back to work."

"Work? Daddy, you work too hard. Sit. Relax." There appeared to be a small commotion in the hallway as Lena, Louisa, and Joe entered at the same time. The girls bounced up and down, not sure who to hug first. After tackling their father, they embraced Lena is warm hugs.

Louisa turned to move out of the fray, and gratefully accepted a glass of wine from Angela. She made her way towards Victor, her lips were frozen in a smile. "We need to talk," to which Victor responded with a slight nod.

"Mi famiglia!" Lena exclaimed. "Angie, the scampi smells great."

"Thank you, mama." Her father and husband disappeared down the hallway towards the home office. She thought to follow, yet that would mean Lena was taking over in the kitchen, and like in the old days, Louisa assisting with setting the table. Neither idea sounded appealing.

Joe led Victor down the hall and shut the door to the small home office behind him. He poured out two glasses of scotch, neat, and took a seat behind his desk. Victor sat back on the couch and took a sip. The liquid burned the back of his throat.

"Louisa wants to talk to me," Victor's voice rose.

"You shouldn't have Enzo blow his cover."

"I didn't. Bruno set it up. Honestly, Joey, I completely forgot little Enzo was up at that school." Victor raised his glass to his lips. "You know, though, this is a break because I got one less family member to worry about." Joe started to speak, yet Victor interrupted with, "And to me, Louisa is still family."

"To me too. Neddy is an idiota." Both men raise their glasses and drink. Victor's smile turned serious.

"Joey, what I got to tell you isn't good," Victor stated.

"If it was, we'd be out in the living room, and you'd be playing with your granddaughters."

"To the princesses," Victor raises his glass. He emptied the amber liquid and leaned forward. "Joey, your brother is a dumb ass."

Joe burst out laughing. "No, kidding! Tell me something I don't know."

"He owes a hustler who calls himself The Pirate King about a hundred grand, best I can figure."

"He owes what?" Joe sat with his mouth open. He started mumbling something in half Italian and half English. "Are you serious? I guess this explains the missing money. Who is this guy?"

"Joey, relax. I'm going to take care of this. Family—"

"Family does, I know. But Vic, this isn't your fight." Victor met Joe's gaze yet didn't speak. Giggles from Gia and Amelia came from behind the door. They could hear Angela instructing the girls to be quiet down, or Nano and daddy would stay in the office all night. "Vic, what am I missing here?"

Victor took in a long breath. "This is a little more complicated than the Pirate King." Victor opened and closed his mouth several times. He gestured in all directions, "We've established your brother is a dumb ass, right?" Joe agreed. "You've met his new one, what the number five--"

"Don't call her that in front of my mama—"

"No, kidding. Well, number five comes with, how do I say this, baggage."

"What kind of baggage?" His son-in-law's fist open and close.

"Here's the whole picture. There is this pirate king guy who shows up every night after you leave. He stays around fifteen minutes and exits with a paper bag and a cup of something."

"Vic, it could be a to-go order."

"To-go order every night from your fancy pants restaurant? Joey, I thought you were a smart man."

"Okay, so what do you think it is?"

"I think he is picking up payment or drugs or both. There is a spike in drug arrests in the city in the last two weeks. This could be related." Victor paused. "Do you think Neddy could be dealing or letting someone deal out of the restaurant?"

Joe thought about the money, "My heart says no, but my gut..." Joe heard the girls laugh. *Protect the family.* "Vic, I think Neddy could be into something." He explained the missing money. "But I want to give the guy the benefit of the doubt, you know because he's —"

"Your brother."

"Exactly. Now I don't know what to think."

"My guys are keeping an eye on this Pirate King character. We should be able to do something soon. If nothing else, I will get him out of your life," Joe shuttered to think what this could mean. "As far as the girl —"

"You mean number five." Joe closed his eyes as the words slipped out. "Crap, now you got me doing it! Mama's going to pitch a fit!"

"Yes, number five," Victor laughed. "Ah, Joey, I can't make this shit up! Number five is part of something, yet I am not sure what. My men have taken pictures of her with, how do I put this, ah, people who we are watching."

"What kind of people?"

"The usual," Victor shrugs."

"Jesus, Mary, and Joseph."

"Not quite, but you get the picture. Try to avoid bringing the kids around Neddy's new gal."

"Avoid bringing the kids around family? Ah, Vic—"

"Yes, yes, I see your point. Maybe we should let my Angie in on this part."

"Oh, crap. Angie's going to kill both of us."

"No, just you. She loves me." Vic laughed, yet his face showed no happiness. "Joey, we need to keep an eye on the family. Just avoid Neddy's, new lady. That is all I ask."

"Easier said than done."

"Joey, I have been doing this for years. You remember when you first started dating my Angie. My friendship with your father only went so far."

"You had us followed…"

"That's right, I did. I had you followed, and you were a perfect gentleman, because if you weren't," Victor brought his finger across his neck, "well, we wouldn't be sitting here, now would we." Joe let out a nervous laugh. "The girl lives in a costly building and doesn't make any known income we can find. Neddy drove her home multiple times. We are working on the connection. There is one thing about your brother I never understood…" Vic brought his voice down, "He's an okay-looking boy, but Joey, he's not really good looking. I mean, the guy is probably a seven, maybe an eight. So how does he get all these women?"

A soft knock prevented Joe from answering the question. Louisa poked her head in, "I am the only one here brave enough to interrupt you two," she joked. "Angela said to tell you if you don't get your butts to the table," Louisa shrugged, "her words, not mine, the pasta will be mush, and you will officially ruin dinner." Someone shouted something in Italian. "Mama said to add something, but I can't understand her," Louisa smiled and shut the door. "No capire, mama."

"We'd better go," Victor rose. "I know better to mess with an Italian woman's cooking."

"Vic, you know better than to mess with your daughter, we both do."

Victor smiled, yet he stopped by the closed door. "Joey," he said, "our conversation today is family business, meaning it is between you and me."

"I understand."

"I know Neddy is your brother—"

"I get it, Vic, family business," Joe let out a sigh. "Let's eat!" Joe moved out of the door as Louisa stepped to the side. As Victor exited, she moved to block his path.

"We really need to talk now," she didn't move, adding, "about Enzo." Victor nodded.

"Eat first. Talk after."

Lex Oxford followed a wiry, disheveled man do the main street. His target paused to take in a 360-degree gaze at each corner. He would turn to walk south, yet instead, continue straight at the last minute. Lex thought he had been spotted until he stopped to create distance, only to see the mannerisms continue.

He chuckled as he thought about his target's moniker, The Pirate King. "What the freak does that mean?" Lex said to no one. His walk continued for a few more blocks, ending in front of a rundown brick building. He ducked into a doughnut shop across the street.

"Hey, boss. What goes it?" Lex had one of those hearing devices he ordered off the television. For twenty bucks, he could hear any conversation within fifty feet. He thought it was a good investment. The King answered, "It's going. Did you do the pick-up?" The other man nodded and handed over a brown paper bag.

"Could they get anymore templated?" The few sitting at the counter turned in his direction. He pointed out the window and let out a cackle. His audience turned back to their coffees. *Yes, I am just another crazy in your neighborhood,* he chuckled.

If any had asked his name, the situation could become more humorous. People always asked, "Lex? Like in Luther?" He would laugh as he explained how both his parents had been fans of Superman, and yes, he was named after the villain of the series.

Lex always thought his parents foreshadowed his current employment when choosing a name for their only son. He was, after all, produced after they conceived four females. Thoughts of his long-gone family popped into his head. As he visualized each sister (Ivy, Harley, Quinn, and Talia) along with his parents, Bruce and Robin. He greeted each with a grin and waited for each face to disintegrate within minutes before his eyes.

A coffee cup shattering across the floor brought his attention back to The Pirate King, who was making his way across the street towards where he sat. The man arrived whistling and proceeded to give a quick head nod to each of the six people, Lex included, who sat nursing coffees. He walked around the side of the counter, only to disappeared into the back room.

"Putz," Lex heard someone mutter. He jotted down a couple notes. He placed his full cup of coffee into the bin by the door. The sign above reading: *If You Want Cheap Coffee, Clean Up After Yourselves.*

Lex walked out laughing. The world was full of inept crooks, and he loved every single one. He turned in the direction of downtown and sauntered away, unaware of the other following his path.

Victor stood outside the restaurant, smoking a cigar when Joe arrived for work. "My staff didn't offer you coffee, Vic?" he said in the way of greeting. The fact his father in law came to visit at such an early hour caused his stomach to hurt more than eating his wife's leftover scampi for breakfast.

"I got a cappuccino down the street." Vic followed Joe inside. The staff scurried to set tables, cut fruit at the bar, and restock liquor and glasses. Joe waved as he walked straight to his office. "Is this the way you always greet your workers?" Victor inquired. "Joey, you should be nice. Then they take care of your interests."

Joe let out a laugh. "Is that the way you get your crew to do work?" Victor shrugged. Joe closed the door behind them, "What's up? I doubt this is a social call." Victor sat down and placed his cigar butt in the clean ashtray on the coffee table.

"Joey," Victor began, "Remember our conversation from last night. I'm going to let you into what a dumb ass your brother is. The guy who takes the bag at night. He goes by the name of The Pirate King—"

"The Pirate King? I thought Neddy was the Pirate King?"

"We wish. Neddy apparently borrowed money from this small-time crook…"

"Jesus," Joe ran his hands over his face. "What a freaking idiot!"

"Although we can't figure out why…"

"This is Neddy. Who knows!"

"Okay, so we can take care of the King for you. No worries there. Think of this problem as a non-problem."

"So if the Pirate King is a non-problem…"

"Okay, problem number one. Problem two is a little more complicated."

"Problem two?"

"Yeah, this one is bad."

"Worse than extortion?"

"Oh yeah. This one will involve having possible protection for the family." Joe didn't say a word. He glanced at the photo of Angie and the kids on his desk. He clenched and unclenched his fists. "Possible, Joey, possible. Neddy's new friend, we believe, is involved in the drug ring I recently eliminated. If our theories are true –you'll need a little escort for about a week or so."

"And if not?"

"If not, you guys are in the clear, and she is yet another female to fall for your brother's weird charm." Victor let the last part sink in.

"Are we still in the family business stage?"

"Yeah, about that. We—"

"We?"

"I had a conversation with Louisa on the way back to her hotel—"

"Victor!"

"I was dropping her off, nothing else." Victor threw his hands up. "Is that all you Vaffanculo's think about is sex?" His son-in-law's grinned, "Remember I am Angie's father. You only had sex twice; once time for each princess." Joe let out a laugh. "Louisa was concerned about the relationship between Enzo and me."

"She drove all the way here to talk with you?"

"I asked the same question and was told she is a trained professional, and body language is important."

Joe rolled his eyes and crossed his arms. "What does this tell you?"

Ignoring the jibe, Victor continued, "I explained to Louisa that I still thought of her as family and figured because she was new to Ithaca having a friend there could be, ah, helpful."

"Vic, you pulled the part of the family act?"

"Louisa informed me although she appreciated the gesture, it was not necessary. Enzo would be getting no special treatment by her. And could I let him know she wasn't his responsibility."

"And?"

"I told her I would." Joe broke into a big smile. "So, I lied. If the situation changes, we may vacation at the beach house."

"Oh, crap…"

"I'll let you know." Vic took a sip of his now cold coffee. "Now, as I think about this, you should probably let Angie know what is going on. Can we trust Lena?"

"We did in the past," Joe responded. "Vic, don't you think mama is getting too old for this shit?"

"I'm the same age as your mama…"

"Yeah – about that…did not you promise Angie you would retire after you took down the last drug guy?"

"Well, Joey, I did. But there is no one to take over at this point, and the drug slime had friends. Maybe after this one, I'll retire and spoil my grandchildren. Speaking of which, maybe you and Angie could think about one more…"

"I know I'm in trouble when you switch to additional grandchildren. I'll talk to Angela."

"Thank you, my son."

"Yeah, you need to talk to my mama. I think I got the better end of breaking bad news to stubborn Italian women."

"Maybe." Victor got up to leave and repeated, "Joey, family business," to which he got a nod. "I'll let you know the plan as soon as I put it together."

Joe picked up the phone and hit speed dial. When his wife said hello, he smiled. Even after all these years, hearing her voice made him happy. "Angie, Vic was here this morning. We need to talk." While he waited for her response, he came up with a plan to kill his brother and make his life so much easier.

Neddy finally hushed the last of the bar crowd out for the night. It had been a long one — three fights over a woman and one with two guys fighting over a third. The city police visited all four times. After the third fight, Neddy gave the cops free lunch certificates and bought a round of drinks for his "nice customers."

Then the guy fight happened.

"Go get an espresso," he instructed to the last two women who stumbled out. His staff moved in their own rhythm, wiping down tables, rearranging chairs, and restocking the bar. The room smelled of stale boozes and piss.

"Who's got bathroom duty?" Neddy shouted. When no answer came, he yelled again and waited. He swore under his breath and went back to his office. Two register tapes, along with a stack of cash, lay across the top. The door to his office opened without a knock. "Don't you believe in knocking," Neddy commented as he guided some of the money into his top drawer.

"I don't need to knock," the voice gruff, his words slurred. "And is that all of my money?" The Pirate King stood in full regalia, purple robe, and all. He rested one hand on a sword while the other gestured with glee. "How much?"

Neddy stood still. "I haven't counted it yet," he explained.

"Counting, smouting. What does the tape say?" the Pirate King reached over and grabbed the register tape out of Neddy's hand. "Ah...nice...this is perfect," he muttered. A purple string bag appeared in his free hand. With once scoop, he moved the money from the desk into the bag. "This feels light. You ain't holding out on me now, are you?" With one motion, The Pirate King brought his sword's point to Neddy's throat. "You don't want to cross me, Neddy."

"Please just move that thing," Neddy quivered. He opened the top drawer then piled on another more bills. "This is all of it, I swear."

"This includes the restaurant?"

"No, NO...because my brother takes and makes a deposit. So, this is the club..."

"Your brother, huh?"

"We have a deal."

"We have a deal as long as I say we have a deal!" The Pirate King waved his sword around, just missing the photos on the desk. He grabbed the bag and held it out, mentally weighing the contents. "Only a bit more after this," the conversation more thinking out loud than directed at Neddy. He turned and walked to the door adding, "Neddy, don't get any ideas. This is a good partnership here," and with that comment, he left.

Neddy rested his head in his hands. His desk now completely cleared, along with its open, empty drawers. In the next drawer, down, Joe kept a pistol. *Joey is going to kill me. I should just tell him, but...he can be such a righteous jerk!* His family photo stared back at him. All smiled brightly. *I did this for you!* He pointed at the picture. *You! Because family comes first.* Neddy went back to resting his head. A knock on the door jolted him.

"What?" he screamed.

Santos poked his head in, "There's someone here to see you, and the crew is pretty much done."

"Who's here?"

"I am," Rayleigh pushed the bartender aside and waltzed into Neddy's office.

"Yeah – the crew is done."

"Rayleigh now is not the right time."

"Neddy, what's wrong?" With two steps, she appeared by his side.

"Nothing, I just—"

"Oh, Neddy," Rayleigh engulfed Neddy in her arms. Even though she shouldn't be here, Neddy didn't move. Rayleigh rubbed his back. When he brought his eyes to meet hers, tears ran down his face. "Neddy, talk to me."

Neddy broke the embrace and moved to sit on the couch. Rayleigh followed. "I'm fine. It is all fine," he whimpered.

Rayleigh rose to get two glasses and a bottle of tequila off the shelf behind Neddy's desk. "You need a drink," she poured two shots. She handed one glass to Neddy and without ceremony, "To a better life," before downing the liquid in her glass. Neddy hesitated, yet followed. Rayleigh poured two more. "You want to talk about it?"

"Naw," Neddy downed the second shot. "I'm good." Rayleigh sat with one hand on Neddy's thigh. When she leaned in to get another glass of liquor, she moved it closer to his crotch. Neddy didn't move.

"One for the road," she proclaimed. Rayleigh tilted her head back to swallow. She let a trickle of booze escape her mouth. Neddy's eyes follow the thin stream down her neck into her cleavage. She took her hands and pulled his head into her chest. His hot breath warmed her nipples. "Things will get better."

"No, they won't," Neddy spoke into her breasts.

Rayleigh lifted his head, so their mouths lined up. "Yes, Neddy, they will," she whispered as she brought her lips to his. With a fierce hunger, she moved her body close, rubbing her breasts against his chest as her mouth took what it craved. Rayleigh's free hand stroked his zipper, and she delighted the area underneath lay hard and at attention. "Tell me what's wrong," she begged. "I may be able to help."

She unzipped his pants and took him into her hands. Neddy shook as she touched with her fingers. Rayleigh brought her head down into Neddy's lap, her mouth again taking what she needed. She heard Neddy gasp. She peered up to a relaxed smile and closed eyes.

Rayleigh brought her head back down and counted to ten. "Neddy, you're right," she said through sniffles, "this isn't going to solve anything." Neddy opened his eyes. His erection lay still in Rayleigh's hand.

"So close," he muttered.

"Neddy, tell me what's wrong. I feel this weird connection, and it makes me want to help you."

Neddy took in a deep breath. "It started with the construction of this place..." A half-hour later, Neddy had told her the entire Pirate King story.

"Holy shit," Rayleigh commented. She got a faraway look in her eyes while her hands massaged his shaft. "I need to think," she proclaimed as she took him in her mouth. Neddy lay back, mentally exhausted. Things were getting better. He could see the light coming in his direction. *Yes, it would all be okay. It would be okay because of Rayleigh. Rayleigh. Rayleigh.*

"Oh my god, I got it," Rayleigh exclaimed prior to Neddy reaching contentment. "I know how to fix this!"

Neddy looked down at his now soft manhood. Disappointment showed on his face. "Fix what?"

"The Pirate King silly," she answered.

Neddy had forgotten he told her about the Pirate King. The gun in the middle drawer appeared a better alternative than having to confess to his family he got hustled. "What?"

"You know the Pirate King...Dude taking your money..." Rayleigh poured herself another shot and downed it with one motion. Neddy's head began to ache. "I'm not crazy. I want you to know this upfront because what I am about to suggest," she giggles, "it is a little wild," he nodded. "You said he comes in every night and cleans you out, right? Except you had been hiding cash, which he found tonight, right?" Neddy could feel his head getting ready to explode. When did he tell Rayleigh all this? "And no one questions the dude because, in the beginning, you made it look like you two were friends —"

"Rayleigh..."

"Okay, I am getting there. So when he comes in tomorrow night," she paused for effect, "we kill him. Problem solved."

Neddy slipped down the sofa a bit more. *She didn't just say that...* His mouth hung open, and eyes blazed in her direction. "You're nuts," he slurred.

"Yeah. So are you. We are both in therapy, you know." Neddy waited. "Darling, hear me out. You said he used to come in at the start of your shift, but now he's showing up after you close the club. So – next time he comes in, you shoot him, and I'll help you dispose of the body." Rayleigh took in a big inhale, "you know, I explained how I'm amazing at doing that sort of thing."

Neddy tried to remember any conversation mentioning the disposal of body parts and came up blank. He moved his butt so he could zip up his pants and sat straight up. "Rayleigh, I'm not sure about this…"

"Fine," Rayleigh stood up. "I'll just," she leaned over to grab her purse as Neddy grabbed her hand to pull her back down. This time on to his lap.

"Let me think," he instructed. "Come back tomorrow, and I'll let you know." Rayleigh opened her mouth to speak. Neddy reassured her, "Our secret."

"Our secret," she repeated. "Oh, and Neddy, let me know if you want the cashback he got tonight?"

Neddy arrived back home as the sun began to rise. From his youth, he knew what stairs squeaked, so he jumped and swerved to arrive at the apartment door unnoticed. Once inside, he removed his shoes and went straight to the bathroom. Here he stripped naked, threw his clothes in the hamper, and washed with a nearby towel, also adding the cloth to the hamper.

He caught his image in the mirror and smiled. *Everything would be okay. This is all a minor inconvenience. The situation would go away, and life would be normal again. I can tell Joey after how I fixed this one, not him. Rayleigh promised to fix her problem…*

Victor slammed around his office, throwing anything within his reach. The photographs in the middle of his desk told it all; Rayleigh O'Connor appeared to be involved with Lex Oxford. Of all the people! To make matters more complicated, a photo of her and Neddy leaving the club last night at four in the morning lay on top of his pile.

"How freakin' stupid is this guy!" he exclaimed to no one. Victor stared at the images as he paced. He clenched a released his free hand. "Neddy, you are a complete and utter idiot," he murmured. His voicemail had five angry messages from his Angie. The last, the most hurtful. "Daddy, you don't need this crap, and neither do we. Retire for crying out loud."

Her words haunted. *Except now, he couldn't retire because he had to take care of Neddy's mess. That's ok. Neddy will owe him, which could be more lucrative than a 401K.* Victor snorted at the thought. A single bang on his door brought his attention to Bruno, who kept looking over his shoulder as he spoke.

"Did you see the photos?"

"Couldn't miss them." He again picked up the picture of Neddy and Rayleigh.

"She's in with Oxford," Bruno pointed towards the image.

"No, shit."

"We watched her place last night. Englishman came by around eight and stayed for about an hour or so. If the shadows in the window indicated anything, they are close." Victor stared. "Neddy got there around four-fifteen, four-twenty this morning. He stayed until a little after five. We are not sure what they were doing because the lights appeared off." Bruno waited for a beat, "If she was a guy, we'd be envious…"

"Yeah," Victor responded without any enthusiasm. "Except she's not, and she's very dangerous, at least to our operation." He walked over to the bulletin board covered with photos. "Bruno, take a look at this. If Rayleigh and Lex Oxford are connected…" He pointed to a picture in the upper left corner of a man and a woman walking near Steak.

"Boss, you don't think?"

"I don't know what to think at this point." Victor ran his hands over his face. "If my son-in-law's dumb ass brother is involved." He shook his head. "Joey is such a nice boy. I promised his father I would watch out for the family. Now, look what his dipshit brother got us all in to!"

"Speaking of family boss, did you tell Angie?"

"No, I let Joey take care of it. Which is why I have all those nasty barks on my voicemail. My daughter is not happy with me right now."

"I can understand. What about Mrs. Vaffanculo?"

Victor gaffed. "I haven't told her yet. Today. I will tell her today." Victor walked to the window. A white van is parked directly across the street in front of Steak. "Ah, Bruno," Victor called and pointed to the vehicle.

"Not ours, boss."

"Do we know who it is?"

"Not yet, but we are working on it." There was a slight nod. "By the way, I disposed of our old van and its passenger."

"Good work," Victor smiled. "At least something today went right."

Victor strolled up the walk at the Vaffanculo residents like he had so many times prior. The geraniums along the walk stood at attention. He noticed Lena's plants next to the house had a few ripe tomatoes. He picked one and bit into the sweet fruit. He reached for the other and pocketed it.

The Vaffanculo house had been his sanctuary. When Angie's mother left, the first people at his door were Giuseppe and Lena offering to help. Angie spent many nights here as a young child when his work took him to other places.

When Giuseppe passed, Victor took on the role of an older brother with Lena. He protected her from the shady characters who tried to date the beautiful widow and the hustlers who wanted to steal her money. She had Neddy off god knows where and Joey away at school. Victor visited once a week and took her to dinner at least as many evenings.

Next to the tomato plants grew a large bush of basil. He snipped off a leaf to smell the pungent aroma. Victor raised his hand to knock at the door, only to be greeted by a familiar face out the second-floor window.

"You a steal my tomatoes again, you poacher, and I will pour the hot espresso on your head!" Lena's smile stretched across her entire face.

"Oh, Mrs. Vaffanculo, please forgive me. Your tomatoes are so ripe and beautiful." Victor couldn't tell for sure, yet his old friend appeared to be blushing. "And your basil—"

"You stay away from my basil!" Lena's laughter resonated. "You coming up?"

"As soon as you unlock the door." Victor reached for the door handle. As he did, the door opened into the hallway. "Lena, how many times do I need to tell you and the kids to lock this thing!"

Lena greeted Victor with a hug and a kiss on each cheek. He followed her through the open door of her apartment into the kitchen, where she already had two cups of coffee and a plate of homemade cherry biscotti on the table.

"Lena, you really need to start locking the door," he said while adding cream and honey to his coffee. Not hearing an answer, he turned to find Lena pointed an antique Saturday Night Special at him.

"Don't let Angie or Joe see you," he proclaimed. "I got a lecture from both for having my gun on the desk in the office.

"That's a because the princesses came by."

"They could stop in here anytime."

"The gun is in its secret hiding place. The girls will never find it," Lena's laughter filled the room. She took a saucepan off the wall to reveal a tiny shelf. She placed the gun on the shelf and repositioned the pan.

"How do you know they won't use the pan for cooking?"

"Because these are Nana's special pans and only Nana gets to use them. If anyone else uses these while I am alive, then I stop cooking. Plain and simple."

"No one would want that to happen."

"Damn straight." Lena sat across from Victor. She fixed her coffee the same way, with a splash of cream and a squirt of honey. Lena used a piece of biscotti to stir the hot liquid. She took a sip and stared at Victor right in the eye. "This isn't a social call."

"No."

"So?"

"Ah – that is what I love about you, Lena. Straight to the point. Giuseppe married a perfect woman." Victor saluted her with his coffee.

"We both know that. Victor..." Lena reached across the table and placed her hand on his.

"It's not good, Lena."

"Are you sick?"

"Not me —"

"Am I sick?"

Victor laughed. "No, you are not sick, either."

"This can't be about your retirement. That would be wonderful news for the entire family..."

"You're right. It would be. I am going to retire," Her smile grew wide, "but there is one more situation to take care of." Her smile vanished. "And it involves family."

"Family? Who would be so stupid in this family — " Lena's hand flew up to cover her mouth. Victor reached over and took both her trembling hands in his. "I'll kill him myself, and I know how."

"No need. At least not at this point," Victor glanced up at the pan. "Remember the English people who were playing games with us? Apparently, he has a brother. I'm still trying to figure out why this brother is over here, but I think it's got something to do with me." Lena snickered. "Seriously, no ego. I think the brother wants revenge because…"

"Oh. So how is the family involved? In the past, you managed…"

"Yes, I managed to keep you all out of my affairs, but this time is different. A woman is working with him. She is stunning and manipulative."

"Neddy," Lena muttered under her breath.

"She has taken a shine to your son, yes, but I believe she will use him to get to the rest of us."

"Does the idiot know?"

"Probably not. He seems to attract pretty girls all the time—"

"This is why I have papers in my drawer Louisa delivered signed. This is why my jewelry is scattered over three states. This is why…"

"Lena, stop. We both know Neddy's issues."

"Of course!" Lena paused and asked, "So what do we need to do."

"Nothing. Well, no. I need you to be more aware of your surroundings. I need you to lock your freakin' doors. If the situation changes, one of my guys will visit you for coffee and company." Victor takes a bite of this biscotti. He savors the cherry vanilla flavor a moment, adding, "If it comes to that, please do not give him these. You will never get him to leave."

"What about my Neddy?" Lena had no patience for jokes. "What about the rest of the family?"

"We are watching him, and don't worry, the family takes care of the family. As far as Joe, Angie, and the kids," Victor held his hands out in front, "Joey knows what is going on. He said he would let me know if they needed back up, and he would not put any member of our family at risk. Lena, my babies are safe, and so is yours…"

"No matter how stupid?"

"Exactly. No matter how stupid."

"Vic, what is the worst case?"

"You take a vacation to the beach."

"Always the freakin' beach…" Lena takes a bite of her biscotti and chews, thinking about the beach house.

Lex Oxford stood off in the distance from Steak's entrance. He watched the cleaning crew enter and leave, jotting down the times for both. He observed the kitchen staff arrive. He made notes of delivery times and who greeted each vender. The brother showed up around eleven. He chatted with a few of the delivery people on his way in.

The rhythm stayed the same during his week of observations. When he noticed nothing out of place, he relaxed a little. No deviations meant no concerns, for him at least. The plan is simple. Rayleigh cons the dumb brother into killing off his nemesis. She probably broke up his marriage for sport.

He glanced at the tan line from his missing ring. *Rayleigh is very good at breaking up marriages*. At least she is skilled at revenge too.

The lunch crowd began to arrive. The valet attendants moved each car with the precision of a dance routine. His stomach growled. The idea of a nice steak enticed his palate, yet the practicality of eating at the restaurant wouldn't work.

Instead, he walked in the opposite direction, towards the deli that had become part of his daily routine. This better be done soon.

Bruno watched through the apartment window with binoculars. Oxford appeared again today, right on time. He needed to call Victor, yet he would wait. His boss was with Lena Vaffanculo. He knew enough not to disturb their meeting, at least he learned not to…Victor was a tough boss, yet Lena took toughness to a whole new level.

He should at least tell someone to follow Oxford. If he only had a partner. Bruno sneered. He had warned the guy many times about screwing up like he warned the guy he replaced, yet no one listens. Bruno knows firsthand of Victor Cuzzuto's temper.

A few years back, he was working with a so-called friend of Victor's. The friend was robbing Victor blind, and when Bruno found out, he offered him a cut of the action. He declined. The friend upped the ante. Yet he refused again. The friend threatened Enzo, who was in high school.

Victor flipped out. For almost an hour, Victor ranted in half Italian and half English. Bruno, who spoke both, could not understand a word of the rant. When he finally finished, after throwing an ashtray through the wall, Victor looks at him and asks, "Why didn't you tell me when you first found out?"

Bruno answered, "Because it was none of my business. Victor punched. Lights out. He got rid of the friend and left him with a warning, "Don't ever go against the hand that feeds you." Bruno took this to heart and became one of Victor's trusted allies. Victor talked about him taking over when he retires, although word on the street keeps saying if he retires.

Lesson learned. No one crosses the boss. Ever.

Victor picked up the phone on the first ring, "What?"

Bruno gave a detailed report of his observations and waited.

"Nice job." The phone clicked off.

Neddy arrived early at the restaurant. He worked the dining room, greeting customers, asking about their families, and leaving each table smiling as he moved to the next. Breezy observed her dad, wondering, not for the first time, why he had the club shift and not Uncle Joe, who vanished the minute her father had arrived.

"How is my princess?" Neddy asked in between tables. He may be the owner, yet his daughter was the star of the restaurant. She addressed customers by their name and made sure to remember something about each repeat, so she could ask how did Bobby do on his spelling test or is Jeri still into gymnastics. Even with a line out the door, Breezy made everyone's visit a little better.

"Good." She surveyed the room before bringing her attention back to her father. "What's going on with you?"

"Nothing," Neddy's smile stretched across his entire face.

"Hum, what does this mean?"

"It means that you will be picked up at eight—"

"No need —"

"No need?"

"Yeah, I have a date."

"A date?"

"With Harry. We both want to talk to you too."

"Oh, boy."

"Dad, what does that mean?"

Neddy laughed. "Anytime a boy wants to talk with a girl's father, it means trouble, either for the girl or her father."

Breezy returned the laughter. People glanced up from the dinners. "Daddy, I am a woman, and this is serious, but you will like this. I promise."

Neddy observed his daughter, all grown up. Mama did an excellent job with this one. God finally blessed my mama with a daughter. She always wanted a daughter. Actually, we could have made Joey the girl. "Call Nana and let her know." He kissed Breezy on the forehead and went back to chatting with customers.

Joe stewed in the office. Just seeing his brother made him want to punch him. Plain and simple; Neddy is an idiot. He checked the time and went out to empty the bar and dining room register. Although the restaurant took credit cards, most of their customers still paid with cash. This was an advantage for quarterly taxes, bad for leaving uncounted bills around for his brother to pilferage.

"Hey, Joey, what's shaking?" One of the bar regulars asked. Joe answered with a shrug. "Nice to see you so happy," the guy came back with. "Man, I never have seen anyone who was making money looking so miserable!"

Joe shoved a pile of twenties along with a few fifties and hundreds into his front pocket. "Give the mouth a drink on me," he instructed and pointed at the customer, "This one is on me. Break out the old wallet and tip my bartender proper." The guy howled with laughter.

"Thank you, Joey."

Joe went around to behind the hostess station. Here he lifted out a pile of bills from the register. He reached under the shelf and threw the money into an already two-thirds filled metal box. Joe went to the register, punched in a code, and waited for a long slip of paper to submerge. He glanced at the total on the bottom while he held the box in his left hand.

He gestured to Breezy and disappeared back into his office. Joe stacked the bills in three piles. He counted out each collection. Instead of putting the cash in the safe, he got a to-go container off the shelf and shoved the bills in until no more could fit. He fitted the foil top on and got ready to leave.

"I'm taking off," he told Breezy as he strolled passed.

"Aren't you going to talk to daddy?" she asked. When her uncle didn't reply, Breezy shouted, "Have a good night," in the same voice she used for customers.

"Where's he going?" Neddy came up from behind.

"Damn if I know. Uncle Joey had a to-go container for Angie and left," Neddy turned to walk towards the kitchen.

"Yo, chef," As Neddy entered the inner sanctuary, he heard a knife hit a cutting board loud. His head chef, Pedro, gave a warning glance, yet Neddy just continued, "What did my brother get to-go tonight. I'm feeling a little hungry and want the same."

SLAM. The knife hit the cutting board. "Joey, no get take out," one of the waiters answered. The knife came down again. This time a tomato burst all over the counter. Without a word, the chef turned his back towards the stove.

"I saw him leave with a container..." Neddy insisted. The waiter nudged him towards the door.

"Maybe he brought home dessert for Angela and the girls. He'll hit the freezer sometimes..." He pushed Neddy out of the service door.

"What the hell?"

"Neddy, Joe warned you. Pedro, for some reason, doesn't like you..." When Neddy opened his mouth to rebuff, the waiter said, "You should be thanking me. I just saved your ass." He turned to go back to his tables. Neddy froze. After a minute of deep inhales, he regained his composure to head into the dining room.

Breezy saw the exchange yet said nothing. She remembered Uncle Joe's warning. Even she stays out of the kitchen. The bar began to get crowded. Breezy noted a creepy guy crawled back on his stool. Why her dad remained friends with him, she'll never know. When he looked directly into her eyes, she shuttered and turned away.

A cold chill stayed. Harry couldn't get here fast enough.

"Hello, love," a very chiseled man with a sweet smile, broke her spell. "I thought this was a dance club."

"It is," Breezy answered, surprised to find herself blushing. "We change over after nine." She glanced at her watch. "Dinner crowd should be clearing soon. You are welcome to take a seat at the bar."

At the crowded bar, his glance stopped at the hunched over Pirate King. "Actually, love," Breezy blushed again, "I think I'll stop by a bit later. Save me a dance?"

Breezy grew redder. "I actually leave after the restaurant closes, yet if I didn't…"

"My loss," he sighed. Breezy stared as he walked away. He held the door open for another person, in walk her boyfriend, Harry. She turned a brighter red and, in an awkward manner, began arranging the menus.

"Hello, darling," Harry smiled as he leaned in for a kiss. "What's wrong?"

"Nothing," Breezy answered, much too fast. She tucked a loose strand of hair back behind her ears. "Nothing at all…" She forced a smile up at Harry yet couldn't figure out why she was off.

"Ah, love," Harry answered. "Everything will go well with your dad." At the word love, Breezy flinched.

Rayleigh showed up close to one in the morning, this time in a tight, red number had both males and females appreciating the view. What had become her stool immediately became vacant, and before she could ask, a glass of the house's finest Chablis is placed in front of her.

Rayleigh loved the attention. She wanted it to last, yet knew it couldn't. Over on the opposite side of the club, she spotted Lex Oxford dancing with two women who appeared half his age. A tinge of jealousy surfaced. He would be gone soon, too.

None of her lovers lasted, ever. Rayleigh used each for her purpose, after neatly disposing of their remains. She had only one she imagined to be permanent, virtually unattainable, yet could be permanent. Everything she did, she did to please him. Secretly she wanted his love and acknowledgment. In reality, all she got a "good job" every once in a while. Delivering Victor Cuzzuto's head on a platter should earn her high praise and maybe a permanent partner.

Oxford caught her eye and gave a quick head nod in her direction. *Amateur,* she thought. *He thinks he's above all this. Little does he know.* Rayleigh gave a small, toothless smile in returning and held her glass in his direction. She took a small sip and turned towards the bar. Many of the reflections she noticed, had been here on her last visit. The few new faces didn't bring any sense of worry.

Her eyes caught with a youngish man off to the side. He was dressed a little off for a nightclub, khaki pants, and a golf shirt, yet seemed harmless. She shook her shoulder back, which allowed one dress strap to fall, revealing her breast. She smiled as the man stumbled, only to spill his drink on a passing young thing. With one motion, Rayleigh brought the strap back up and the dress into place.

She glanced around the bar. Only the nerd caught the action. She snickered, *probably the only boob he'd see tonight*. The man apologized for spilling, yet the girl chose to make a scene. As her voice cut through the crowd, Rayleigh observed the nerd had disappeared.

"That was evil, love," she felt Lex's hot breath against her ear. "Beautifully executed yet very, very evil. Am I going to spank you later?"

Rayleigh turned. Her eyes dead and cold. "Maybe tomorrow, yet tonight I need to work," she said loud enough for him to hear. "If you don't get out of my face, I will cut your balls off personally." She gave a full smile. Lex held his glass up and disappeared into the crowd.

Rayleigh shrugged and waited. She had another target this evening.

Neddy waited for the last of the stranglers to be escorted out the door. A half-hour earlier, the house lights came up, the music silenced, and most clubbers exited. He exhaled relief. Rayleigh still sat perched on her stool. The Pirate King left with the crowd, to-go order in tow. Neddy tried to explain why the package appeared lighter, yet the king stopped him mid-sentence with a hand wave.

"You know the cost of doing business with me," the king just stared. Neddy shuttered. Joe had taken off with the restaurant receipts, so the payment came to about half. Neddy figured by the end of the month they should be square. He really didn't need Rayleigh's or anyone else's help. He had the situation under control.

Neddy walked back towards the bar, somewhat surprised to find Rayleigh gone. "Busy night tonight, boss," Santos commented as Neddy cleaned out his register. "There's only one open tab," he cocked his head towards the now empty stool.

"It's okay. I got it," Neddy moved out into the entryway and reached under the hostess station. He grabbed the metal box, proceeded to his office. He arrived to find Rayleigh, topless, sitting on the couch. "You look lovely yet I don't think my help would appreciate—"

"I'm not here for your help…"

"Yeah, Rayleigh, about that," he turned and placed the pile of cash along with the metal box on top of his desk, stood, leaning against it. "You know, Rayleigh…"

"I know lots of things, Neddy." When he stayed put, Rayleigh rose to strut towards him. "I know you like this," her hot breath circled in his ear as she ran her fingers along his zipper. With one tug, his fly opened, releasing his erect penis into her hands. "And I know you like this," she barely touched him, yet she set off sparks.

Rayleigh stopped and turned to close the office door. She followed Neddy's eyes and, without preamble, dropped her dress on the floor. "Would you like to tell me what else you like? Or I can show you?" She stepped out of the dress. She pulled Neddy over to the couch and straddled him on top.

Neddy could only see Rayleigh's full breasts. He reached up to feel the weight in both hands. As Rayleigh arched back, a knock on the door had Neddy stammer, "I'm busy."

The door opened a crack, yet no one entered. "We are done here, boss. See you tomorrow."

"Yes, tomorrow," Neddy answered. He brought his attention back to Rayleigh's lips, which had found their way down his stomach.

"Did you hear something?" Neddy jumped up.

"Yes, darling. The sound of me pleasing you," Rayleigh cooed. Neddy listened. When silence prevailed, he brought his attention back to Rayleigh.

"Pleasure away," he instructed as he leaned back and closed his eyes. Rayleigh's smile turned to a scowl, yet she continued on with the spectacle.

"Darling, I need to ask a favor."

"Anything," Neddy answered.

"Anything?"

"Just keep doing whatever it is you are doing."

Rayleigh's smile returned. "Are we set for Saturday?"

"Whatever you…" Neddy's let out a groan.

"Saturday night, it is…"

Louisa sat in her kitchen, eating the second of three jelly doughnuts she picked up on the way home. Today she had a tough one. Two students came to her and begged her not to fail them. One she felt sorry for, the other hadn't been to her lectures in a month.

Both got an answer they didn't want to hear.

Enzo had stopped by during office hours, yet since her talk with Victor, Enzo's visits had been less frequent. She found herself missing his tales of the neighborhood and the Vaffanculo family. Louisa consumed the first before leaving the drive-thru. A stack of papers, each containing a letter, sat to her right, the top one smudged with powdered sugar. Her laptop sat open to the college's grading system. With one keystroke, her semester here appeared to end.

Next, she had to find a place to live since she couldn't expect to stay in the visiting scholar's home forever. Louisa looked around Ithaca a bit yet discovered a need for a bigger pond. The city, though beautiful, got too small at times. She had looked into retreats in New

York and L.A., where she might be able to disappear, at least for the summer months.

Ithaca was lovely, yet maybe not for her.

A car pulled up in front of the house. She listened as one door opened and closed, followed by the beep of an alarm being set. She waited for the sound of the front door. Nothing. Louisa walked to the window to pull the curtains back. Across the street, a man leaned against a black car, only visible by the appearance of red ash along with the outline of a white fedora.

She couldn't tell who this was, yet her hand flew to her stomach. The figure flicked the ash off to the side and began to walk towards her house. When the front door slammed, she jumped and hit herself in the head. Lena warned not to leave the door unlocked. She should listen.

A soft knock on her door had Louisa squeal and froze at the same moment. A second knock came louder. "Come on, Louisa, open the freakin' door." She recognized the voice, but from where? "God damn it, Louisa, its Victor. Open the freakin' door before I wake up the whole God Damn house."

"Victor, shush!"

"Louisa, open the door," Lena commanded. She pushed her way passed, followed close behind by Victor. Louisa closed her door, turned to watch Lena put the water on, and take out three coffee mugs. Her mother-in-law took over her kitchen. She placed the last doughnut on a plate, cut it into quarters, stuck a toothpick in each. She shrugged and said something in Italian as she put the plate in front of Victor. He returned the gesture.

Louisa stood in the doorway, more as an observer than a participant. "Sit, sit," Lena pointed to the chair between her and Victor. "Coffee will be ready soon."

"Grazie, Lena," Victor responded. Louisa saw the bags under his eyes. Even his smile appeared exhausted to her. "Louisa," Victor turned his attention, "Do you always dress in black for bed?" Louisa looked down. She had on the clothes leftover from her ventures—all black except for a stream of powdered sugar down the front.

"I, I..." Louisa waited for a beat to catch her thoughts. She shook her head at the doughnut cut up like an appetizer, "I went out for doughnuts." She pointed at the plate for emphasis.

"You needed doughnuts now?" Lena asked. "Are you…" she pointed at Louisa's stomach.

"NO!" Louisa answered with a bit too much force. "I am not pregnant!"

Victor placed a hand on each women's arm. "Ladies," he turned and hushed Lena. "Louisa, how are you?"

"What are you doing in Ithaca?" Louisa's gaze jumped between Victor and Lena.

"We came to see you," Lena took a big bag out of her purse and added a few biscotti to the plate with the donuts. "Mangia!"

"You drove all the way up here to bring me biscotti?" Victor and Lena exchanged glances.

"My idioto son strikes again," Lena muttered in Italian. "you know Vic, I liked this one. She is smart and pretty and …"

"Lena, please," Victor reached out to quiet the old lady. "Louisa, we are here because we want to offer you the beach house for a few weeks…"

"A month tops," Lena adds.

"The beach house?"

"Yes, we thought after your semester you would like a break from…"

"Ithaca." Lena jumps in.

"Yes, Ithaca. What do you say?"

Louisa got up and went to the sink. Her street was bathed in darkness. She took out a glass and filled it with water. After a long sip, she returned to the table. "You came to Ithaca to offer me the beach house, for what did you say, a couple weeks, maybe a month tops?" The two nodded in unison. "Why?"

"Why? What do you mean, why?" Lena frowned. "We can't offer you the beach house?"

The room got quiet. "Okay, Louisa. You are smarter than this. We know." He glanced at Lena. "Here is the situation; Neddy," Louisa flinch at her estranged husband's name, "Neddy he did something stupid—"

"No doubt."

"Hey, there is no need to be mean," Lena injected.

"Fine. Neddy did something stupid," Louisa repeated with an exaggerated eye roll.

"Yes. Very stupid." Victor waited for a beat to make sure he was not interrupted again. "Neddy, he got involved with some bad people."

"They must be really awful for you to be involved."

"Let's just say these are not my type of people and leave it at that."

"What does this have to do with me?"

"Probably nothing, yet I will rather be safe than sorry." Louisa concurred. "These people know a lot about the family, the whole family…"

"Is Meg safe?"

"You keep in touch with Meg?" Lena inquired.

"Lately. Somehow our lives became parallel." Lena had a distant glare. "We seem to be living similar nightmares. When I became suspicious, I called her for the symptoms."

"Symptoms?"

"Signs, Lena. How she knew Neddy was cheating." Louisa took in a breath. "Believe it or not, your son has patterns with women. Patterns go back to, oh, what's her name?"

Lena held up two fingers. "Number two?"

"No, the first one."

"Cloe?" The sound of Victor's voice made both jumps.

"Yeah, Cloe," Louisa repeated. "It doesn't matter. Will Meg be safe?"

"Yes," Victor answered. "Of course, the less she knows about our situation, the safer she will be. As I was saying, We'd like you to stay at the beach house for a few weeks. Angie and the kids will be there too…"

"And me…"

"And Lena. Maybe another friend or two. It will be relaxing. You can take the guest quarters, which will give a bit more privacy. What do you say?" Louisa's eyes volley between Victor and Lena. The room grew more still with each passing glance. The clock above the stove movements became more prominent — the birds out the window louder. Lena took a long sip of her coffee while Victor's bites of biscotti could be heard in the room.

"Is there a choice?"

"Of course, you do. Go. Don't go. This is your choice." Victor took a sip of his coffee, now lukewarm. He rose from the table and placed the cup into the nearby microwave. All observed his coffee turning in silence as the timer lowered into a single beep. Victor removed the cup and took a sip. Satisfied, he sat back down. "Louisa?"

"I don't want to go yet my gut tells me I must—

"Good thinking!" Victor shot Lena a glare.

--So, by default, I guess I will meet you there?"

"Why meet us there when we can take you now?" Victor smiled. "Pack an overnight bag. Bruno will bring back the rest of your things when he comes up for Enzo."

"Enzo..." Louisa repeated. She got up from the table and placed her mug in the sink. Outside the window, mountains stretched down to sinking valleys. She glanced out at Victor's car. A man in a driver's uniform stood smoking a cigarette while conversing with a campus police officer. The cop appeared to be laughing at something the driver said. *Does he have people everywhere?*

Victor motioned to Lena, who stared back. *What?* He pointed again in her direction. "Louisa, would you like some help?"

"Help? Oh yeah, packing. No, thank you, Lena. I got this." Louisa disappeared down the hallway. Banging, slamming, and objects hitting the wall could be heard in the distance. Lena and Victor could not make out what Louisa said, yet parts came through more apparent than others.

"Freakin' Neddy. I gave up everything for that twit and now look!" Crash! "I am being banished into some sort of hell hole at the beach. The freakin' beach." Thump! "Where is my summer of adventure? When do I get my new life?" Bang! "It is not bad enough the bastard cheated on me, now I am tied to his family. Jesus!" Louisa stopped to make the sign of the cross. "Dagnabit!"

Louisa emerged from the hallway with a computer case on one shoulder, pulling a suitcase with the opposite hand. She blushed as she entered the kitchen. "Ready?" Her voice carried a monotone.

"Ah, Louisa, we are so happy you will be joining us," Lena rose from the table as she spoke. "The princesses will be thrilled to see you!" Louisa forced a smile in Lena's direction. "Let us go."

Victor moved to help Louisa with her bag. He leaned in, "Louisa, this will be the last favor, I promise."

Lex Oxford sat on a bench across from Steak and waited. A few minutes later, Neddy and Rayleigh emerged. Neddy turned to lock the door. Rayleigh glanced across the street to meet his stare.

She gave a slight nod and pointed up to the sky. He rose and began to walk in the opposite direction. He glanced in time to see a shadow move across one of the apartment windows facing Steak. He crossed the road and disappeared from street view around the corner. From his pocket, he brought a thin scope to his eye. The image brought a smile to his face.

"So, Victor Cuzzuto, we meet again," he whispered. Lex Oxford watched for a few minutes before walking in the opposite direction as he whistled, *Goodbye Earl*, substituting Victor for Earl in his head.

Rayleigh followed Neddy to his car and waited for him to open the passenger's door. She slid across the seat, allowing her dress to slide up to the tops of her thighs.

"Shouldn't you fix your dress?" he asked as he entered the driver's side.

"Why darling," Rayleigh pulled it up higher to reveal her lack of panties. "Don't you like it?" Neddy started the car. He drove towards her penthouse. Rayleigh slipped her dress back down. Neddy stared straight ahead. "Is something wrong, darling?"

"I'm not sure," Neddy chose his words then just blurted out, "Yes…"

"Oh, darling, do I make you feel better?"

"Yes, but I shouldn't do…"

"Do what Neddy," Rayleigh created distance with their bodies.

"Do this," Neddy pointed at Rayleigh's crotch and up at her breasts. "I was supposed to be faithful. My god!" he shouted as he slammed the breaks. "Maybe this is why I have been married four times! Maybe I can't stay faithful?"

"Or maybe you just need to meet the right person to stay faithful to…"

"But I thought at the time they were all the right person." Neddy stuck his free hand in his mouth and began to chew on his fingers. An old habit every woman he dated found a turn-off. Rayleigh cringed before taking his hand in hers. She attempted to ignore the spit and where the hand had come from.

"Darling, we are never sure when the right one will be there. Before you, I never had sex out of marriage. I spent the last week going to Saint Francis every day to pray for forgiveness. If anyone should carry guilt in this situation…"

"Rayleigh, oh my gosh, I forgot about your problem. Now I feel even worst. I cheated on Louisa and, in the process, made you sin. Maybe she was right. Maybe I do need a different therapist. It seems I screwed up royally with this one."

"What does therapy have to do with all this?"

"Think about it; I was a married man. Each time I cheated on the one, I'm supposed to love. Wouldn't Doctor Von call this another pattern?"

"Screw Doctor Von!"

"Screw Doctor Von?"

"Neddy, I am going to tell you something. Something about our prestigious doctor. Yet you can't tell anyone, okay?" Neddy waited. "He is in with Louisa."

"Doctor Von is in with Louisa? Are you crazy?"

"Neddy, think about it. Doctor Von put you in a group with how many females? And what does your wife do? She watched from the observation window..." Neddy stopped the car and stared at Rayleigh. "Yeah, I saw the figure moving around in there too. I figured it must be her because you would get all quiet. But did you notice Doctor Von ignored this? I mean, come on, Neddy! I am not a psychiatrist, yet I saw it, and he didn't?"

"You think they set this up?"

"I wouldn't be surprised if they were in cahoots with the Pirate King too." Neddy burst out laughing. "Seriously. Where is Louisa?"

"I don't know. Teaching at some college upstate."

"Really, Neddy. You don't know. Wait, don't answer." Rayleigh held up her hand. "You said the Pirate King took how many extra dollars?"

"A lot." Rayleigh smiled. The Louisa angle hadn't been planned yet if she was to bring in the doctor, why not the ex, too. "A real lot. Do you think he is sending her money?"

"I think this is all for revenge." More real words were never spoken. "Neddy, you need help. Maybe now is the time to tell your family."

"No! I will not do that!" He let out a loud sigh. "I, no we," he took Rayleigh's hand in his, "we are going to eliminate the Pirate King and…"

"And what, darling?"

"And…let me think." He leans over and covers Rayleigh's mouth with him. "Yeah, and," Neddy repeated.

"Not coming up tonight, darling?"

"I think I need to go home." Rayleigh sighed. "There is too much on my mind."

"Neddy, about the Pirate guy…"

"What about him?"

"My offer stands. I think we should take care of him sooner than later. You are going to need every cent you make."

"Why?"

"You have five ex-wives!"

"I have three ex-wives and, oh hell!" Neddy threw his arms up. "You are right. I have four ex-wives, and whoever I marry next will end up being number five. I'm such a —"

"Lover, Neddy. You are a lover. Soon the Pirate guy will no longer be your problem. I promise darling." Rayleigh blew a kiss in the window. "Your other problem, you need to take care of, probably not in the same manner, but you need to take care of her all the same."

"And what?"

"And maybe our number fives are looking into each other's eyes right now." Although he didn't feel it, Neddy smiled up at Rayleigh anyway.

Rayleigh turned and sashayed towards the door. When she got inside, he made a U-turn to head for home. He glanced back at the building as the lights in the penthouse flashed on. He needed to go clean up his mess, yet a critical detour was in order.

"I need a dozen jelly doughnuts," he instructed at the drive-thru.

"Bonjorno, Joe. Espresso?"

"Si," Joe responded. He turned to glance around the small café, surprised to see his father-in-law in the back booth. He recognized Bruno from behind, yet couldn't identify the other man who faced away. He said, "Grazie," as he accepted a small, fragile cup of hot, brown liquid. Victor gestured with his fingers for Joe to come over. As he approached, the three men leaned in as Victor said something.

His arrival is met with silence.

"Bonjorno," Joe greeted. He stood by the side of the table.

"Joey, please sit down," Victor gestured towards the opposite side of the table. Already occupied by two large men, Joe slid in on the same side as Victor. When he began to protest, Joe shrugged. "Kids," Victor responded, "They lack respect."

The occupants pretended to laugh, which morphed into an awkward silence.

"Joe Vaffanculo," he extended his hand to the stranger. The man glanced over at Victor, who gave the nod.

"Jimmy," he replied, extending to shake Joe's hand.

"Does Jimmy have a last name?" Joe directed the query to Victor.

"Jimmy works with me," Victor shrugged. "And he's going to help us fix our Neddy problem."

"Our Neddy problem?"

"Yeah. Bruno, would you share with Joe what went on in his establishment last evening."

"Sure boss," Bruno leaned forward on the table and repeated what he saw to Joe. Joe cursed under his breath yet did not show any emotion on his face. "Then, the boss had to get involved."

"You were there?"

"No, Joey. I was upstate yesterday. We went to visit Louisa and to invite her to the beach house for a week or two," Victor shrugged. "Maybe a month."

"We?"

"Yes, me and Lena."

"You had my mama in on this?" Joe ran his hands over his face. His impatience showed.

"No, no, no, Joey. Lena made a little coffee. She helped get Louisa out of there before she blew the whole operation."

"God forbid that happens."

"Joey, please understand. I was going to retire—"

"Save the speech, Vic…"

"But I need to fix this one thing. So we all be able to rest easy."

"Is anyone with Louisa?"

"Not yet, but," Jimmy interjected. Victor shushed him with a wave of his hand.

"Where is Louisa from, Joe?"

"Damn if I know. Neddy…"

"Yeah, Neddy. Speaking of which. Neddy left the club again with what's her name. He didn't stay at her place, yet he never came home."

"Neddy is missing?" Joe let out a loud laugh. "Well, if it doesn't…"

"Not missing. Neddy slept at the club." Joe's head began to nod. "We think he's waiting to talk to you."

"That would be different."

"Joey, we think Neddy is going to confess or ask for advice or something. To clean up his mess, you can't help him."

"What? Vic, family—"

"I know, family, we told Louisa we like her better—"

"Right now I do—"

"Joey, if you help him out, we won't be able to take care of things on our end, which means…"

"No retirement."

"Exactly. Bruno here, or maybe Jimmy, one of these two will take over after this is settled." Victor takes Joe's hands in his. "Joey, I really need you to tell Neddy to handle it. Tell him he needs to fix this, and you are done bailing him out…"

"But I've always bailed him out."

"I know, Joey. Now it is his turn. Trust me on this." Victor was both respected and feared throughout the neighborhood. Yet, in Joe's eyes, he always did what appeared best for the family.

Joe rose from the table. "I would say it's been a pleasure, but I would be lying," he said before departing. Victor waited for him to leave.

"I think we are okay," he focused back on his guests. "Joey will do right by us. Now Bruno, are you sure we are set?"

"Yeah, boss," responded Bruno, "Oxford has been spotted in the area of the club. We are working on a fix of his location."

"Yes. Good work."

"He follows this Pirate King guy every day. Drinks coffee at the front he uses," Jimmy filled in a few more details.

"Well, well," Victor smiled. "We may be able to kill two problems with one bullet." The group snickered. "Bruno?"

"We are ready to roll. Day after tomorrow."

Angela sat at the kitchen table. She closed her eyes to relish both her cinnamon coffee, and the magnificent silence followed her girl's daily departure for school. She hadn't slept well last night. The clamoring of those climbing the stairs kept her awake. She nudged Joe a couple times, only to have him mumble it was nothing and to go back to sleep.

At one point, she swore she saw her father's car parked across the street. She knew her imagination went into overdrive. Even so, she had checked on the girls, who were both fast asleep, and took a look around the apartment for her own sanity.

The sound of the front door closing brought Angela back to the present. She got up and opened the door in time to catch Lena climbing the stairs.

"Bonjorno, Mama," Angela called.

"Bonjorno, Angie," Lena called back. "Are the princesses off at school already?"

"Already, mama," Angela replied. "It's after ten! Where are you going so early?"

Lena hesitated before she replied, "Out," as she disappeared into her apartment.

"Out?" Angela repeated. "Out?" Angela placed her cup in the sink, grabbed a few of her biscotti and a plate. She walked down the stairs and knocked, a bit too aggressive, on her mother in-law's door. "Out you say," Angela held the plate in front of her. "Do you have any coffee?" Lena always had a pot ready to go. Angela followed Lena into the kitchen. On the table, she already had two cups set up along with a plate of her homemade biscotti. "Expecting company?"

"I figured you'd be down soon." Lena filled the two cups with hot brown liquid. "There was too much activity around here for you to miss."

"I told Joe—" she muttered.

"Excuse me?"

"Nothing, mama. I heard some ruckus, but Joey said it was my imagination and to go back to sleep. What went on?"

"You should talk to your father—"

"Daddy's involved?" Lena nodded. "Damn."

"It's okay, Angie. He gotta everything under control."

"As usual. Is Joe involved?" Lena went over to the cookie jar. She took her time selecting a pignoli cookies to add to the untouched biscotti. "Forget it. You actually answered my question."

"Angie, this isn't Joey's fight yet he is involved," Lena swore under her breath. "When my Giuseppe went to heaven, he left me with two boys to raise. Both are beautiful in their own way. One uses his looks and brains, while the other," Lena shrugged, "not so much."

"This all has to do with Neddy? Again? God damn trouble follows that boy."

"Angela!"

"Sorry, mama, but Neddy gets into more jams than anyone I know. Is that why Louisa went away?"

"Ah, Louisa…"

"Mama…"

"Your father and I went upstate yesterday to see Louisa. As you know, Neddy was, how can I say this, getting his cookies somewhere else …"

"Poor Louisa…" Angela repeated.

"Poor Louisa found out. She had got a job at a college upstate…"

"Mama, I knew all this. Why did you and daddy go see her?"

"Because now Neddy is involved with someone from his stupid therapy group…"

"Rayleigh. She was here for dinner, remember?"

"Yes." Lena gazed into her mug. "I remember… Anyhow, Neddy got himself into another jam, and your dad thought it would be a good idea if Louisa went to the beach."

"Louisa is at the beach house? Shit!"

"Angela!"

"Oh, excusie mama. Louisa is at the beach house…" Angela fiddled with her cookie. "Mama, what does that mean for us?"

Lena took a bite of biscotti and chewed. She shrugged. When her daughter in-law's stare didn't budge, she took in a deep breath, "I'ma going to the beach. Would you and the princesses like to join me?"

Angela burst out laughing. "You are kidding, right? My father or my husband couldn't speak this conversation to me?" Angela got up from the table. "Excusie, mama, I have a few people to see." Angie bolted out the door. A few minutes later, she heard the car start-up in the driveway. Lena got up and reached for the phone. When she heard hello on the other end, she said, "Oh my dear, your shit just hit the fan," and hung up.

They will know the meaning soon enough.

Joe walked back to Steak. He shook his head and strolled through the unlocked front door. "My brother is an idiot," he muttered. The place appeared quiet, except for snoring sounds waffling from the office. Joe proceeded to the kitchen to start a pot of coffee. He opened the walk-in refrigerator and pulled out a large container of heavy cream.

Joe helped himself to a few of the chef's biscotti from a bowl next to the wait station. He took a big bite. The cookie had little taste. He threw the rest in the garbage and considered following with the rest of the bowl. "Mama should teach his staff how to make these things." The smell of coffee caught his attention. He filled his mug before he walked back to the office.

The place was a mess. Papers typically stacked in orderly piles lay scattered across the floor. Empty beverage glasses lay on tables. Chairs appeared organized around the coffee table instead of the desk — the sounds of someone with sinus issues emulated from a blanket on the couch. Joe watched the rhythmic movement of what he hoped was his brother's body.

He placed his mug on the desk, not sure of what he wanted to happen next, Neddy to wake up or to enjoy the moment as is. With a deep inhale, Joe walked over and kicked the lump on the couch.

"What the—"

"You tell me," Joe screamed in his brother's ear. "I got missing money, a father-in-law whose pissed, a mother who is more pissed than Vic, and there's..." he gestures towards his brother.

"Glad those aren't my problems," Neddy replies. He repositions himself to a sitting position as he rubs his ribs. "Nice shot, by the way.

"Neddy, your problems don't even come close to the sanity of mine. Why are you here?"

"Dear brother. Unlike you who met the love of his life in third grade, I am still exploring possibilities. It seems now that Louisa and I are officially over, it is time for me to commit to my true love."

"Really? Because Louisa was your true love a year ago."

"I know. But I met someone new. Someone who I feel gets me a bit more than Louisa…"

"Someone who gets you more than a renowned psychologist? The woman who wrote papers on people like you to help others understand. The woman — "

"I get what you are saying." Neddy threw the blanket off and stood.

"Jesus, Neddy!" Neddy looked down to see he only had on his briefs.

"Whoops," he smirked, reaching behind the chair for a pair of wrinkled khaki's. "You think Louisa is my perfect soulmate because she can analyze me six ways to Sunday and knows what's going on up here?" Neddy slaps the side of his head. "I disagree."

"You disagree?"

"Yes, because I met my soulmate, I think, and I plan on asking her to marry me on Saturday."

"Huh."

Joe reached over to slap his brother on the side of the head. "That's all you got to say? Huh? Your bride, yes, under a year they are still brides, leaves you and now you want to marry someone else. Neddy, what the freak is wrong with you?"

"Nothing. I just… Louisa left me, maybe she went with another guy—"

"She left with Victor Cuzzuto."

"Victor? Wow, I didn't think she liked them old." Joe smacked Neddy again, this time harder. His smile didn't vanish.

"She left you, you idiot, because of something she saw, perhaps here… any thoughts?" Neddy's face turned bright red. With a quick peek at the couch, his smile widens.

"Not a clue," he pushed passed, Joe.

"Conversation is not over," Joe called after. "You need to explain a few other things for me."

Neddy strolled in the direction of the bathroom. Once out of view, he went straight to the house phone to dial Rayleigh. No answer. He took a deep breath and dialed her cellphone. She picked up on the first ring.

"Darling," she sighed. "Good morning, love."

"Good morning back at you," Neddy smiled. "I called to hear your voice."

"You made my day."

"Joe is really pissed about missing money."

"We have a solution, darling."

"Yes, we do. Rayleigh, I know this isn't very romantic of me, yet, will you marry me?" Neddy waited. The silence, on the other end, sunk into his stomach.

Finally, she answered, "Of course I will, darling." Neddy let out a hard breath. "Will you be coming by to celebrate, perhaps with a ring, later?"

"Of course, let me finish up here, and I will be there in a couple hours."

"Can't wait to see you!" Neddy turned towards the kitchen.

"Yeah, that is a great idea," Joe's voice made him jump. "You used the house line, idiot. It lights up when in use." Joe turned and walked back inside the office. He slammed the door behind him.

Rayleigh lay in her bed, Lex Oxford's quiet snores coming from the other side. She took a look at the incoming number, set the phone to mute, and snuck out of her warm nest. She listened carefully to Neddy's babble and responded with what he expected. In the end, she did a fist pump. This appeared to be a new record. The Englishman lying next to her, took about a year and a half for her to manipulate. The one prior around two. Neddy just set a new record.

She couldn't wait to tell her connection. He will be pleased. Maybe now she would be elevated to his inner circle. Perhaps he'll see she should be taking on a more substantial position in the organization. Possibly Neddy will be her catapult into the big time.

A loud snore broke her revelry. She glanced at her current partner. *There will be at least three corpses to dispose of this time.* Rayleigh cackled out loud.

Angela knocked on the beach house side door. She jumped when Jimmy, instead of Louisa, opened the door.

"Didn't know you were in town," Angela said as she pushed passed him into the house.

"Nice to see you too. How's Joe doing?" When she didn't respond, he added, "I saw him today at the coffee shop with Victor. Things are still going strong between you two?"

"Last I checked." Angela peeked around the corner. Outside on the deck, a large hat covered up someone typing feverously on a laptop. "How are you doing?"

"I'm good. The kids are good. Martha depends on the day." He shrugs. "The job is tough on the family, but you know already, don't you."

"He says he's retiring. Said he's getting too old for this crap."

"That's why I'm here. So, he can retire in peace. She's out on the deck, and I am certain she would like to talk to you. God knows she wants nothing to do with me."

"You're a man."

"Yeah. You know, if Louisa is as good as you guys say with this psychology stuff, we might consider hiring her in the—"

"Bite your tongue! When she gets done with the horse crap about to happen, she'll probably want to disappear in a nice quiet town teaching other psychology people. Maybe she can even live happily ever after with a counterpart Prince Charming." Jimmy stood there, not saying a word. "Anyway,' Angela gestured towards the door.

Louisa kept typing as Angela made her way to the table. Angela peered over at the screen to see an updated resume. Louisa went between the resume and another document. Angela tried reading over Louisa's shoulder, yet couldn't quite grasp what the second document contained.

After a few minutes, Louisa shouted, "It's my paper on serial daters and my conclusion about not venturing into marriage with one!" She surged into tears. "That rat bastard," she slammed her hands down onto her computer keys. "I never understood the phrase until now." Angela put her arm around Louisa, who leaned into her touch. "Rat bastard," she repeated again.

"You know for a doctor, I thought you'd come up with better insults," Angela joked. Her words received a blank stare in return. "Still too soon?"

"I don't think this is funny."

"Neither do I," Angela scooted into a nearby chair. "Neddy is an idiot. I got the right Vaffanculo brother. I'm here to help you."

"That's what the guard said, too," she nodded towards Jimmy's shadow in the kitchen.

"Eh, Jimmy," Angela pointed in his direction, "He's a good guy. Works with my father. Jimmy's going to make sure you are safe."

"People keep saying that…safe from what?"

"Oy. My father didn't tell you anything, did he?"

"Not really. He and Lena helped me pack my stuff up at the college and brought me here. He said Neddy's in trouble, and he doesn't care. I am divorcing the ass. I am still family as far as he's a concern. He said he needs me to stay here to be safe."

"Yeah, thanks, Daddy," Angela murmured. "He does this, you know. My dad and Lena, they only tell people part of the story and forget not everyone understands what they do." Angela took a deep breath. "You're updating the old resume?"

"Don't change the subject, Angela. Yes, I am. I was upstate and had started to get my life back. I got my undergrad in Ithaca and was familiar with the area. Now I'm looking for another research teaching position somewhere else. Did you know Bruno, who works with your dad, his son goes there? Where do I need to go to get away from all this, Canada?"

"Canada, you should be fine in Ithaca."

"Now tell me what my idiot ex did besides screw a jezebel."

"Where to start...where to start. Are you comfortable being here for a bit?"

"I agreed to stay for a month. That is all the time I am guaranteeing this cause."

"Okay, then," Angela rose up and sat back down in the chair. "Do you need anything? You know, essentials: clothes, doughnuts, tampons? Whatever you do, don't ask Jimmy to go and get you Kotex. He won't even do that for his wife!" Louisa retorted.

"Did you look in the frig? Milk and jelly doughnuts. There's green tea in the cupboard, and Jimmy has to-go menus from every restaurant within ten minutes of this place."

"The menus are my dad's. He hates to cook when he's on vacation. This place," Angela looks around the deck, "was my grandparents. My dad made a few improvements, and when he finally retires, he wants to move here permanently. He said the ocean calms him down, yet he'll only be twenty minutes or so away from his princesses."

"I'll miss your kids."

"You won't go for long. We are coming out as soon as they finish school. You, me, the kids, and mama. What could go wrong?" Louisa choked back a tear. "Louisa, you are more family than Neddy right now. How a man could be this stupid baffles me yet, he is a man, so I suppose this explains at least part of it. If you would indulge me a few more minutes, please let me explain what happened." Angela proceeded to tell the story about how Rayleigh seduced Neddy and why. "As far as I can figure, this bitch is basically using Neddy to get to daddy. Not to say Neddy hasn't done some stupid things, but by this point, he should know better than to think someone in their late twenties, with model looks, would chase after a man like Neddy. Maybe ten years ago, but now? Huh!"

Louisa listened with intent. She always wondered what Victor Cuzzuto did and why he appeared to be so overprotective of the family. Now his actions all made sense. She got more upset with herself as she listened to what Rayleigh's con is and how everyone in the family, including her, fit. "Do you think Doctor Von has a stake in this somewhere?"

"I cannot answer, but I wouldn't be surprised. Rayleigh and her kind are power-hungry, and they won't stop until they get what they need."

"I had a feeling..." Louisa said.

"What kind of feeling?"

"When I saw her as an addition to the research therapy group, I inquired about the late entry. Doctor Von said it was his research, and he knew what thesis he was proving. He never justified adding her presence. My supervisor wouldn't allow Neddy to leave the group either. Both seemed to get a bit too superficial for me."

"Interesting. Do you think the place is a front?"

"Who knows. They are both ivy league educated." Angela rolled her eyes, "I know this doesn't mean a lot to you, but in my circle's, it is the top ranks."

"Interesting," Angela observed Jimmy staring at a computer screen back in the kitchen. His hands stopped moving with their silence. "Are you okay with hanging low? You can't contact anyone, especially once me and the kids arrive."

"Why not?"

"Because we want —"

"To keep you safe. I get it." Louisa turned and began typing again. After a few minutes, Angela left.

Jimmy observed the entire interaction from the kitchen, the phone against his cheek. "Looks like everything here is a go boss." He listened for a moment, "Yeah, Angie is a pro."

Lena placed a pot cover over the steaming dish filled with homemade gnocchi and sauce. The meatballs simmered on the stove while a fresh-baked loaf of Italian bread, half gone, sat next to the pot. She had the princesses set the table over an hour ago, each glance at the clock got her stomach going. She hated it when the family had troubles.

At a quarter past six, she called the girls in. "Are you two hungry," she asked, already knowing the answer. "Sit. We mangia!"

"What about mommy and daddy?" Amelia asked.

"And grandpa?"

"They are late," Lena looked over at the door as if expecting the rest of her family to arrive with her words. "And they can eat leftovers if we leave them any." The girls laughed. "Okay, whose turn is it?" Gia's hand flew up in the air. "Okay," Lena gestured.

"Dear God, thank you for nana's cooking, and may the rest of the family get here before it is all gone. Amen."

"That works," she began to fill plates of gnocchi and meatballs. Her granddaughters dump a heaping spoonful of fresh shredded Romano on top. Their parents would scold saying the amount of cheese to be excessive. Lena could care less.

"Nana, you are the best!" Gia said between mouthfuls.

"Way better than Daddy's restaurant," Amelia smiled then added, "Don't tell daddy." The sound of someone entering through the front door caught their attention. Everybody stopped eating.

"Oh, look at my beautiful princesses," Victor's voice boomed in the room. "Buena noches, Lena."

"Bueno noches, Victor. Sit. Eat. I made gnocchi and sauce."

"Ah, my favorite. Do you young ladies know how much I love your nana's gnocchi?"

Both girls laughed. "Papa, you say that about all nana's cooking."

"That's because all your nana's cooking is my favorite," he leaned towards the girls. "Don't tell your mama because she will be disappointed." The girls nodded with agreement. The meal continued in comfortable silence. The girls got up and placed their plates in the sink.

"May we be excused, nana?"

"Of course. Grazie for putting your dishes away." The girls skipped off into the living room. Soon the sounds of the television resonated through the house. When Lena was sure the girls were occupied, she asked, "How is Louisa?"

"Angie went out to see her. According to what Jimmy heard, she decided to move again. She is giving us a month to get this all straightened out."

"Do you think she knew anything before all this?"

"I don't know, Lena. I think she knew something was wrong, but I'm not sure how much. But she is very organized and seemed to have pieced together. She'll be okay."

"I hope so. Neddy and his freakin' woman," she threw her hands up. Lena got up and started to clear the table. "Coffee?"

"Gratzie." She put on the coffee and loaded the dishes into the washer. She put the food away in the frig and produced a cake of some sort. "I got bored today," she shrugged.

"Ricotta?"

"Is there any other?" Both granddaughters peered around the door frame. "Come, come. You ready for dessert?" Both girls jumped up and down. "Sit." Lena doled out slices of the rich cake, served herself, and Victor coffee. She sat to wait for the comforting sound of the door opening again.

Neddy walked out of the restaurant. He moved in the direction of the back parking lot.

"Where the hell do you think you're going?" he heard Joe bellow behind him.

"Out."

"Neddy cut the crap."

"Joe, I need to go take care of something. I'll be back for my shift." Joe watched his brother get into his car and screech onto the main street.

"Dumb ass," he said to no one.

Neddy drove by the house only to find Victor's car parked out front. The driveway was empty of cars and activity. He continued around the block and parked on a side street. Just like in his teenage years, he went through the neighbor's yard, over the fence, and up the fire escape. Neddy peeked into the first-floor windows to catch the outline of his nieces sitting in front of the television. He took notice of the empty plates in front of both.

Mama's ricotta cake. Neddy wondered what the occasion would be. He moved to the next window to catch a glimpse of his mother and Victor sitting in the kitchen. Luck was with him.

Neddy moved up the metal stairs and as quiet as he was able, slid the window open in his living room. He tip-toed into his bedroom, heading straight for the closet. Under a pile of clothes on the floor, he opened a metal box, removing a small, black box off the top. He picked up a necklace containing a single diamond, placed it back amongst the papers. With care, Neddy closed the box, slipped it back under the pile of clothes. He stood, closed the door, left the way he entered.

After he reached his car, he headed into downtown traffic. Neddy parked in front of Rayleigh's building. A familiar-looking man, though Neddy could not place from where, pushed opened the front door and ascended onto the street.

He waited until the other person got out of sight, left his car in the tow-away zone, and proceeded into Rayleigh's building. "Good afternoon, sir," the doorman greeted. "May I ask who you are visiting?" Neddy takes note of he had the phone balanced in his right hand.

"Rayleigh O'Connor," Neddy stated.

"And your name, sir?" Neddy enunciated his given name just to hear the guy attempt to repeat it. As usual, once he got passed his first name, the doorman was all mumbles. Neddy hid his laugh with a cough. "You may proceed," the doorman instructed.

Neddy winked back at the doorman as he disappeared into the elevator. He began to whistle. Neddy found when things get bad, they can only get better. Maybe Louisa wasn't his soulmate. Perhaps Rayleigh came into his life to save him. Hell, if she really does kill the Pirate King, this could all be worth it. The family met Rayleigh. They seemed to like her or at least pretended. He had to explain the advantages of this whole relationship with all parties involved. Once they all understand, this will make sense. Rayleigh fits the family.

The elevator door opened to the penthouse suite. Rayleigh stood in the shadows. "Darling, what are you doing here?"

"Are you not glad to see me?" Neddy had a flash of life with Rayleigh. He felt the box in his pocket. Yes, they would be in all this together.

"I'm just surprised," Rayleigh said.

"Hey, why don't you come over here and give me a proper hello." Rayleigh emerged from the shadows. She wore a torn t-shirt and shorts. Red bruises lit up her arms and left cheekbone. "My god, Rayleigh. What happened?" Neddy took steps to close distance. With a light touch, he stroked her cheek. She responded with a wince. "Rayleigh..." his voice husky.

"Your friend, the Pirate King paid me a visit," she sobbed. "He said...he said..."

"Tell me what he said!" Neddy's face was now a brilliant shade of red. He clutched his fists down by his side. He squinted his eyes shut, only to see Rayleigh's bruised face again and again. He stroked her with restraint, asked again, "What did the king say?"

"He said if I go near you again, he will kill both of us. He said I need to leave or else," Rayleigh buried her head in Neddy's chest, coughed out what sounded like a sob. "Oh, Neddy, I was so scared!" His arms tightened around her.

"This is unacceptable," Neddy's voice started to break up. "I will...I will...I...I will kill him!" Rayleigh hid a smile. "My darling, I will take care of this. Let me make a call—"

"No!" Rayleigh separated from Neddy's hold. "He threatened me. I need to take care of this." Neddy didn't speak. Rayleigh paced, her red bruises flash between light and shadows. "Look, Neddy," she turned. Neddy's eyes opened wide. Rayleigh pointed a small, silver gun in his direction. "The king is dead. When is his next pick up?" Neddy hesitated. "Neddy," Rayleigh's voice rose. "When is his next freakin' pick up?"

"Rayleigh, I really think—"

"Don't think."

"But murder?"

"Look, Neddy, the guy beat the crap out of me?" She held out her arms as proof. "Now, he pays."

Rayleigh went into the freezer to pull out a box of bullets. She loaded eight into chambers, replaced the box back behind a container of Haggen Das Honey Vanilla. She turned back towards Neddy.

"When is the next pick up?"

"Tomorrow night. After we close," Neddy turned away. Rayleigh came up by his side. The gun dangled in her left hand while she wrapped her right around his neck.

"We will be free, darling," The gun brushed against Neddy's side. "We will be free."

Victor sat in his office, staring up at the corkboard of photos. All except one had a name, country, and place of photo scrawled across it in red. The new photo appeared to be a man, around six feet tall, in decent shape, smoking a cigarette. The Steak sign seemed to be clear in the background. Victor walked over and marked the photo *Main and Elm.*

Attached to the side of the picture, a handwritten list of agencies had the F.B.I., C.I.A., and the Russian Foundation crossed off. Both Homeland Security and M16 had significant question marks next to their names. He threw the pen across the room. Grabbing the phone on his desk.

"This is Victor Cuzzuto," he spoke slow and enunciated each syllable with care. "I will hold." While he waited, Victor stood closer to the photo, willing his memory to come up with a name. "Yes, I am waiting for the identification of a person of interest. Yes, I can hold." Silence prevailed.

Victor glanced out the window to watch the little activity on the street in front of his office. For an urban area, he was surprised at the lack of people. He went back to the open file on his desk. Rayleigh O'Conner proved to be more interesting than he anticipated. Her records showed one marriage, not the three she claimed to Neddy. Her country of registration came up Argentina, yet the authorities there show no record of her presence.

"Oh, yes, I am still holding. Okay. No problem." At least they were checking back. Yesterday they left him on hold after two hours. "Yes, this is Victor." He stared at the photo while the other person spoke. "Really?" Victor smiled. "Please say you are not yanking my chain." He waited for the additional details. "Thank you. I owe you guys big time." Victor hung up the phone. He picked up the red Sharpie and on the photo in quotes wrote *Lex Oxford.* Next to that, he made a small chart with Rayleigh's name. He put Oxford on the same level as a big, bold question mark.

"I'll be damned," he said and went back to Rayleigh's file. Here he drew the same chart. Again, he picked up the phone, "Joey, we need to talk. My office. Yours isn't secure." He hung up the phone, burst out laughing. "I'll be damned," he repeated.

Joe cringed at the sound of his father in-law's voice. "What fresh hell is today," he cursed as he grabbed his keys and wallet. He purposely locked the office when he exited. "I'll be back in few," he called out to his day shift. Joe got escorted into Victor's office upon arrival. Bruno met him at the elevator.

"This can't be good," Joe reached to shake Bruno's hand.

"It's not, but there is progress, which is positive." Joe knew Bruno would give away nothing. He avoided Victor's wrath as much as anyone could. Both men knew this was not an easy task.

Victor's door appeared open. Bruno entered without knocking. He took the seat next to Victor's desk and gestured for Joe to do the same. Victor arrived a few minutes later, almost skipping through the door.

"Ah, Joey, thank you for coming," Victor's smile didn't match his demeanor. He moved around the two men and sat in the chair behind his desk. Victor leaned forward on his elbows. "I got some good news and some not so good news," he began.

"Just lay it on me," Joe responded. "What is my idiot brother involved in now?"

"Glad you asked." Victor opened the file labeled Rayleigh O'Connor. He pushed out a photo of Rayleigh and Neddy, leaving Steak. Joe visibly recoil. "This is your idiot brother, as you say, and Rayleigh O'Connor. Apparently, Ms. O'Conner met Neddy at therapy—"

"Come on, Vic," Joe said. "Tell me something new."

Victor's smile widened. "Ms. O'Connor states she was married three times. She has been married once, and may still be. She is a native of Argentina, yet their government posses no record of her. She associates with," Victor pulls out the photo of the Englishman standing on the side of Steak, "this gentleman, who goes by the name of Lex Oxford. He is wanted in six countries for espionage and in another three for attempted murder."

"He wants to kill Neddy?" Joe asked.

Victor let out a loud laugh. "Neddy, no. Why would you think someone with his credentials would want to kill your idiot brother? This situation really has little to do with Neddy. He is a, what is the word I am looking for?"

"A player," Bruno inserted. Joe had forgotten entirely about the man sitting next to him.

"Yeah, Neddy is a player. Oxford and I guess Rayleigh is in on this too are after," Victor paused for a moment, "me."

"You? Why you?"

"Remember that case I was working on maybe a year ago? You know, when I sent the family to Disney?" Joe looked up to the ceiling. He crossed his arms and gestured for Victor to continue, "Apparently, I missed someone in the round-up…"

"Ever think about retiring boss?" Bruno had his eyes shut and missed Victor's glare.

"Every day, but that is beside the point." Victor brought his attention to Joe. "What I know is this involves the same case. I left something I shouldn't."

"How does this involve Neddy and the family?" Joe's impatience showed.

"Simple. They are using Neddy to get to me. As far as the family goes, Jimmy is out at the beach house with Louisa, mostly to keep an eye on her. I have a couple other guys taking turns with Lena, my Angie, and the princesses until they go to the beach tomorrow."

"Sounds like you got everything under control."

"Yes and no. We need to get these people off the street — "

"So…"

"We need to wait for them to screw up and get caught," Bruno repeated his boss' words.

"Joey, I need you to talk to Neddy — "

"He's off until tomorrow. I won't see him before, and he won't take my calls because I don't understand him," Joe threw his hands up.

"When will you see him?"

"He is supposed to be there mid-afternoon to go over the books again. He knows I am pissed about the money — "

"Yeah, the whole thing, Whole different circus."

"What do you mean?" Joe asked.

"I mean the disappearing cash has to do with either extortion or a loan shark. Either way, it is only a small timer. Neddy's latest is a whole different ballgame. For the record, I don't think they know we have a line on them. That is good news. The bad news is your brother's cooperation is imperative to finish this up."

"So, he can retire," Bruno snorted.

"Yes, so I can retire."

"You are lucky. I am still crazy about you," Joe said. He had just finished telling Angela the update. She sat, silent, a sure sign she is pissed off. "Kidding aside, I really do, Ang. And I hope Vic can retire after this latest hurdle…"

Ange sighed. "Your idiot brother,"

"According to your father, it is only a small piece of the puzzle."

Angela threw her arms up. "He is a prime example of the male ego! Not great looking yet every woman in the world wants him." Joe sat in silence. "Joey, what about mama? What is she going to do?"

"Vic said he talked to both of you about hanging out at the beach house with Louisa."

"Vic said," Angela's voice rose, "Why must daddy get us all involved in his business?"

"He said —"

"I know what he said. Damn it, Joe!" She hesitated, "What do I tell the girls this time?"

"I don't know. Ask your father." Joe stood up to pace the room. "Supposedly, the whole thing will be over tomorrow. Vic said we should stay away from the club. His guys will take care of the situation, and we can all get back to normal."

"What about Breezy?"

"Victor arranged for Harry to take her out of town for a few days."

"You got the night off?"

"Not the way I want, but I do get to stay with you and the princesses." Joe put his arms around his wife.

"You always find the silver…"

"That is because I am surrounded by gold."

Lena puttered around the beach house kitchen. She chopped up tomatoes, and fresh basil then threw the mixture in a pot to simmer. From there, she began pounding chicken breasts on a wood cutting board. The banging sound disturbed Louisa, who had quarantined herself out on the deck. Louisa's focus wavered with each loud bang.

Her computer screen had several windows open. She flinched between changing her resume, apartment listings in Ithaca, and the email from her attorney. She re-

read the correspondence several times, yet couldn't fathom why, with a divorce rate over fifty percent, that the process would be so tricky, especially when she didn't want anything from Neddy.

She wanted out.

The smell of fresh sauce made its way out to her, and her stomach responded. She hadn't had anything to eat since before Lena's arrival. Louisa had tried to be courteous, yet that ended right when Lena started to defend her son. When she told Louisa this whole thing was her fault for letting Neddy go to the stupid therapist, Louisa lost it.

Since then, Lena made noise in the kitchen cooking up a feast, and Louisa sat planning her escape. Jimmy sat at the kitchen table, sipping a cup of coffee and nibbling on Lena's homemade biscotti. Mama Vaffanculo walked in with a giant suitcase, instructing him to get the few bags of food she had out of the car. Three trips later, grocery bags covered the table and all the kitchen counters. Lena had gone out to talk to Louisa. He heard the shouts as he shut the front door.

Lena stomped in the kitchen. She took out the tomatoes. The rhythm of a knife hitting wood took over as the waves crashing moved to the background. Louisa turned her chair to face the ocean. Truth be told, both women scared the crap out of him. And he was a retired seal! Lena walked by and refilled his cup. She kept walking out towards Louisa to do the same. To his surprised, she sat in the chair next to her. Jimmy watched the dynamic with fascination.

"I'm making chicken parmesan for dinner," Lena announced.

"Wonderful," Louisa replied. Both watched the movement of the waves.

"I like chicken parmesan too," Jimmy muttered. Neither woman turned to look.

"What do you want for lunch?"

"I'm not hungry," Louisa's stomach growled, adding, "mama," as an afterthought.

"Louisa, you got to eat. I'll make a salad, maybe add a little salami and cheese…" Lena moved before Louisa could answer. The old lady flew around the kitchen. In a matter of minutes, she produced three plates piled high with artichoke hearts, olives, salami, and provolone. A large piece of crusty Italian bread topped each. "Follow me and bring the silverware and napkins," she instructed.

Jimmy followed close behind. Lena placed a dish in front of each chair and ran back into the kitchen. She then distributed ice water with a lemon slice floating. "Mangia," she instructed. With the roll of the waves for background noise, lunch had begun.

Victor sat in the apartment across the street from the club. He had his team stationed both inside and out, waiting on his signal. Joe paced behind him, muttering, "That freakin' idiot better not screw this up…"

"Joey, stop, or I'm going to need to replace the carpets here," Victor said. "I got this under control—"

"Vic, if you had it under control, my mother, wife, and daughters would not be under guard at your beach house."

"Joey, that's what I mean. Everybody's safe and sound. My guys are all in place. We get O'Connor and Oxford tonight. Of course, we'll need to pick up Neddy too, just a minor detail." Joe popped an antacid in his mouth. "What's the worst that could happen."

That thought concerned Joe the most. He had been on jobs with his father-in-law in the past. Victor appeared too confident for Joe's liking. Plus, if anything happens to Neddy, he'll have to explain how to mama, and that is a conversation he'd rather avoid.

Bruno walked in without a knock. "Everybody's in place, boss. The girl is at the bar, and the other sleaze bag arrived. Only one problem…"

"Only one?" Victor replied.

"There's no sign of Lex Oxford. We had him on our radar earlier but lost visual inside."

"Santos hasn't seen him?"

"Nobody."

Victor considered this new information. He needed both Rayleigh and her accomplice to make this all stick. She would rat him out in a heartbeat, at least that is what the current plan states. "The place is starting to clear out. Have someone check the men's room, hell check the ladies too. He didn't leave. My guys are on all the exits. Make sure to get back to me with his whereabouts and Bruno," Victor paused, "Stay safe."

Bruno disappeared. Joe noticed Victor had bags under his eyes and, for the first time, appeared like an old man. He didn't say a word. Maybe this time, the old guy really is ready to retire.

Rayleigh sat at her usual spot at the bar. She noticed many new faces amongst the crowd, yet her eyes darted back to the same couple dancing in the corner. She couldn't put her finger on a reason, yet each time she glanced over, they seemed to spin out of view, yet their eyes met in the mirror several times. *Victor Cuzzuto's people couldn't be so ignorant not to see the mirror,* Rayleigh thought. Yet, the dance between the three of them continued into the late hours.

Lex Oxford pushed his way through the crowd next to Rayleigh's stool. Santos appeared in an instant. "What will you drink?" Santos barked over the loud music. "Gin and tonic, with a lemon," he called back. He threw the man a ten on a seven-dollar tab. "Keep it," he gestured towards the money.

"Big spender, are we?" Rayleigh joked. Her mouth was hidden by her wine glass.

"After tonight, I won't be needing any of these dirty American money. I expect a deposit by morning."

"Oh, you'll get what you are owed," Rayleigh responded. She turned away to add, "You'll want to get in and hide out in the office somehow. Victor's guys are all over the place."

"I saw them arrive. Not very effective at hiding, are they?" Rayleigh snickered. "Are we sure Victor will show up?"

"Once I shoot Neddy, the whole family will be present," she let out a full blow laugh. Santos made a note of the interaction. He gestured to Bruno, who sat at the opposite end of the bar, then the gesture repeated itself throughout the room.

Rayleigh scrutinized in the mirror and counted at least six repeats. She then turned towards Lex, "I count at least six men who repeated the signal."

"I got eight, love," he responded. "None of them Cuzzuto," Lex raised his glass then disappeared into the crowd. A minute later, Rayleigh smiled as she pictured Lex behind Neddy's desk with his feet up. She should have a clean shot at him when the fun starts.

Neddy worked the crowd like a salesperson. He bought some drinks while he danced with others. Rayleigh made a mental note of each person he came in contact with and what his response appeared to be. In back, almost into the restaurant, there seemed to be a group he was careful to avoid. He gave the table a wide berth, nearly tripping over others to avoid contact with its tenants. Upon further inspection, she saw an older man seated in the middle.

"Hello, Victor Cuzzuto. So, we do meet again," she whispered. The Pirate King arrived to take his seat at the other end of the bar. This time when the bartender approached, The King waved him off. A glass of water was placed in front of him, yet he didn't touch it. He also gave her no notice. "Love this."

"Oh, hi," Neddy approached with caution. He kissed her on the cheek, his eyes darted around the room after. He pointed towards the Pirate King at the same moment, Rayleigh grabbed his hands.

"No need to be direct, darling," she cooed. "I know who will die tonight." She half-smiled, then bent over to open her purse. Neddy peeked inside, a small silver revolver sat in a side pocket. "All memorable things, my love," Rayleigh said as she placed her purse up on the bar. "How long until closing?"

"About a half-hour," Neddy replied.

"Oh goody," Rayleigh slid off the barstool. "I will have just enough time…" She rose and headed in the direction of the Ladies' room. Neddy waited for her hips to sway out of sight, then moved to the other end of the bar.

"Go in my office at closing," he instructed The Pirate King.

"That's not how we do business."

"Tonight, it is," Neddy walked away.

"Neddy, my guys are crawling in this place. There better be no funny stuff." The Pirate King's stare sent a jolt up Neddy's back.

The Pirate King then ran a finger across his throat. Neddy backed away.

Rayleigh turned towards the dance floor then walked around the parameter of the room. She had one hand inside her purse, resting on the gun. Her adrenaline carried her towards the opposite side of the room only to find an empty booth. "Crap," she muttered. A group of twenty-somethings pointed in her direction, yet none approached. She turned to go back and slammed into a wall.

"Excuse me," she heard Bruno's low voice. "Are you okay?"

"Just get out of my way, you imbecile!" She shouted as she pushed Bruno aside. She stomped off and let out a laugh.

"Yeah, she's got a gun in her purse," he said into a small shoulder microphone. "I don't know this for a fact, yet I am completely certain the thing is loaded." Bruno just shook his head. "No problem, boss."

Lex Oxford opened every drawer of Neddy's desk. "What a bore!" he exclaimed as he found only papers and pens. He walked around the office and waited. Each time someone came close to the door, Lex jumped into Neddy's chair. He wanted someone to come in. His gun rested inside his waistband.

He rubbed his hand on it often. "You haven't been used in a while, baby. Tonight, I have plans to make up."

Angela balanced two suitcases along with a cloth bag filled with groceries up the front stairs of the beach house. The girls followed with their backpacks, filled to capacity with books, make-up, and stuffed animals. Angela hiked up the bags, then knocked on the door and waited. Her foot tapped. "Angela," Jimmy greeted her with a hug. "I'm not surprised you are here again."

"Amelia and Gia, go put your stuff in the room, then find nana and aunt Louisa." The girls ran off down the hall. "First time they've listened to me today." Jimmy laughed. "Daddy said —"

"You are relieving me, and I need to get to the restaurant. I just had a three-way with him and Bruno."

"Was Joey on the line?" Jimmy shook his head. Angela swore under her breath. "I want him safe."

"He will be. Your father likes Joe. That was always his advantage."

"Yeah, and my dad and Giuseppe's relationship." Both nodded.

"Do you have —"

"In my bag," Angela dropped the suitcases to reveal a small black sashay case. "Yes, it is loaded too. I don't fool around when it comes to my kids."

"Lena's probably packing too, although every time I ask, she waved me off. Are you ready for the conversation?"

"Daddy thought it would be better coming from me. How are they getting along?"

"They are speaking food – nothing else."

"That is better than not at all." Angela and Jimmy stood in silence. "Well I guess I should — "

"Yeah. Let me carry those to your room, at least."

"Thank you." Angela walked out towards the deck. As she passed the kitchen, Lena had both girls sitting at the breakfast bar. She already had cookies on a platter, and both her daughters had scattered crumbs in front of and all over. "Mama don't spoil their dinner," Angela instructed as she walked through. Lena gave her the hand wave to which both girls covered their mouths with their hands. Lena brought a finger up to her lips. Both her granddaughters nodded. The kids loved her cookies.

"Angela, are you here?" Louisa called from the deck.

"Live in the flesh," Angela took the seat across for Louisa and took notice of the bags under her eyes and pale color to her face. "How's it going?"

"Interesting question. I finished my paper on relationship studies and started a new one on perpetual liars. I've updated my resume. Lena's cooking has probably added ten pounds to my frame. I am confused, pissed off, and," she paused for a beat, "lost. And how are you?"

Angela moved up and down yet did not speak. She watched the waves roll in and out as she recited a silent prayer for Louisa to be okay. Then after a deep breath, "I'm sorry about the divorce thing. Neddy is an idiot—"

"No, shit."

Angela laughed. "I've never heard you swear before."

"Swearing isn't very intellectual, although I did pick up a couple new ones at the college. For me, it's a sign of real frustration."

"Me too."

"Is this a social visit, or are you quarantined too?"

"Quarantined. Interesting word choice. Me and the girls are here for a while, probably a couple days depending."

"Depending on what?"

"Depending on what happens tonight. Jimmy went to help my father, and I'm—"

"His replacement?"

"Yeah, his replacement. I don't work with daddy often yet when I do…"

"I'll be damned. I always knew you were bad-ass." Louisa looked away towards the water. Angela went inside and came back with two glasses of wine. "Am I going to need this?"

"Sip as I speak. You decide." Angela took a long sip. She listened as Lena hustled the girls downstairs to the rec room. "You and Neddy are completely done, right?" Louisa shook her head. She then took a long sip of her wine. "Just checking. Is there a plan?"

"Sadly, I have had a plan since day one. Something about Neddy…"

"Yeah, yeah, yeah, okay. What is this plan?"

"I am looking for another research facility, probably academic…"

"I thought you already found another academic place?"

"I did, but Bruno's son goes there and…"

"And what?"

"I feel like having Enzo up there makes this all," Louisa swept her hand in a half-circle, "too close for comfort."

"I understand. Have you talked to Bruno or Enzo about this?"

"Funny you should ask," Louisa drained her glass, "about halfway through the semester Enzo introduced himself and started visiting during office hours, a smart kid by the way," Angela gestured for her to continue, "then when I asked him to stop and explained knowing his dad had no influence on his grade, he told me he was just keeping an eye on me and if I needed anything…"

"He did not!"

"Oh, yes, he did." Angela burst out laughing. "I called your father…"

"You talked to daddy?"

"Yes, I talked to daddy, and he said he would take care of it." Lena came out with a bottle of wine. She refilled both glasses and gave Angela a wink before disappearing back into the house. Louisa sat back and took a sip. "Thank you, Lena," she said towards the sliders.

"And what did daddy do?" Angela now sat forward in her chair.

"He took care of it, I guess. Enzo finished my class, and I haven't seen him since. Although…"

"Although what?"

"When Lena and Victor came to pick me up, they said Enzo would pack up my stuff and deliver it where I wanted…"

"Where is that?"

"Storage unit in Ithaca. I really don't have a clue what is next."

"You should talk to daddy. He has contacts at Ithaca, Skidmore, and UVM. There are others. You pick." Louisa didn't respond. "Look, Louisa, for us to get out of this and you settled, we are going to need a small favor."

"There's always a price," Louisa's head started to spin. The wine was making her fuzzy.

"You need to do a speech, Louisa. It's straightforward. I will get you details."

As if she hadn't heard Angela, "I can't believe Victor has contacts at Ithaca. I guess that's how I got the job so easily." Louisa brings the wine glass to her lips then stops. "Skidmore would be too small, although I like the location. Let's start with UVM, although it gets freezing up there…" Angela reached over and moved the wine glass out of reach. "Hey!" She reached to pull the glass back, "I have a request," Angela waited. "Doctor Von started this whole charade. I want him taken down. Fraudulent grants, I don't know. He is somehow responsible for ruining my life."

Angela hesitated. Her father taught her long ago to only tell people what they need to know. She debated on sharing the whole connection, yet when she looked into Louisa's eyes, the rage reflected back, shown Angela all she needed to know. So instead, she asked, "Could you send me some links, so I can get on that?"

"No problem." Louisa shut her eyes and leaned her head back. "How did my life come to this?"

Angela sat yet did not speak. *Only tell people what they need to know,* echoed in her head. Instead, she closed her eyes, pictured her, Joe, and their girls walking on a beach. She had done this so many times she had the scene fine-tuned down to the cobalt blue shade of the water and the powder blue shade of the sky.

Neddy hustled out the last customer and turned to see his wait staff walking towards the exit.

"What's up, guys?"

"We're done. Everything is put away, and Santos is taking care of the floors."

"Santos is taking care of the floors?"

"That's what he said." Neddy held the door.

"Santos!"

"Yo," the answer echoed from the dance floor. Much to Neddy's surprise, he had the floor mopped and was in the process of handing the bucket over to one of the cleaners.

"Santos, why are you doing extra?" Neddy stood with his arms folded.

"Not extra. I lost a bet to Carlos, and this was the payoff. This or a C-note, and I am one cheap…"

"Gotcha. Okay. Finish up. Where is the girl who was sitting at the bar?"

"I think she left. She had a word or two with the guy who sits at this end, and I lost track of them both. Hey, I'm all done…"

Neddy panicked and ran towards his office. He heard shouting and a gunshot.

"Crap…crap…crap, crap," he repeated. Neddy paced outside. He needed to call someone. He ran back to the bar and picked up the phone. "Joey, I think Rayleigh just killed The Pirate King in our office," he shouted.

"Neddy, are you doing drugs again?" Joe responded. His voice carried a sense of calm.

"No, I am serious. I think Rayleigh—"

"Who's Rayleigh?"

"My fiancée—"

"Neddy you are still married to Louisa—"

"She left me. We filed the papers months ago. But that's not important. The Pirate King—"

"You told me the Pirate King was a figment of my imagination—"

"Joey, get here and bring Victor. I think we need him too…" Neddy hung up the phone. He went back to his office and listened. He heard Rayleigh speaking with someone. "Maybe she didn't kill him, just scared…" Neddy kicked open the door. His breath came fast; he got a dizzy spell.

Someone lay slumped over his desk. He didn't know who, just it wasn't the Pirate King because he lay on the floor in front of the office. A movement to his left brought Rayleigh into view. She sat perched on the couch, gun pointed at Neddy.

"Hello Giuseppe," Neddy recoiled at the sound of his given name, "The Pirate King will no longer be a problem," her laugh echoed back.

"Who is that?" Neddy pointed to the body on his desk.

"Oh, that," Rayleigh cackled. "My now ex-lover. He came to kill you, but you know, I wanted the pleasure." Neddy cocked his head to one side. "Yes, you heard right, darling. As soon as Victor Cuzzuto arrives to try to save your ass, then my work here is complete."

"What does Victor Cuzzuto have to do with this?" Neddy took a step towards Rayleigh at the same moment she raised the gun higher. He stepped back.

"Everything," Rayleigh threw her head back.

"Rayleigh, love?"

"Neddy, you didn't think this was all about you, did you?" His face sagged. "Oh, my gosh, poor baby, you did." She stood. "Oh, Neddy, all you men are alike." She started to pace. "You see, Victor Cuzzuto is my mortal enemy. His last drug deal, Victor Cuzzuto, got one associate killed and one rotting in an American jail. There is no recourse except for the death penalty."

"Say what?"

"My associates will compensate me well for this one. That piece," she gestured to the body now bleeding on his ink blotter, "thought he could bypass me to get ahead in the organization. He couldn't." Rayleigh's laugh sent shivers down Neddy's back. "He also thought he was my only lover, yet we both know he was wrong there too. That guy was not a good judge." Rayleigh glanced at her watch. "When did you call your brother?" Neddy's eyes opened wide. "You are predictable. All men are. When did you call?" She raised the gun again.

"Right after the first shot."

"Huh. They should be here by now. Okay, Neddy," Rayleigh pointed towards the door. "Let's meet at the party outside." The gun waved in the air, then shuffled out into the hall. The glow from the lamps above the bar brought little light to the area. He moved towards the door. "Stop," Rayleigh commanded. Neddy stood still. "Stay there until I say move."

"Rayleigh, this is ridiculous—"

"Neddy, trust me. You don't want to piss me off—"

"She's right, you know," Victor's calm voice came out of the darkness. "Rayleigh put the gun down."

"Oh, Vic. Really?"

"I'm here. I see you took care of Lex—"

"Not me, Neddy…"

"Hey!" Neddy shouted.

"Shut up!" both Rayleigh and Victor responded. Neddy stood perfectly still.

"Look, Rayleigh, I didn't kill anyone, but I can help you get who did."

"I saw you—"

"No, you saw someone else. Rayleigh, let me help you. I'm on your side. Remember, there are interests in your native country."

"Not anymore, you don't."

Victor took a step out of the dark. "We both know I do. Come on, Rayleigh put down the gun." A commotion broke out behind him, yet Victor kept his focus on Rayleigh. Her eyes darted towards the door and back to focus on him.

"Can you guarantee me immunity if I tell you about this one?" She gestured towards Lex.

"Rayleigh, you give me Lex Oxford plus one, and I can guarantee you get home safe." Neddy listened to every word. Did Victor really say he would let Rayleigh off if she gives more information?

"Are you kidding me," Neddy responded. He heard a rustle behind him and felt a sharp pain in his side. His knees buckled. The last thing he remembered was hitting the floor.

"Where did she go?" Victor shouted as he stepped over a slumped Neddy. "Santos, Jimmy! Where is O'Connor?"

A breathless Santos appeared from the side. She got out the back, and boss," Victor glared in Santos direction, "Jimmy has been shot."

Victor ran his hands over his face. "How bad?"

"She blew out his knee."

Victor paced in front of the bar. With each passing, he would glance at Neddy's slumped body. "We need an ambulance or two. And call the coroner, call Les, not the other one. He hasn't been informed about our business yet."

"Anything else, boss?"

"Don't let Joey in until we clean up this mess. I'll be right back."

Rayleigh watched from the shadows a block away as the activity around the restaurant increased. She saw Victor leave by the front door. He spoke to someone in a black van and moved across the street. He entered the building opposite the club. She waited to see if any apartments lit up. When none did, she narrowed her choices to two.

She reached for her cellphone. "Hey, it's me. Oxford is dead." She waited while the person at the other end swore a few times. "I had to shoot Giuseppe Vaffanculo in the process. I believe he is dead too."

"You done well, my love," the words made Rayleigh's heart swoon, "Yet you missed the big fish." In the background, she heard someone mutter if she had slept with him he would be dead like all her past lovers.

Rayleigh made a note of the voice to handle them later. "He offered me immunity if I can state Oxford planned the whole thing, and he was my contact." Silence, on the other end, made her nervous. "I did not accept his offer."

"Oh, my love, this is fabulous news," the voice purred. "You will accept his offer, yet you will need to meet in person. Then you can do the job I paid you to do."

Rayleigh's hand shook. "Yes, yes. I will do my job," she disconnected. Down the street, the commotion had grown. She counted three ambulances, someone loading a body-size bag into a black van, Rayleigh let out a laugh and several unmarked vehicles. The local police were visibly absent.

With one last glance, she turned in the opposite and walked away.

Victor entered the dark apartment. He saw his son-in-law sitting at the kitchen table — two glasses of scotch in front.

"Are one of those for me?" Victor asked as he sat in the opposite chair. "Salute'" he raised his glass and downed the brown liquid.

"Do you have to tell mama we are planning a funeral, or do I?" Joe responded. He hadn't touched his drink. Victor reached across the table, repeated the gesture with his glass, and downed the other shot.

"Neither of – wait a minute Joey. That's a great plan. We could bury Neddy!"

"Is Neddy?" Victor shook his head. "Too bad," Joe poured two more.

"Too bad?"

"Victor, look where we are! I only got one question," Joe leaned forward, "Tell me you can retire."

"Almost."

"Jesus, Mary, and Joseph, what is it going to take?" Joe slammed his glass down.

Victor sighed. "Joey," he said, "tonight I made strides towards retirement. I am almost there."

"Good to know, Vic." Joe turned away.

"I need to get one more piece taken care of." Vic glanced out the front window. "Okay, maybe two. Then I am done. I will retire to the beach house or maybe me and you will go into business, ay? A legitimate one this time."

"I have a legitimate business…" Victor didn't respond. "Oh man, is the restaurant on fire?"

"No, Joey, the restaurant is not on fire. The place has bad juju, you know?"

"Bad juju?"

"Yes, like a bad vibe. Maybe you sell it? Start over?"

Joe stared at his father-in-law and wondered, *What did he and Neddy do?*

By morning the only talk on the street was of the shootout at Steak last night— snippets of theories scattered like leaves. Speculation ran wild. Was this a drug bust that went bad? Did something happen to Victor Cuzzuto? Does anyone know who is responsible?

Victor asked many of the same questions as he paced in his office. With a red Sharpy, he drew lines threw the ones who had died or sustained injuries. His eyes moved between the now identified Lex Oxford, who was in a body bag somewhere in Jersey, and Rayleigh O'Connor, whereabouts unknown. He thought by offering immunity, she would stick around. Yet, she had disappeared sometime between their meeting inside Steak and Santos announcing Jimmy had been shot.

Off to the side of the photo displace, Victor wrote a list of those involved in his organization. The family appeared in blue, others in gray. Some names, Bruno, Enzo, and Jimmy, had a blue underline, while Santos had yellow highlighter over his.

"Come on," Victor whispered. "Show yourself you rat bastard." The photos sat, not sharing any secrets. A knock brought Victor back to reality. He slipped a sheet of paper with *Other Notes* written across the top over the list of names. "Enter," he instructed.

"Hey, boss," Bruno handed over a paper cup. "Thought you could use this."

"Gratzie, Bruno," Victor gestured Bruno to join him.

"Still staring at those photos," he observed.

"I am missing something. Tell me, Bruno, what do you see?" Bruno stared at the collage on his boss' wall. He read each note, then either moved yes or no after. Victor sat sipped his cappuccino, grateful for the liquid boost.

Victor finished his drink and waited. Bruno's eyes focused on one particular photo. Victor moved to get a better look.

"What is it, Bruno?"

"This," he points to the distorted photo, "This can't be right." Victor waited. "Because here is Oxford, see?" Bruno pointed with his coffee cup. "And over here is who, O'Connor?"

"That's what I thought. Do you think it isn't her?" Victor moved closer for a better look.

"No, I think it is O'Connor..."

"Huh. Because besides the photos in the club, this is one of the few connecting the two."

"No, look here, Vic. They are meeting with a third person. See?" Bruno points into the background of the picture. "You can see the head and the outline, sort of, in the shadow. I can't make out who it is, but there is another player."

"Crapola!" Victor exclaimed. "Damn it! I bet whoever is the one who shot Jimmy. I will send this back to the lab. Maybe the boys can get an ID." Bruno nodded. As Victor pulled the photo down, his notes paper fell to the floor. Bruno stared at the list, yet didn't say anything. "I wanted to list everybody. You know, get a full picture." When no reply came, Victor continued, "Okay, so how do we get these freaks in the same place?"

"That is the question." Bruno took a long sip then pitched his cup in the wastebasket across the room. "By the way, how is the family?"

"Pissed off. I know it is not funny, yet they are all pissed off. Joey is pissed because I suggested he sell the restaurant. Angie is pissed because I am not retired and as put it 'making the family put up with this bullcrap,' and don't forget about Louisa…"

"How is Louisa?" Bruno turned his head, yet Victor caught the red tint rise on his face.

"Louisa is mad at me for getting her the job in Ithaca," he shrugged. "What was I supposed to do?"

"She's probably mad because you sent Enzo up there too."

"I did not!" Victor exclaimed. "Enzo was going there anyway. You told me! I just asked him to watch out for her." Bruno's lips turned up into a smile. "You're the one who told him to introduce himself."

"Anyway…how is Neddy?"

"Ug! Neddy! The idiot is recuperating in a hospital crosstown. I had him registered as Mr. Ivy Idiota," Victor laughed, "You know, for fun."

"I bet Lena doesn't think it's funny."

"No, Lena has no sense of humor. You know what she suggested?" Bruno waited. "She suggested we should give Neddy a funeral. Then everybody will come out to see the body, and we can get all the bad guys at once."

"With a closed casket? That wouldn't work. Neddy's people would want to see the corpse, make it real."

"You are right. There are trust issues in this community."

Bruno started to speak then shook his head. "Do you think I could get Neddy to go along?"

"He wouldn't really need to agree. See Lena's been on the internet again," both men did an eye-roll, "and she says there is this stuff, Tetrodotoxin, we can give him. He'll be out for about four hours…"

"Four hours sleeping?"

"No, four hours like a corpse."

"What if he wakes up?"

"Not an issue. We just give him another shot."

"Huh…" The two sat in silence for a beat. "You know boss if we wrote up a fake obit and paid off the priest, I mean, make a donation to the church…"

Victor smiled. "We could probably draw out our mystery man in less time than the agency could ID him." He sat back in his chair. "Bruno, I think we have a winner." He reached forward for the phone. "I will explain this all to Lena, would you start the rumor, please."

"Of course, boss. I am just suggesting we keep the news quiet, right?" Both men recoiled with laughter.

Lena listened as Victor lay out the plan. Every few words, she'd look up at the ceiling to make the sign of the cross. Both Angela and Louisa watched from the deck. The princesses were down below on the beach, building something out of the sand with Enzo.

Enzo had shown up late last night with the news Jimmy had been shot. He said he was there to help, yet both Louisa and Angela had doubts. He played with the girls as they waited for Lena to hang up with Victor.

Joe arrived around five a.m. and left again after he woke around nine-thirty. Both Lena and Louisa had peppered Angela with questions, none of which she answered.

"Have you had enough coffee?" Louisa inquired.

"Yes, why?"

"Earlier you said you needed coffee to deal with all this and now," she gestured towards her empty mug, "you drank your coffee." Angela didn't say a word. She rose and opened the sliders, meeting Lena's glare as she did. The old woman began to respond in perfect Italian. As Angela refilled her mug, she caught the words *funeral* and *soon.* According to Joe, the only corpse was from one of the guys they were after. *Don't tell me we are throwing that crook a funeral!* She shuddered.

Angela walked back out, shutting the slider behind her. She strolled over to the rail and to watch her girls playing on the beach. Amelia, still innocent, poured sand from a bucket to sculpt into a castle. Gia lay off to the side in a skimpy bikini containing a woman's body with a teenager's mind. Enzo, being wise beyond his years or had been warned by Victor, kept his focus on her younger daughter, as he assisted with reinforcing the walls.

"That one's going to give my Joey fits," Lena observed as she joined the two with a mug in hand. "Angie, make her put some clothes on!"

"Mama, her bathing suit is on. That is the style. Enzo is a good boy," she smiled, "besides daddy will kill him if he touches her." Both women giggled and burst into full out laughter as Louisa's eyes opened wide. "We are joking!" Angela cried as she tried to catch her breath.

"I wonder about you two..."

"Oh, Louisa, you are going to wonder more after this conversation." Louisa creased her brow. She sat back and folded her arms across her chest at the same time, crossing her legs. If she could wind herself any tighter, she would. "Are you ready?" Lena asked. She had witnessed this routine before. With a head nod, Lena began to explain her chat with Victor.

In the end, Louisa bursts out, "Are you kidding me?" When Lena or Angela didn't respond, "Isn't this against the law?"

"Look, Louisa," Angela started, "Daddy knows what he is doing. We need you to participate and be real, so the others will not pick up on what is going on."

"Others?"

"Sure," Lena jumped in. "The rest of his wife's will probably show up. Friends of the family. You know others…"

"So, Meg?"

"Will be there, and you can't tell her what is going on," Louisa drifted off. "Seriously," she took Louisa's chin and brought her face back to focus. "You can not tell a soul."

Louisa waited for a beat. "What is in this for me?"

"What do you want?"

A normal life. "I want…" her thought interrupted by the slider moving.

"Good afternoon, ladies. I brought lunch." Bruno stood in the doorway, two large grocery bags in his arms. Lena jumped up to help him. Louisa's eyes moved from her coffee cup to Bruno's smiling face and back.

Bruno returned the attention as Lena grappled with the bags of food. A slight crimson tint made its way to both of their cheeks. "I know what you want," Angela said.

Joe paced in his shirt and tie. An Armani jacket lay across the bed. Angela emerged from the bathroom dressed all in black.

"My god, Angie," Joe exclaimed, "You are beautiful."

"Gratzie, love," Angela leaned in for a quick kiss. "You ready?" Joe nodded. Angela yelled, "Gia, Amelia, let's go!" Their two girls walked towards the front door, both dressed in black. Both as beautiful as their mother.

"There is a limo out front," Amelia noted.

"Ah, the car is here. Gia go see if nana is ready." His oldest vanish out the door. Turning towards Amelia, he asks, "Are you going to be okay, my love?"

"We are only saying good-bye to Uncle Neddy, right?" She shifted on her feet. "That is what nana said."

"Yes, my love. We are saying good-bye to your uncle." Angela walked passed Joe and placed her arm around her daughter. "Then we are going back to the beach for a while."

Amelia smiled up at her mom and wrapped her in a hug.

"WE ARE WAITING!" Her sister's voice echoed through the house. The family walked out into the hallway. At the bottom of the stairs, Gia towered over her grandmother, dressed all in black, including the traditional veil.

"Oh, mama…"

"Let's just get this over with," Lena interrupted. She grabbed hold of Gia's hand moved towards the door. The car moved with ease through the city streets. They parked in front of a large stone church. "Oh, Jesus," Lena muttered. "Here we go." The driver opened the door and helped the old woman on to the street. "Gratzie," she gestured as she waited for the others.

Joe took Lena's arm on one side and his wife's arm on the other. The girls followed close behind. As they approached, the doors opened. "Let's get this over with," he repeated.

Lena stomped around the kitchen of her new bungalow overlooking the blue water of Islea's Inlet. Her eldest granddaughter posed on the beach in front as she flirted with a bare-chested boy. The sun in Lena's eyes made it hard to see. Yet, the muscular outline of a man's body made her wonder how old this boy could be and how did he get onto the family's private beach.

The boy's movements, the way he pointed to the water and tilted his head to the side while Gia spoke, brought a sense of the familiar to Lena. Could one of the neighborhood boys find Gia here? She moved further into her house until the two receded in view.

Her new kitchen stretched into the living room, creating a massive space for the family to gather. Lena liked the way the sun came in, and she did admit the view didn't hurt, but she missed her old house in the old neighborhood. Her friends called, yet it wasn't the same as sitting across the table from someone drinking a cup of coffee. Of course, she had most of her family here, yet having to move because her eldest son is a *stunad* didn't sit well.

Joe and Angie and the princesses stayed close. Just past the in-ground pool lay the door to their house. Now instead of having her family on top, everybody was alongside each other. It's the new house style, so everyone said. She liked the old style with stairs that squeaked, so she knew when they all got home.

Joe and Angie on the far side of the pool, Victor, had his place down a short pathway, this appeared to be cozy for all. Vic proclaimed the area safe, yet, they built a big wall separating the family complex from the rest of the street. From what Lena experienced so far, the neighbors were a bit full of themselves. Everyone had names that someone recognized, everyone except her family. The goal is to keep the life that way.

"Mama, what are you doing? Come out and sit by the pool with me," Angie walked on to her patio and called.

"I'm keeping an eye on your Gia," Lena replied. Angie came closer. Her eyes followed her mother in law's finger. "She's out there with a boy."

"Oh, mama," Angie pointed. "That is not a boy! That is our Enzo!" Lena leaned closer yet still couldn't distinguish the older boy.

"That is Enzo, huh?" She went into the kitchen to produce two coffee mugs and a plate of biscotti. "Sit, Angie." Angie sat in the chair, facing the water. "I have questions. I want to know where is our Joey? I haven't seen him today."

"Joe is out with my dad," Angie observed Lena's shoulders tighten then relax. "Mama, don't worry. Daddy retired. He promised it was real this time." When Lena didn't respond, Angie tried another tactic, "So Bruno is bringing Louisa to dinner. How about that?"

"That is the only enjoyable news to come out of this mess." Angie opened then closed her mouth. "Besides Vic's retirement."

"Amen." They fell into a comfortable silence. "Mama, are you okay here?"

Lena took a bite of her biscotti. "I am okay." She continued to chew. "I did not like leaving the old neighborhood…"

"But this place is beautiful!"

"Yes, Angela, it is. But it isn't home. I miss our house and the smell of the bakery down the street…There's no bakeries or real cafes here. Just those Bucks places that pretend to serve our coffee." Lena enjoyed a long sip from her mug. "I miss my garden and the basil growing along the walk." She played with a piece of biscotti. "I miss...a lot."

"I understand what you mean. But we are family, and we are still all together. That is a blessing, no?" Angela waited, and when Lena didn't say anything, she continued. "The girls adjusted. Their happiness and safety is what is important." She took a bite of the biscotti before adding, "That and my dad retiring. That alone is going to save us so much stress."

"We are almost altogether."

"Mama, that couldn't be helped. At least he is alive."

"Alive for now, until the *stunad* does something stupido again."

"Mama, Neddy might have learned his lesson. Daddy had him debriefed, and when Joe sold the restaurant and the house, he set him up with a business even Neddy couldn't screw up!" Lena gazed up at the ceiling. "No, really, mama. How much trouble can he get into running a food truck?"

Lena thought for a moment. "This is my Neddy..."

"Your Neddy, who still comes for dinner every Sunday, like a good son." Lena smiled. "He's really not supposed to do that. Daddy made the arrangement with the program." Across the pool, Bruno and Louisa emerged from the guest house. Adding the new building was one of Lena's better ideas. "For company," she had insisted. Of course, she never dreamed company would include one of Neddy's ex-wives and Victor's right-hand man.

Bruno was always like a son and Louisa, well she helped get them out of a jam. Bruno got promoted to Vic's old position, and he talked Louisa into moving from Ithaca back to Connecticut. Lena noticed Louisa sporting a Wesleyan t-shirt. Could this be a new situation for her?

"I didn't know your father knew people at Wesleyan."

"He doesn't." Angela caught a glimpse of Louisa and Bruno relaxing on the lounge chairs by the pool. "Louisa must have done that one on her own. I wonder if Enzo will transfer?"

"He doesn't need to with his father keeping an eye on Louisa, no?" Bruno caught Lena's eye, and he waved in her direction. She returned the gesture with a smile. "Ah, mi famiglia."

"See mama, this is not so bad. Maybe you get a grandchild from Louisa after all."

"Oh, Angie. Make no mistake. I love Bruno like a son, but he is, how you say, adopted family. If he stays with her, fantastic, but the child---"

"Will be just like Enzo…" Lena turned back to the beach to watch as Enzo kicked a ball with Amelia. Gia stretched out on a blanket nearby. Enzo called over to her periodically. Gia raised one hand to wave him off.

"Enzo is a good boy," Lena slapped her hand on the table. "What time is Joey and your dad returning? I'm making risotto for dinner, and I don't want it to be sticky."

"They should be back soon, mama. Come," Angie opened the slider, "Let's go sit by Bruno and visit."

Joe sat on Victor's left. In front of him sat a cold, half-finished espresso. His leg bounced. All morning people stopped by to wish Victor well. A few had asked where the family decided to go. Joe laughed at each response, then broke into a coughing fit to hide his amusement.

"Oh, we are moving to Orlando because the princesses are going to work at Disney," he told the first person. The second guy heard Disneyland in California, while the next got Hollywood. Each time Joe covered his mouth with his hand, so no one would see his smile.

When a break happened, Joe excused himself to the men's room. When he returned, Victor sat alone. "You okay?" Joe asked. Victor indicated an agreement. "This is going to be a big change for you, Vic, yet you've been saying for years…"

"I know what I said, Joey. I figured when I did retire, I could go between the beach house and here. The only difference is I wouldn't be involved anymore, you understand?" The pace of the café slowed as the day grew. "I figured I would fill in for Breezy at Steak when she had the baby…"

"Your retirement plan was to play host at my restaurant?"

"You know," he gestured with his right hand, "to keep busy."

Joe laughed. "I'm sorry, Vic, but I can't picture you seating people and bringing them menus."

"Oh, I would bring menus too," Vic considered this. "Then, I'm out because you know I couldn't handle that." A lone tear drifted down his cheek.

"That's not what I meant. I mean…"

"Forget it, Joey." Vic took a sip of his cold coffee. "Besides, I can't completely retire because of your idiot brother, so…"

Joe waited for his father in law to continue. When nothing happened, he wiped his hands over his face, scrunched his eyes, "What do you mean by can't completely retire, Vic?"

"What do you mean, what do I mean?" Vic's eyes darkened as he moved to meet Joe's. "What I mean, Joseph is someone must keep an eye on your idiot brother. If by some chance, he keeps his end of the bargain, I will see him every Sunday," Vic made the sign of the cross, "God willing, the agency decided to pay me a stipend to be his…" Vic took a minute to look around the room, "his, like his parole officer, but he's not under arrest."

Joe let this sink in. "The agency didn't let you retire," Vic shook his head, "although your daughter and the rest of the family think you did," then broke into a smile, "does Bruno know this because he thinks he is in charge?"

"Bruno is in charge of the office up here. And right now, he is in charge of keeping an eye on our family because I am not there. If not Bruno, then Enzo will take over. I only picked the people your mama trusts…"

"Vic, Angie is going to kill you, and mama is going to help her dispose of your body!"

Vic viewed the time on his Rolex, a retirement gift from the agency. "Speaking of which, we got to go. How long should a game of golf take anyway?" Joe shook his head. He followed Victor out to the waiting town car. A short time later, they boarded a private plane out at a small airport outside of Hartford. "Should we visit your idiot brother or leave him be?"

"We'll see him Sunday." Victor closed his eyes and slept away the short flight.

The warmth of the sun sparkling off the clear blue water made South Beach the place everyone wanted to be, everyone that is except Neddy. He lay outside his coffee truck, *Café de Ignaro,* counting the seagulls sitting on the fence across the way.

"Having fun?" Jimmy, his new best friend, at least per Vic, poked his head out of the serving area.

"Time of my life," Neddy smiled.

"Look, you might as well enjoy this while you can. Vic got you a sweet deal." Neddy closed his eyes. "And you know it. Come on. How many people get to hide out in paradise until their trial?" He paused as two women in matching Brazilian bikinis stopped to look at the menu. They smiled in Neddy's direction then continued to sway down the stretch of beach.

Neddy opened his eyes to follow their path.

"Hey, idiota," Jimmy brought his attention back. "This is the kind of crap that you were warned about." Again, Neddy shut his eyes. "You, my friend, are not that fine-looking…"

"My mama thinks I am."

"Your mama is wrong."

"You are a brave man, Jimmy, to say that my mama is wrong, especially out loud. She'll know, and she'll poison your biscotti." Neddy rose to walk in the direction of the ladies. Jimmy called out after him. "I am only going to use them," he pointed towards the beach facilities, "don't worry, I will come right back."

Jimmy watched Neddy until he reached the building. A couple approached the truck to order to iced coffee. "Yes, we will have two Frappuccino with low-fat almond milk, one squirt of simple syrup, and maybe add a little cocoa."

"This ain't no, Starbucks," Jimmy answered back. "We are the real deal. Authentic. Here try this." He had poured two iced coffees sweet with local honey. He poured in a bit of cream and chocolate sauce.

"Wow, that is delicious," the female exclaimed after one sip. "Pay the man, darling." Her companion handed Jimmy a ten, then muttered, "Keep it," before he produced the change.

"Ah, gratzie," Jimmy smiled. "Here, you must try one more thing." He broke one of mama's biscotti's in half and offered a section to each. "Come back again."

"Now, you are giving away mama's biscotti?" Neddy pulled himself into the truck.

"They'll be back," The two sip their drinks and hold the biscotti up in front as they spoke. "They are marveling at the taste as we speak. And now they sit to enjoy." Their conversation paused only for tastes of the biscotti, "Now where is Tucker?"

Tucker was a new guy who Jimmy traded shifts. Victor had instructed that Neddy was not to be left to his own devices. He needed constant watching. Jimmy had asked why place a serial dater in an area where women wore very little. When he thought about Victor's answer, he still laughed. "Because," he said, "the bad people wouldn't think to look there. I mean, what kind of idiota would put a person like Neddy around all these beautiful women?"

Jimmy watched the parade during the day. Tucker's responsibility included closing up the truck and getting Neddy back to a safe house. They both had rooms there, so they took turns with the overnight shift. Tucker worked in judicial and, like Jimmy, served as a Seal at one point.

He took no crap from Neddy.

"Late again, huh?" Neddy said to no one. "If it was me, I'd be pissed."

"When you had the restaurant, you were late every night to switch with your brother," Jimmy pointed out.

"That was different. That was family. You are allowed to screw up every once in a while. Of course, in our current situation, I wasn't the screw-up, was I?"

Jimmy wouldn't take the bait. "I need to get out of here."

"Jimmy, you know me for how long? I wouldn't do anything stupid. Especially not now. I mean, think about it; my family is quarantined. My business is gone. My next long term relationship will be number six…"

"You didn't really marry the last one." Neddy didn't answer. "Are you crazy? You married her?"

"Sort of. We did the paperwork at the town hall but never the ceremony."

Jimmy stared up at the ceiling. He made sure to enunciate each word clearly. "Does Victor know?"

"I don't know. What happens to those papers anyway?" Jimmy raised his hand, opened his mouth, and stop. The pattern continued so did Neddy. "Doesn't matter. What matters is my," he points down at his crotch, "got me in trouble many a time. Too many to discuss here, and I am more aware now. Jimmy. Think about it; I did not get up to talk to the beautiful ladies in the skimpy purple bikini's today, did I?"

Jimmy shook his head.

"Nor did I make a move on the luscious brunette who was obviously flirting with me…"

"She was half your age and asked for sugar for her coffee."

"Sugar, right. We both know what she wanted."

"Sugar," Jimmy repeated.

"You can trust me. I know women. She wanted more than sugar. Look, Tucker just pulled in. He's talking to some guy over there." Jimmy observed Tucker talking with one of the skateboarders who frequent the beach. Earlier the same person left with one of the bikini babes whose visits to the truck coincided when Jimmy took his break. Jimmy took out a pair of binoculars, then began to take note of the approximate age, gender, and other features. He observed his partner slip something into the stranger's hand.

"Don't do anything stupid," he instructed, adding, "I'll see you at home tonight." Jimmy walked towards the exchange. The skateboarder took off in the opposite direction as he approached. "Friend of yours?"

Tuckers shrugged. "Isn't everybody?" He turned his attention towards the van. "How is the prima Donald today?"

"He's okay," Jimmy waited for Tucker to react. "I would keep an eye on him because I can't figure this out, the ladies keep coming by and flirting with him."

"He appears egotistical, and they want free stuff," Tucker explained.

"Yeah, probably. Just an easy mark. But we can't be too careful" Jimmy hesitated a moment before adding, "Did you know that he and number five got married?"

"No, shit? Does Victor or the boys in Witness Protection know?"

"I doubt it, but isn't there a rule about testifying..."

"I think there might be. Are you calling Victor, or should I?"

Jimmy turned to find Neddy talking with another bikini-clad female. "I will make the call. Victor is used to me delivering bad news."

Tucker's arrival signaled the end of the day. Neddy began to move cups into storage bins, bottles of flavored syrups into the metal drawers, and containers of cream into the refrigerator. Tucker set up a lounge chair under a tree. He sat to face the truck.

Neddy waited for him to get settled before calling out, "Hey, Tuck, I could use a hand." The man hesitated, then stood to walk towards him."

"Tucker," he greeted without preamble.

"Whatever." Neddy turned his back so he couldn't see his smirk. "Listen, bud, either you or I need to take the empty pots and swirl the salt in them to clean." Tucker glared at Neddy.

"Why can't we do this at home?"

"It only takes a few minutes. We can have the truck ready to go tomorrow instead of us getting home and having to clean all this stuff. Just dump everything in the sink and rinse. If you do this, I can do the rest, and we could get out of here." Tucker grabbed the pots from Neddy.

"Don't do anything stupid," he instructed as he moved towards the facilities.

"Oh, I won't," Neddy sung back. Once Tucker disappeared, he wiped down the counters with the commercial spray, then leaned on his elbows and enjoyed. Neddy stopped cleaning to watch the parade of sunbathers who were packed up to head home. Off by the facilities, he watched Tucker converse with a young lady. He couldn't make out who, just that she curved in all the right directions. The two turned towards Neddy. Tucker pointed towards the truck.

In a flash, something blinded him. All Neddy saw dots. Big dots. White dots. His hands rubbed against his eyeballs as they watered. "Damn it," he blurted.

As his eyesight recovered, a figure came into form. Tall, curvy, her long brown hair was flowing in the slight ocean breeze. He dismissed a tug of familiarity as she swayed towards the truck in a model's strut. Her light, purple bikini covered ever so little.

Neddy smiled. He looked around for Tucker, who appeared nowhere in sight. When he brought his gaze back, she stood in front of him, full, real.

"Hi." Neddy felt his pants tighten.

"Hi, yourself." Vic's words popped into his head. *If she is too beautiful, you are not that good looking. Bullshit,* the voice in his head screamed, *I am.* Neddy half-closed his eyes. He let his smile, the one that usually gets him in trouble, freeze upon his face. In front of him stood the same woman who had stopped for coffee every day since he parked the truck. The one Jimmy said he didn't have a chance with.

"This may seem forward," she glanced around. Her right index finger hung in her teeth, "but would you like to get a drink with me?" Neddy looked around. Tucker appeared nowhere in sight.

"Two sugars, no cream?" he answered.

"You remember my combination?" Neddy's eyes moved up and down her body. "I was thinking about something besides coffee. Maybe a glass of wine?"

"Oh, yes." He placed the keys on the driver's side floor, jumped out of the truck, and walked off into the sunset thinking, *number six?*

Ah, gratzie writer. You finally did something right. That goddess in the skimpy bathing suit is named Maria, and her people come from my hometown in Italy.

My mama would approve.

Gentle reader, let me tell you what parts the writer purposely left out because right now, you are thinking that I am a stunad, yet you must know, Maria is the love of my life. How do I know this, you ask? Simple, she just loves me.

Ah, let me back up a little, so you know that I am not a married fool committing a sin. I did learn something here. Rayleigh and I filed the paperwork at the town hall to get married a couple of days before that mess at the restaurant. Rayleigh thought it would look better if something went wrong if she and I were actually married. Once I told Jimmy, then I had to explain again to Vic and Joey, and let's just say they are not very happy right now.

I guess there is some law, or how did Vic put it? I don't know, but there is something that says that if you are married, your testimony is tainted, so now Rayleigh's lawyer is trying to get her case thrown out. Joey says I put the family in more danger with one stupid move, but I don't know-how.

I think the whole thing was made up. Not the Pirate King part but going after my sweet Rayleigh. I know, reader, she shot me. But she was trying to protect me from the other guy she shot. Why would a gal like Rayleigh want to waste her time going after Vic? Yeah, you can't answer that, can you?

Okay, so they talk me into the fake funeral thing, and I go along. It took a couple of days for that crap they gave me to wear off. And then when I do wake up, I am told I must testify against Rayleigh and say that she planned the hit on the Pirate King. Oh, and the Pirate King's real name, Marvin Smith. Seriously, that is the dude's name. He is not even a pisain!

Between you and me, that is the most embarrassing part of this whole story. I got taken by a con man who wasn't even from the old country! WTF!

Okay, so we go through with the funeral, and then I get whisked off to a safe house down here in Florida. For the next month, I meet with these people who tell me things about Rayleigh and Victor that I didn't know.

I believe about half of what they say because they are trying to convince me to testify in a federal court against the woman I love. I refused. So, then they bring in my family and tell me how much my not testifying would put my mama in danger. They give me a scenario where someone will come and kill my mama. So now I need to testify because you know, we are talking about my mama. Except for all this time, they don't know about the marriage.

Here is when things get weird. Vic starts showing up and taking over these meetings. He decided that I needed to see the shrink because these people kept telling me that I am not that good looking. If beautiful women came on to me, they wanted something. I know what they want. Come on, so do you, gentle reader... Seriously, look at me!

Now here is the even stranger part. My entire family gets put up in this compound over in Palm Beach, in a really lovely area. Their place is in between a retired New York Yankee and some A-list Hollywood actress. Don't get me wrong; the restaurant did okay, but nowhere near New York Yankee money good.

I'm wondering how they afforded it myself. My family gets this beautiful oceanfront compound, and I get a coffee truck, a babysitter, and a house that, let's just say if I called it a shack, that would be an improvement. Rayleigh is off in prison, so I am told, and the Pirate King is dead. Someone else died in my office too. I didn't know the guy, so he really doesn't matter.

Now I got Jimmy, who is pretty on the ball. He used to hang around the neighborhood, and I'd see him in the café at times. This other guy, what's his name, Tucker, is an idiot. He hangs out, talks to chicks, and if he's supposed to be watching me, he failed miserably.

That's how I got together with Maria. I am so happy that the writer included her. Maria says she wants to move back to Italy and I plan to go with her once this whole thing is straightened out. She told her family about me, and she said they are looking forward to meeting me in person, especially her boss, who is also family. I am not sure what she does, but really, who cares!

I think mama would understand, don't you?

Thank you's

I'll start with the obvious; thanks to my family for their love and support. Although I find the family stories interesting, none appear in this book.

Thanks to my beta-readers: Robert Calegari, Evelyn Pampuro, Terri Meigs, and Stephanie Fischer. Your feedback was perfect, and changes were made!

Thanks to When Words Count – Writer's Retreat. You fed me gourmet meals and homemade cookies, put me in the middle of the beautiful Vermont Green Mountains, and gave me three blissful days to just write. I finally nailed that landing (ending) while in your presence.

Thanks to the folks of CoLoNY for peace, love, and understanding. You ladies rock!

Thanks to The Harmony Café for the best breakfast sandwiches and homemade Chai tea. The creative vibe comes alive in your place.

My ongoing thanks and appreciation to Chris Archer, Kay Janney, Jamie Cat Callan, and Jim Parise.

And finally, thank you to Sean Carlin for the subtitle, "the king of bad decisions."

Also, by L.M. Pampuro,

Dancing with Faith

Maximum Mayhem (Zack & Maxi's 1st adventure)

The Perfect Pitch

Passenger: the only game in town

Uncle Neddy's Funeral

Maximum Trouble

Harlot's grace

Harlot's fire

Visit her at Pampuro.com